Sardinian Silver

Also by A. Colin Wright …

Mikhail Bulgakov: Life and Interpretations

Sardinian Silver

by

A. Colin Wright

iUniverse, Inc.
New York   Bloomington

Sardinian Silver

iUniverse books may be ordered through booksellers or by contacting:

iUniverse
1663 Liberty Drive
Bloomington, IN 47403
www.iuniverse.com
1-800-Authors (1-800-288-4677)

ISBN: 978-0-595-48100-2 (pbk)
ISBN: 978-0-595-71601-2 (cloth)
ISBN: 978-0-595-60199-8 (ebk)

Printed in the United States of America
An earlier version of Chapter Four appeared as "From: Novel-In-Progress," in *Nebula*, 18 (1981), pp. 43-48.

The author acknowledges the Cantina Sociale della Vernaccia in Rimedio, Oristano, Italy, as former producers of the wine *Sardinian Silver*. Three lines are quoted in translation from the song "Legata a un granello di sabbia" by Fidenco-Marchetti (1962).

Author photo by Andrew Wright.

For Tina and John, and for former friends in Sardinia

Acknowledgements

I wish to express my gratitude to Rachel Derowitsch for her assistance with the preparation of the manuscript for publication. I should also like to express my sincere appreciation to my wife, Mary Anne Wright, not only for her help with proof-reading but above all for her patience and understanding during the writing of this and many other works.

One

A quarter to seven on a fresh, blustery morning in February. I went out on deck thinking it should have been warmer, warmer at least than Genoa, some five hundred kilometres behind to the north. The *m/n Torres* had come to calmer water since passing a long peninsula that jutted out from the Sardinian mainland, now finally in reach after twelve hours of overnight tossing. In the ship's bar, I'd found a few unshaven figures sipping at strong black coffee, but in the world of sea and wind outside the door I was alone, except for those who'd been sick.

I leaned on the rail, staring at the sea and the distant coastline, featureless in this pale morning. I recalled how yesterday evening I'd stood watching the lights of Genoa disappear into the night behind; then, with the still gentle plunging up and down of the black Mediterranean beneath the ship, I'd set about exploring, immersing myself in its atmosphere. A small cabin shared with incomprehensible, rough-looking strangers. Sard handicraft in showcases in the corridors. In the bar, I'd studied a map of the island on one wall and then sat watching television, something novel against the incongruous background. For the first time I realized that another language was being spoken around me besides Italian: Sard, which I, a scholar of languages, hadn't heard of until a month ago. In fact, I'd known nothing about Sardinia at all, except that it was an island below Corsica, shaped almost square, like a distorted shoebox stood on one end. And now I was being taken, impossibly, to a place that didn't exist outside an atlas.

This morning Sardinia existed, stretching in a thin wedge of grey over the horizon. Somewhere ahead was a place that would have people, its own colour. No longer would it be just a black dot on the map labelled *Porto Torres*.

I'd worked in a travel business for two years, not counting my summers as a rep during my university vacations—which meant staying at one of the company's resorts, meeting tourists on their arrival, seeing them into their hotels, and generally being available if they had problems. I immediately thrilled to the idea of Sardinia when my boss in London told me I was to go there, although, at twenty-four, I was too sophisticated to admit it.

He didn't seem worried about my unfamiliarity with the place, or that I didn't speak much Italian. "You've got a degree in languages, haven't you? You can learn Italian when you get there. Sardinia's going to be the fashionable place for tourism in a few years." He was right. I learned Italian well, and Sardinia would later become fashionable.

At the time, of course, my youthful romanticism about exotic countries was inextricably bound up with the idea of involvement with a local woman—the best way of getting to know a place, I told myself. But with my inborn fear of appearing anything other than an English gentleman, this was difficult. Particularly in Sardinia.

The journey there was trying enough. In the 1960s flying was a luxury, and the company sent me by rail, second class, which meant a Channel crossing from Dover to Ostend, followed by a night of travelling south across Europe, trying to sleep sitting upright in a crowded compartment. A routine trip, until I was jerked awake the next morning at the first stop across the Italian border. Domodossola, I read on the dull brown station signs, a name I knew well from my days of working in the office.

I was about to close my eyes again when I saw a pile of luggage being unloaded onto the platform—and there was my suitcase, which I'd sent through to Genoa. A phlegmatic British Railways official at Victoria had assured me it would travel on the same train as myself, but had said nothing about it being taken off at the border. I jumped to my feet, pushed past the slumbering forms in the compartment, struggled into the corridor, and made for the door.

On the platform I was about to grab my case when a man in a plain grey suit appeared before me, holding up an arm with a red band tied around it. Italian customs, I understood him to say.

I had to open the case while he rummaged through it, taking his time.

I'd just got it closed again when I heard the clanking of wheels behind me. My train was leaving—with my briefcase and coat still on board, en route to Milan, where I had to change to the only train that would get me to Genoa in time to catch the evening ship to Sardinia.

Trying not to panic, I lugged my heavy suitcase into the station to find the departures board. A local train for Milan was due in half an hour, but it would leave me a mere twenty minutes to make my connection. It was late, of course, and by the time it finally pulled into the Milan station I was standing impatiently with my hand on the door, ready to make a run for it, with just six minutes to retrieve my briefcase and coat from some lost luggage office and then find the other train.

Still dragging my heavy suitcase, I plunged along the platform, and to my relief saw the office straightaway. After bursting in, I found the man in charge was talking on the phone. At least my coat and briefcase were on a luggage rack behind the counter.

I hadn't enough Italian to explain. "*Deux minutes!*" I shouted in French, gesturing urgently.

Then I was running desperately across the station, struggling with all my luggage to the platform, where the Genoa train was pulling away. A young man lifted my cases from me as I heaved them aboard, and then seized me by the arms and pulled me inside.

*   *   *

That was all behind me, I thought, as I stood by the ship's rail in the morning breeze. Now, the same young man joined me.

"Oh, the Englishman, good morning!" He was taller than I, with a rather triangular, intelligent face and an attractive shyness. We'd started to talk on the train—his English wasn't bad except for the stilted intonation—and he'd turned out to be Sardinian, the first I'd ever met.

I asked his name.

"Gavino Palmas." His face was all activity as he explained that his surname was Spanish, since many Sards were of Spanish descent; that Saint Gavino, a martyr in Roman times, was the patron saint of Porto Torres.

"Arthur Fraser," I introduced myself.

He didn't catch it the first time, but laughed loudly to be sociable. "Mister Arthur, then. And you call me just Gavino."

I grasped the hand he'd offered but then, uncertain, partially withdrawn.

He shook mine warmly and smiled, eager that I should be happy at our arrival. His words came falling over themselves. "You have seen Sardinia? The island we have passed, Asinara. It is—how do you say it?—a prison place. You know, bad men, robbers, bandits, murderers. We get them here in Sardinia. Alas. At Alghero it is more beautiful."

"How do you know I'm going to Alghero?"

"All the foreigners go to Alghero. I myself, I go to Sássari."

The second largest town on the island, where I had to change trains yet again. Stressed on the first syllable, not the second: knowledge I'd acquired in my local library.

"And the capital's Cágliari?" I said, careful to stress it on the first syllable too.

"Cagliari. The Sards say it is the most beautiful city in Italy. Those who've never been there. To Italy, I mean." As though it were a foreign country.

As the ship groaned on toward the land, my companion told me he worked in a lawyer's office. He laughed, making a joke of it. "It's very dull. Life's like that for us Sards. I ought to have left for the continent before it was too late. There's no future in Sardinia."

He explained that he'd been away on a study tour of the continent— Rome, Florence, Bologna, Milan, but not outside Italy—and his sombre face brightened. He spoke hastily, with the long, drawn-out explanations of a child. "This was my visit first to the continent, imagine. I have often wished that I was born Roman instead of Sard, but only now I know what is wrong. We're really very backward. You'll see for yourself once you've become tired of the easiness and—how do you say it?—superficial pleasantness of life here."

As the coastline became more distinct, Gavino's enthusiasm returned. "But look there, you can see the port! Come to the other side, you'll see more." We pushed through the ship's vestibule, crowded with people and luggage. "That is where the beautiful beaches are, along that coast."

The superficial pleasantness of life. Wide sands against a background of low hills. Sun. Blue sea. Ahead of us was a long harbour wall with a tower and a light on top, and the masts of fishing boats clustering behind it.

"Porto Torres."

The crowd on deck was growing. The tower approached ever closer until the sea carried it past. In the harbour mouth a tiny boat came out to meet us, almost disappearing behind a wave, then reappeared, dangerously close. The *Torres* lowered a thick noose of rope to be seized from under its bow. Engines stopped, the tug made off in the other direction, engines started again, and we were swinging round, toward a quay surmounted by a huge gantry looming up from the side. Down below on the dockside another crowd was shouting and waving, with women in shawls and porters in blue uniforms in front of piles of crates and enormous bottles in wickerwork casings. A surge from the water below, and the gantry was already lifting one of the gangways to place it against the ship. I struggled down it, pushing through the people thronging on the quayside, busy with their own, Sard, lives. Porto Torres.

I followed Gavino to another train. Climbing high steps, finding room for cases, sinking back into soft yet unbearably cramped seats. The ship, the last surviving link with the continent, was now only part of the background, giving pride of place to the stone walls, cacti, and sea through the window.

The doors rattled shut, and the train started to move lazily, stopping again at the town station. When it left again, Gavino started jumping back and forth to point out the Roman ruins on either side of the line. "Look, if you turn back now you will see the Roman bridge, with the sea beyond it."

The barren green countryside, the stony land beside the railway, and the huge cacti made everything seem exotic. I loved it all.

A couple of men passed down the central aisle, and Gavino shouted out to them with the peculiarly Italian "O-ui" sound. A brief exchange of enthusiastic, meaningless words as the men continued down the train.

"*Ciao*," Gavino shouted after them.

He let his shoulders slump and his mouth drop. He was disappointed not to be able to introduce his English friend. Suddenly his mood had changed, and I was embarrassed for him, recognizing perhaps but not yet accepting that Italians had little of the Anglo-Saxon reserve about expressing their feelings.

For a while he was silent, and I, too, said nothing, content to watch out the window and listen to the strange sounds of Sard from the other passengers.

Around the shaking train stretched miles of olive trees. Gavino took a card and a pen from his pocket. "I will give you my address. When you are in Sassari you will come to visit me. And I will show you something of Sardinia. I will take you to Porto Torres properly, to Castelsardo, Tempio, and La Costa Smeralda perhaps. And this is my office address and phone number."

I took his card and he gave me another so I could write down my address in Alghero as well. Gavino put it away with a glow of pleasure. "Oh, but we come to Sassari. Here you change, and I must leave you."

I'd been aware of the town we were approaching and of a skyscraper that stuck out incongruously from its centre, with other buildings clinging onto it. The train drew into a station surprisingly large for an island I hadn't imagined to have railways at all. Gavino led me through a surge of Italians on the platform to another train, chocolate-brown and more bus-like than the first, bearing a large yellow placard "Sassari—Alghero."

Gavino was serious, bowing over my hand. "Mister Arthur, I thank you infinitely for your company. It has been a great pleasure, and please, when you come to Sassari, I shall be delighted to have the honour if you come and call on me."

Two

When I arrived in Alghero, I was surprised to find a young man with a neat little moustache waiting for me on the platform. From his clothes and casual sportsmanlike manner, he was clearly English.

"Arthur Fraser, I presume," he said, offering his hand. "My name's Jim Fielding. You probably won't have heard of me."

I hadn't and was a little annoyed that my private excitement at arriving in a strange place had been intruded upon. "Don't say our firm's got someone else here I hadn't bargained on!"

It turned out that he worked for a rival company. "We were ahead of you there, you must admit. Not that I give a damn for it anyway. I'm only doing this to have a year's break from college. Decided to come out a few weeks early, have some time wandering around by myself. But come along for some coffee. I presume you haven't had breakfast?"

"What about my cases?"

He strolled over to a taxi, had a few words with the driver, and returned. "He'll look after them. Your hotel will sort it out."

I followed behind him to a bar across the street, where we remained standing as he casually ordered two coffees.

"How did you know I was arriving?"

"Hmm? Oh, I had a letter from Maurice."

"Maurice?"

"Maurice Winter, your Italian manager." He distractedly filled his coffee with sugar. "You know him surely? A good friend of mine."

I explained that I'd never actually met him. Taking his time, Jim dug into his pocket, took out a whole pile of things he placed beside him, and finally handed over a grubby typewritten envelope. "Maurice gave it to me when I saw him in Rome. Asked me to come along and meet you. Look after you a bit, like." He leaned his elbows on the bar and started fiddling with his moustache. "You'll enjoy it here. Not too many hotels to bother with and ideal for having a good time. But then, I can tell you all you need to know tomorrow."

"You're just an amateur in this business, then? Still at university?"

"Hmm? Graduated last year. Just missed a first. Italian language and literature. I'm going back to do a Ph.D., but I wanted some practical experience first. You speak Italian?"

"Sort of."

"It's a wonderful language. *Beautiful!*"

It turned out we were both from Cambridge, and I soon decided that his know-it-all manner was only a pose. He was justifiably proud of having got himself a Sard girlfriend in defiance of local custom.

"But we must go. These women, they don't like to be kept waiting. Marcella in particular."

We plunged into a maze of narrow streets between houses several storeys high, where tiers of washing hanging out over the street excluded most of the light. Jim mentioned casually that this was typical.

"Oh, but I forgot to tell you." There was another long pause as he sauntered along. Someone perhaps had once told him to create expectancy in his audience and he'd never forgotten the advice. "The Americans are here too. Their rep's called Isabelle, or Isabella—I can never make out which. She's quite a character. Everyone in the island knows Isabelle. You'll meet her soon enough. But this is your hotel, on the corner here."

After introducing me as though I were his new assistant, Jim quickly departed, leaving the manager to make the more lengthy introductions.

Expressions of good will, enthusiasm over what a wonderful country England was, listening to a long list of the places the manager knew—boring, but important. It was half an hour before I was in my room, pleasantly large, with one tattered carpet on an otherwise bare tile floor.

I sat down on the bed and took out the letter from Maurice Winter, a friendly note to wish me good luck and give some useful background information. Then I looked up and saw the ceiling: a magnificent blue, with yellow and red stars and a number of plump angels floating ponderously across it, with vegetation entwined around the edges. Sitting on my bed, I reflected that all this was at last Sardinia, which had already been populated for me by at least two characters.

It was still only half past eleven. There was a knock at the door and a third character came in. A maid.

"*Scusi*." She smiled eagerly, speaking loudly and slowly, expecting me not to understand. "You have unpacked? No? Then I will help you."

I was aware of her physical presence. Were her eyes expressing friendliness or mockery? I wasn't sure. Her features were coarse and she was badly dressed. Must have been older than myself, nearly thirty. Her hands were dirty, and so was her tattered red cardigan. Evidently she thought I hadn't understood and came nearer, pointing at herself and then at me: "I ... help ... you."

With my English timidity I refused, afraid of the impression I might make. Here was just the type of girl I'd like to get into bed with, but all I could do was watch her, cautiously.

She laughed, drawing her mouth wide into her cheeks, her teeth half open, almost jeering. Then ran her hand through her tangled hair and pretended to be indignant. "I ... know ... hang up clothes." She scowled, still speaking in infinitives.

I made the excuse that I wanted to rest.

She seemed satisfied but added "I ... do ... very well," drawing herself up proudly. Her bust, I thought, was too large, but her very earthiness—or was it just dirt?— excited me.

She let her mouth open mockingly. "You like me, yes?" She stretched again, her eyes shining. Realizing she'd caught me off guard, she slapped her hands down on her knees, laughed triumphantly, and turned to go out of the door. "Later I help you unpack!"

I recovered sufficiently to call after her. "What's your name?"

She gave another grin and said, slowly again, "Te-re-sa." Then she disappeared out of the door, uttering a stream of words I didn't understand.

Lunch, siesta, strolls around the town, dinner in the hotel restaurant—those first days before the tourists started to arrive soon merged with other memories. Alghero was a typical southern port, with its fishing boats, elegant palm-lined avenue, and the poorer, bare white houses under orange-tiled roofs. Further away were the beaches of white sand and a greenish sea, which, when the sun slipped from behind its filtering clouds, would be transformed into the brightest of ultramarines. It was a lazy life for a while, and establishing professional contacts took little effort. My Italian improved rapidly. Only I felt I didn't quite belong to this country yet and was impatient to do so.

My sense of dignity nearly spoiled things for me. One evening as I went into the hotel dining room, the head waiter announced that I was now to eat with the staff. Insulted and ready to demand my rights, I stalked after him through the kitchen to a large room behind it.

Sitting around an enormous wooden table in a group of shouting, grabbing activity were a number of the younger members of the staff, while a little old woman of about seventy ran around them. I recognized a couple of the porters—and Teresa, whom I hadn't seen since her offer to help me unpack. She laughed tauntingly and shouted out "Oh, the Englishman," letting her spaghetti dangle from her lips.

The waiter was introducing the others before I had a chance to protest. "Carlo and Franco, the porters. Elena, Graziella, Teresa, Maria-Grazia, the maids."

Teresa gave another cackle and placed her hands on her hips, swinging round on her chair ostentatiously.

"And this is the housekeeper, Signora Anna-Maria."

The old woman, smiling up at me respectfully, came forward to shake hands. "I have a fine family, have I not? Beautiful girls, well-made, look for yourself."

One of the porters made a remark in Sard, laughing at the old lady, who almost before he'd finished speaking trotted over to him and cuffed him with her arm, but her eyes were smiling. "To teach you good manners. Don't take any notice of them. They're badly-bred, the lot of them."

"I'm not badly-bred!" Teresa protested.

Franco retorted, "Yes, you are! *Sei mal-educata, mal-educata!*"

He stepped back out of the way as Teresa sprang to her feet, pulling at his hair, laughing wildly, with a stream of words I couldn't understand. Impatient to explain my offended dignity, I still paused to admire her. The side of her forehead was disfigured by what seemed to be a permanent burn mark. In a few years' time she'd be the typical rough peasant woman I'd never look at again, but now I imagined removing her tattered clothes—once I'd established that I should eat in the dining room.

Franco had soon recovered, letting out with his fist and catching Teresa on the arm. Pretending to be afraid, she fled to the other side of the table, flinging chairs in his way as he and the others chased after her. Trapping her in the corner, he pummelled her without mercy while she gave loud, exaggerated cries of pain. But soon she was back at him, clawing in front of her and then skipping out of his reach. Signora Anna-Maria stood laughing, sometimes trying to catch Teresa herself, telling them all to behave. "What will the Englishman think?"

Let me join in, too, my desire whispered, as I imagined how Teresa would fight with me in bed as my hands sought their prize—while my dignity still wanted to make my little speech. Finally, I asked if it was normal for a tourist representative to eat with the servants.

The old lady took my arm. "You're the first guest we've had. You should eat outside, of course, but you're going to be one of us, after all. Although if it offends you, of course you can eat outside."

Dignity relaxed. The old lady clasped her hands together when I said I'd be happy to stay.

Teresa slapped her hands on the table. "Now we can tell him how we decided to invite him."

"Behave yourselves!" Signora Anna-Maria commanded.

Carlo explained. "We didn't know, you see. Then Franco was outside your room this morning. 'He's one of us,' he told us. 'I quite clearly heard him ... in bed.'"

Laughter while the old lady gave a click of disapproval. I was unsure of the verb Carlo had used. "*Scorregiare?*"

Teresa turned her back, bent forward, patted her behind with her hand, blew out her cheeks and emitted a loud rasp through her lips.

Signora Anna-Maria pretended to cuff her once more. "Go away, you filthy girl! *Sei mal-educata!*"

Teresa stuck out her tongue and in a gesture of mock gallantry pulled out a chair for me, half curtsying as she indicated for me to sit down.

*   *   *

Jim's moustache looked as if it needed trimming. "Been waiting long?"

"Twenty damn minutes." I'd been filling in time by seeing how often I could make the attractive girl behind the pastry counter look at me. Twice since I'd arrived. Did that represent my prospects for Sardinia?

"That's all right then. In Sardinia it's rare for anyone to be less than half an hour late. Glad you got my note."

He strolled over to the counter, sticking out his chin inquisitively as he gave the order. Avoiding the other patrons, he brought back a coffee and a pastry, then sat down with me and proceeded to light a very English-looking pipe.

"I thought I'd better give you some gen about this place."

His use of slang was old-fashioned. "Is there much to tell me?"

"Oh, no. The main stuff you'll obviously find out for yourself. Sorry, I didn't want to offend you. OK?"

I listened, looking at the long rows of wine bottles behind the counter, with outline maps of Sardinia decorating their labels. Jim had one interesting idea, namely that the three reps—he, Isabelle, and myself—although working for different companies, should pool resources so that individually we might have more time off, all of us looking after one another's tourists. It sounded all right to me, as long as our bosses didn't know.

"What's the talent like here?" I interrupted him.

He grinned. "Well, the tourists are often daddy's pampered little daughters without daddy and longing to have a good time. Unfortunately, though, the local men with their flowery manner of speech and dark adoring eyes are often more of an attraction than we are. Not that it concerns me anyway. I'm lucky in having a Sard girlfriend."

"Yes, you've told me. So how is it with the Sards?"

"Hmm? Well Marcella's modern in outlook, something of a rarity here. You may manage to find someone if you try hard enough, but with a respectable girl it's almost impossible. I've just been lucky." He made his customary long pause. "All women indoors by nine, and if you go out with a woman more than once—if you manage to go out with one at all—you're engaged to her. If you object, you'll have her brother standing behind her in church with a shotgun to make sure of it. Even the few modern ones daren't offend tradition too much. Marcella's usually spoken of as 'that girl with the wicked continental ideas.' No brother, luckily."

"It's that bad?"

Jim puffed away complacently on his pipe. "Marcella told me about a girl who asked her priest if it was wrong to kiss her fiancé. He said it was OK as long as she kept her teeth tightly closed, but if she parted them it was a mortal sin. It was in a small village, admittedly—and the church, thank God, has less influence in the towns. But even there the attitudes are still pretty strict."

"What do the men do then? Prostitutes?" I asked casually, so as not to show my interest. I'd never had the courage to go with a prostitute, but the idea of it excited me.

"Hmm?" Another long pause. "Yes, if they can't get hold of some English or German girl. All the men go with prostitutes, I'd say, without exception." Jim screwed up his eyes and gave expression to an odd fastidiousness. "That's something I find rather distasteful. A lavatory act, I'd call it. But it's a recognized profession, though no 'nice' girl will admit she knows of its existence."

I was about to ask about a girl like Teresa, but we were interrupted by a sudden shout from the doorway. "Hi there!"

The whole café stopped to stare as a tall, haggard-looking woman of about forty in an off-white raincoat made a theatrical entry and launched herself toward us. "Now I guess you must be Art Fraser!"

"Arthur his name is." Jim had evidently remembered that I didn't like being called Art. "This is Isabelle."

"Isabella Schwartz," she said loudly, pronouncing it as 'sworts' and grabbing hold of my hand. Then she let go and flung out her arm in what seemed to be intended as a gesture of patriotism. "American to the core, in spite of my name. Great to meet you, Art!"

The others in the café were exchanging glances.

Her pose changed and she looked flustered. "Look, I'm in one hell of a rush. You didn't see Alberto, did you, Jim? It's damn rude of me, but I'll see you this afternoon, OK?" She seized my hand again and released it before making an equally dramatic departure.

"Exit Isabelle," Jim announced. The audience relaxed. "We're due to meet her later, to show you something of the countryside. Her boyfriend's got a Giulietta, which she drives at about a hundred and forty."

"Sounds fine. Who's Alberto?"

"No idea. He's not the one who owns the car. Which reminds me ... " He waited for several puffs of his pipe before telling me the two of us had a chance to get a secondhand car if I was interested.

"I'll think about it."

"The trouble with this place," Jim said as we wandered back through the narrow streets, "is that most of the inhabitants have never been out of the island. You just can't tell them that life's different elsewhere, in England, for example. England's the same as the continent, and the continent's 'immoral.' 'We're more honest than the continent,' they'll say, 'if we go out with a girl we marry her.' It's a fantastic place. It depends a little where you are, though. Sassari, for example, is terribly dull. Alghero's a bit more liberal because it's 'contaminated' by the tourists."

I returned to the hotel for lunch, but it was quieter since the staff all came in at different times. I didn't see Teresa at all.

Isabelle turned up screeching in the Giulietta early in the afternoon. I sat next to her, while Jim struggled into the space behind the two seats.

"Where are we going?" She flung the car into gear and drove off, only to come to a violent halt the next moment as she nearly hit a cyclist.

After a stream of ludicrous Italian she set off again. We took the coastal road to the west, and soon we were following a narrow reed-lined isthmus between the sea and an inland lake that shimmered like a watercolour painting. "Fertilia," Jim's voice came from the back. "The Roman bridge."

Halfway across a channel from the lake into the sea stretched a low stone bridge over several arches, but then it stopped short, as if some catastrophe had overcome it, its last column rising in sharp relief from the blue and green below. The typical Roman brick, the red of the tiles, the prosaic strangeness of the past—its eternal stillness soon shattered, however, by the American desire to reduce antiquity to a photograph. Three shots with Isabelle standing up in the driver's seat (a muffled "goddamn it" as she pressed the button on the second of them), and the car jerked forward again.

After passing the main airport, little more than a single runway, we left the highway for a white, chalky road leading among cactus-hedged fields emblazoned with the stumps of vines. Past hamlets with impossible names—Palmadula, Biancareddu, Casteddu—until we reached the northern coast and headed back toward the east. Now Isabelle got into an argument with a farmer, whose cow had the effrontery to stop the car and then, in grand style, relieved itself against the side. Her argument consisted largely of gestures and the words "*Io … carabinieri*," pronounced as though they were the name of a Chicago gangster, while her unshaven protagonist defended himself in Sard. Neither understood the other and the conversation ended in another roar of the Giulietta's exhaust.

"Second Roman bridge," she yelled.

It was the one I'd seen before, from the train. Soon we were in Porto Torres, driving through streets where shawled women outside their doors warmed themselves over bowls of sand with little piles of glowing charcoal in the middle.

"What you might call an underdeveloped country," Isabelle pointed out. "You see the DDT painted on the houses? They only stamped out malaria a few years ago—the good old Rockefeller Foundation. Sure glad they did. My arm got lousy with mosquito bites last year."

"Isabelle came to Sardinia last year, too," Jim explained. "Beat all the other firms to it. Come to think of it, it's the one place the Russians didn't get to first! Pity really. Communism would do a lot of good to this place."

He started talking about the theoretical advantages of communism. There was something placidly reassuring about Jim: God was in his heaven and all was right with the world, as long as it could be reduced to a formula of words. He was still talking long after we'd left Porto Torres.

Olive trees and stone walls guarded us from the road, then more cacti and open countryside. "You see that?" Isabelle shouted, swerving violently. "A new rag!"

"A what?"

Jim chuckled. "The tower. She means a nuraghe."

It was no more than an unheeded symmetry of stones in a field, like a ruined Martello tower, but mysterious, exciting. I'd read how there were several thousand nuraghi in the island, towers whose purpose remained unclear, the remains of Sardinia's earliest known civilization. As always it was the atmosphere, not the historical details, that appealed to me. I could almost have waited for a nuraghic warrior to appear on horseback from behind it, but Isabelle, the tourist site having been ticked off, accelerated.

Roman remains, exotic scenery, local customs, a prehistoric civilization—I loved everything. To assimilate the strange and belong, in a society different from my own, had always been my desire. For the first time I realized that one day I'd have to leave Sardinia and, irrationally, it made me afraid.

The top of a rise, then down again. Sassari, the single-skyscraper town, was approaching. Past stone houses, then a sudden corner and the station where I'd changed trains. I remembered Gavino.

We drove up a long narrow street, the top end of which had no room for more than a single file of traffic and was alternately one-way, as controlled by traffic lights. On a wall was another sign indicating the pavements at the side were one-way for pedestrians as well. After a fork in the road, we emerged at the foot of the skyscraper. Through a square filled with palm trees, a barracks on the left, a short, colonnaded street leading to a larger open square—and here was a pompous Vittorio Emanuele II guarded by four sentinel palms with their branches drooping to match the stone feathers of his helmet.

"The Piazza d'Italia, inevitably," Jim commented. "Let's have a drink. My legs are cramped."

We left the car and went to a bar on the edge of the square, just under the colonnade.

"I must say I like Sassári," Isabelle said, stressing it on the wrong syllable. "It's got *atmosphere*, not like Alghero, full of foreigners."

I'd been thinking of Gavino and wasn't really surprised when he walked in. He flung up his arms in amazement, let out an "Eh!" of joy, and came rushing over. I introduced him and invited him to sit down.

He was delighted. He explained where his office was, spoke of all the things there were to see in Sassari, said how friendly the people there were, unlike those in Cagliari, the capital. I had to tell him in detail of my impressions. Then at the first pause in the conversation, he was suddenly anxious he might be keeping me from my two charming friends. I slapped him on the back, reassuring him, at which he went red with pleasure and, changing to Italian, suggested we should use the intimate *tu* form of address. "Oh … but if you will not be offended?" He laughed again when I responded, using the *tu* form myself.

His shyness, his fear of saying something wrong, his self-conscious politeness, reminded me of myself as an undergraduate before I'd learnt to protect myself by a wall of superiority. I felt a vague unease, realizing there was so much I had in common with Gavino, things in myself I wanted to overcome.

"But your friends are getting impatient. I must leave you. But come and call on me whenever you come to Sassari." He left quickly, first paying for all the drinks.

"Nice chap, your friend," Jim said. "The famous Sard hospitality. But would you mind if we made a move? I'm supposed to be meeting Marcella this evening."

Three

"Oh, the Englishman, always he is so quiet, so calm!"

For several evenings I'd enjoyed the same fights, without participating in them, in the room behind the kitchen. Teresa, at the centre of any trouble, made fun of me in front of the others like a spirited Carmen mocking her timorous Don José. She tried to teach me some Sard: obscenities I had to repeat, to gales of laughter, without knowing what they meant. This evening, though, after the arrival of my first group of tourists, I'd come in late and found Teresa alone with the old lady, who always supported me and was a useful catalyst for my silences.

"You don't like it here?" Teresa went on.

"I like it very much."

"It's different in England," Signora Anna-Maria said as she bustled around. "An ignorant girl like you can't understand."

Teresa thought for a moment. "Is England on the sea?"

"Yes."

"The Mediterranean?"

I grinned. "No."

Teresa was annoyed at her own stupidity. "On the Adriatic, of course."

"Ignorant, what did I tell you?" The old lady patted my arm. "You'll soon get used to it here. You look tired, though. I suppose those drunks last night kept you awake?"

I chuckled recalling how Carlo had dealt with them, rushing in pyjamas into my room, jumping up vigorously onto the windowsill, and urinating on them from three storeys up. "No, they didn't bother me. I do sometimes find it difficult sleeping, though."

Teresa wasn't impressed. "And what about when you're married? Will you still want to get your sleep then? Like all these honeymoon couples here, come staggering down all bleary-eyed and feeling dreadful." She straightened herself up and growled at me. "If you were married to me I wouldn't let you get any sleep!"

"I'm not sure I'd let you get any either!"

"Oh, he's not so quiet after all!"

The old lady chuckled. "It's the effect of a dreadful girl like you on him."

Teresa laughed, showing her teeth, and said suddenly, "If I go to bed with you ... will you marry me?" Not sure if I'd understood, she repeated it, speaking in infinitives. "If I ... go ... bed ... with you ... " She paused, with suggestive wriggles of her body as she turned a ring on her finger. "You ... me ... marry?"

Quick, Arthur, find the right reply. "No. I ... no ... marry ... you."

"Oh! Don't you like me? I don't please you?" She came toward me with her hands stretched forward.

"I like you. But I don't want to marry you."

"Why not? If you like me, why don't you marry me?"

"Because you're ugly," the old lady put in. "Who'd want to marry *you?*"

I hastened to keep the conversation going. "In England, it's not enough just to like someone you're going to marry. You have to have something in common as well."

"Oh, in England they're very stupid! Here when two people like each other they come together, so." She joined her forefingers.

"In England too. But why marry?"

"But you like me? Yes?" Teresa placed her hands on her hips and swung round, arrogantly showing off her body. She ran one hand down her front. "Doesn't this ... suit you?"

It suited me very well, but the terms were unacceptable. "Oh, yes. Not that I've seen it yet, of course."

Teresa was delighted. "You can see it if you marry me!"

"It's ugly," the old lady repeated. "I've seen it and I know."

Teresa took no noticed but laughed provocatively, throwing her hands forward. "Why not marry me? When I'm dying of love for you!"

The old lady pointed at Teresa's crotch. "You're interested not in Teresa, then, but in this."

"Oh!" Teresa shouted again as I smiled my agreement. With her hand in an enormous curve out in front of her, she patted her stomach and continued in a warning tone, "If you put anything in my belly and don't marry me, I ... you ... bang-bang!" Now she pointed with her fingers in the shape of a pistol. "Bang-bang! I ... you ... bang-bang! No more Mister Arturo!"

Franco came in. "Oh, run away. You'd never know how to use the thing!"

"Oh no? You'd be the second one I'd use it on!"

Franco laughed as she flew at him trying to pull his hair. Calmly, he seized hold of her nose between bent fingers and twisted it, then started to drag her around the room until she screamed with pain. The others came in, too, and my one promising encounter turned into yet another general fight. But I went to bed looking forward to the next evening.

I was so uncertain, though, how I should behave with Teresa. The next few evenings brought little change. She would ask me again when I was going to marry her, but it was only a joke, and I failed to suggest she might simply get into bed with me. Once I clumsily joined in the fighting with the others and actually slapped her on the behind, but then she got annoyed and shouted loudly, "I don't want that, have you understood?" Or was she just pretending annoyance?

She was always shouting, sometimes viciously. On one occasion Signora Anna-Maria told her off for something and she flew into a rage, her shouts coming from a body shaking with anger and her eyes flashing with hatred. Then the old lady started as well, in a high-pitched wailing flood of words, and soon the whole room was in an uproar.

A week later Teresa again mockingly proposed to me when she was in one of her better moods. That night there was an electricity failure, and the old lady, bringing in some candles, offered one to Teresa as a substitute for a husband, while the others applauded.

* * *

Sometimes I went to the pictures with Jim, cheap thrillers and romances, or American films dubbed it Italian, in wooden-seated cinemas empty of women. The advertisements would tell me things like "*Colgate* (pronounced *Col-gah-tay*) *con gardol pulisce i denti*" and seemed less objectionable in Italian. The films started late and ended sometime after one. Jim and I would walk slowly back through the streets and have a final drink at a bar that stayed open late, where we sometimes sat in long, theoretical discussions of a type that appealed to him.

We bought our car, a tiny Fiat 600. When Isabelle saw it she nicknamed it "Pimple," and the name stuck.

Except in the one obvious area, I was beginning to feel that my ideal had become realized: the strange had become part of my life, even if it seemed too impossible to last. In my room I'd look at my blue-and-yellow-painted stucco ceiling thinking how I wanted my time in Sardinia to go on for ever.

I met Jim's girlfriend, Marcella. She was short, dark, attractive in a fairly ordinary way, and refused scornfully whenever Jim suggested she might learn some English. She tended to monopolize him, wanting to be spoilt by an adoring male, while Jim showed a laughingly protective attitude toward her. They were proud of having each other, for different reasons.

By the beginning of March more tourists were arriving, and I received a letter from Maurice Winter, saying the company was to have another rep at Olbia on the east coast and asking me to find a solicitor for some of the legal arrangements. I immediately drove to Sassari. Gavino welcomed me warmly, as pleased to see me as he was grateful for the extra business I'd brought. He insisted on taking the rest of the afternoon off so he could walk me over the city, enthusiastic and proud to act as guide. But as the afternoon advanced and he could find fewer things of interest to point out, he gradually became more depressed. By the time we decided to retreat to a convenient bar, he was showing the same underlying melancholia as previously.

"I could have done so many things if I had been a continental. The continentals know how to enjoy themselves."

"Why not leave then?"

"It is too late now. I'm thirty-two already. No, I'm just a failure." He said it lightly enough: true confessions you pretend to laugh about so as not to be taken seriously.

I'd thought him older. I didn't want to get involved with his problems, fearing perhaps that I would have to reveal some of my own. So I was relieved when Gavino suggested we should make an appearance on the piazza for the *passeggio*.

The square was packed with people parading back and forth, many of them, men included, walking arm in arm. Feeling uncomfortable, I, too, linked arms with Gavino, who greeted everyone he knew with pride. We walked only on the side of the square preferred, he told me, by the better class. I observed some of the girls as they passed, noticing they would stop to talk with the young men or walk with them in a group, but it seemed that only engaged or married couples promenaded by themselves.

"The *passeggio* is the major, traditional entertainment here," Gavino explained. "In fact, it's almost the only one. Except for the local brothel."

"There's a special place?"

He nodded gloomily. "All of the men go there. A few years ago the prostitutes were cleared out of town but given a home of their own just outside, in an abandoned monastery, imagine. Every part of it, every cell, or just holes in the wall—it's all one huge brothel. The whole place stinks, of course, but some of the girls are good. And in a sense they're more honest than some of the high-class whores you can find."

I listened, fascinated, yet refused when he offered to take me there. Now, it seems a pity I didn't at least go to see the place. Even its name I've now forgotten, although I was to hear it many times.

For a while one of Gavino's friends joined us—a doctor from the hospital, a lonely, shy-looking man. Then I had to leave to get back to Alghero. Gavino made his usual farewell speech, adding that a boring evening awaited him. "What an abyss Sardinia is!"

I returned to Alghero too late to see Teresa at dinner, but the next lunchtime I had the pleasure of chasing her around the kitchen—catching exciting glimpses when she bent forward in a low-cut sweater. Then from somewhere across the street there was music, and she started to sing, suddenly serious, almost romantic, in a rough but attractive peasant voice. Until Signora Anna-Maria came in and told her to stop annoying the Englishman and get on with her work.

By the evening Teresa was in one of her sullen moods.

"I know what's wrong!" Carlo announced. "She's thinking that it's the fourth in a few days' time."

The others joined in a loud chorus about the fourth. "She's got guests coming," Franco explained.

"She's lucky," the old lady said to me with a bright little smile. "She's still a young girl. How old are you, Teresa, twenty-three?" Younger than myself, and I'd thought she was nearly thirty! "I'm an old woman now. I don't have guests any longer."

Teresa flew out of the kitchen in a rage.

At least she now treated me as she did the others. I was there for her fights, her tempers, or sometimes her sudden silences—but then I'd go off to bed realizing I'd once again failed to create an opportunity for anything more. In front of the others she encouraged me outrageously, but there was never an opportunity to find her alone. For all my happiness in Sardinia I felt my experience of it wasn't complete.

There were three attractive girls amongst a crowd of tourists who arrived a few days later, and I noted them with interest. I'd had my affairs with tourists who, because of the glamour surrounding my job and the fact that everyone wanted a good time on holiday, were easy enough, although few were willing to go the whole way. But here in an exotic country it seemed a waste of effort to pursue an English girl, like cultural incest.

In any case, for a while I was too busy getting everyone settled into hotels. By the time I'd finished, it was almost time for the Alghero *passeggio*, and I met Jim and Marcella, who'd just returned from a trip in Pimple.

"Oh, but you should have been with us, Arturo," Marcella said petulantly. "I'm sure you drive better than he does." She put on the hurt expression she cultivated, for she was attractive when she pouted. "It's that ridiculous moustache of his. I'm sure it gets in his eyes."

"Hmm? On the contrary, it was all your fault. You wouldn't let me keep my eyes on the road."

"Well, of course I want you to look at me rather than all the other girls! Anyway, you can buy me a drink to make up for it."

"If you insist." Jim was patronizingly, lovingly, proud of her.

We were strolling toward a bar when Jim nudged me. "Isn't that your friend Gavino in front of us?"

"I think you're right. And who's that he's with?"

He was holding hands with a fashionably dressed girl who kept looking up at him, listening intently.

"Gavino!"

He looked round. "Oh, Mister Arthur!" He grasped my hand. "I wondered if I might see you here. Let me introduce you to a friend of mine."

I didn't catch her name but found myself shaking hands with a girl who, from her makeup and elegant clothes, might have lived for years on the continent. I was aware of the slightly hard, brown eyes, conscious of their beauty, looking at me questioningly. Then she shook hands with Jim and Marcella, who greeted her curtly, almost rudely, so that Jim glanced at her in surprise.

Gavino explained they'd just come over for the afternoon and then had a dinner engagement. "Otherwise, we'd have tried to find you." He smiled in relief when I assured him I didn't mind.

"But I didn't know you had such an attractive friend," I told him.

The girl smiled but said nothing. I heard a slight giggle behind me and, turning, saw it was Marcella.

"Oh, we see each other from time to time."

The girl looked at Gavino hastily, as though reminded to show her devotion.

We reached the bar and he was again full of his boyish enthusiasm, insisting on buying the drinks despite Jim's halfhearted attempt to do so first. I had a better opportunity for observing Gavino's partner. She sat smiling obligingly, giving an impression of politeness. Obviously she knew him well, but there was no suggestion they were engaged. Gavino didn't pay much attention to her but chatted with Jim, while Marcella sat almost silent.

"Claudia," Gavino said at last, "we must be going."

She had for a moment been thinking of something else, but her attentive expression returned. "Yes, dear."

Marcella gave another giggle after they'd gone. "How did he get to know *her*?"

"I don't know. I liked her. Why do you ask?"

Marcella shrugged her shoulders. "Oh, nothing. She hasn't got a very good reputation, that's all."

Jim chuckled. "In other words she has up-to-date ideas."

"She's married. The husband disappeared a long time ago."

"And so everyone blames her because she has the sense to go out and enjoy herself instead of sitting at home praying for the rest of her life."

"She's rather well known," Marcella said flatly. "To go out with one man ... "

"And to go to bed with him?"

"Oh, and to go to bed with him if you like. That I understand. Even if no one does it here." As though in agreement with a morality that Marcella didn't herself practise. I wished I could see her eyes behind the dark glasses she often wore. Black glasses, black hair: external symbols, perhaps, of the restrictions she couldn't quite break through. "But with many, that I don't understand."

I was curious. "Paid or unpaid?"

"Claudia? What's the difference? Just likes expensive presents, I imagine."

"And how many men have you been to bed with, Marcella?" Jim asked challengingly.

"Oh, he can actually be jealous!" She kissed him on the cheek impulsively. "Officially, none. Not one, you understand? *Hai capito?* Unofficially, two. You and the old bugger I told you about."

Jim nodded. "And which was better?"

"The old bugger, of course! He had more experience."

We sat talking until it was time for Marcella to leave.

"A wonderful girl, Marcella," Jim said, gazing after her. "Technically still a virgin. Never have been able to persuade her to take the final step. Nor, apparently, could the old bugger. I'm surprised, though, that she spoke of Gavino's friend like that. It just shows that even she can't escape this frightening provincialism."

He took out his pipe and lit it ponderously. "You know each village is virtually a province of its own here. There are lots of them five or six kilometres apart that hate each other like poison and whose dialects are mutually incomprehensible. There are even places in the interior where they virtually speak pure Latin. So they have to speak Italian to be understood. Now if perhaps you could merge all the dialects into one—"

As a linguist, I assured him this was impossible.

That worried Jim not in the slightest. "It would be magnificent if you could."

"But you can't, so why bother about it?"

"But you *might*."

We had many conversations like this. Ideas for Jim were the most fundamental thing in trying to secure human happiness, and one had to strive toward them even when they were impossible—which is why he was a theoretical communist. I, on the other hand, tended to dismiss unrealizable ideas as mere daydreams, although my personal life was probably governed by them just as much. I would dream of love and, endlessly, of sexual fulfillment, turning the worst of defeats into imagined victories, and then later I would be beset by doubts again. It was only in everyday things, in organizing my tourists and in my social views, that I was ruled by the practical.

We strolled back by the sea watching the lights come on one by one as the dark blue sky intensified and blackened. Walking between the clamour of the town and the empty silence of the sea, I told myself again that this was the Sardinia I never wanted to leave.

"England seems such a rush compared with this," Jim said. We reached the corner of the harbour and turned to go out along the short stone pier. "The wonderful thing is that nothing ever happens here. At least, nothing important. A new bishop arrives in one of the towns, so the band turns out and there's a procession. Cagliari beats Torres at football and there's nearly a revolution. Or the sea's slightly rough and the boat doesn't sail from Genoa."

We stood for a while looking over the darkened sea.

"Of course, the biggest thing to happen to Alghero this century has been the arrival of Isabelle. She's really leaving a mark on the place."

"In what way?"

"You haven't heard about her yet? How whenever there's a dance there's a fight to have the honour of dancing with 'the crazy American,' as they call her? Half the male population idolizes her. She picks and chooses, treats them all like dirt, and they love it."

"She's single?"

"A widow. You haven't heard her bragging of how she bumped off her better half? Sometimes she poisoned him, another time she shot him, depending on her mood of the moment. He probably just died as the easiest way out. I guess it's just the foreigners, though, who cause things to happen here."

Inspired by that remark, I tried pinching Teresa's behind in the hotel that evening and was rewarded by a stinging slap on the face and a torrent of abuse.

"You forgot it's the fourth," the old lady said amid general laughter.

Four

Coloured streamers and balloons hung from the ceiling and balcony, boxes of flowers adorned the stage, but the Sassari theatre was still disastrously empty. Gavino and I paraded arm in arm around the bare stone floor, where the seats had been removed to make room for dancing.

"Couldn't you have brought your friend from the other day?" I asked.

"We don't go out often. She probably has other commitments."

Our pace quickened as we rounded a corner and started again on the downhill slope toward the stage.

"We're too early," Gavino said. "I told you no one would be here before midnight."

I'd been anxious not to miss anything. A masked ball, with girls allowed to stay out late, seemed promising. Now I was less certain. A few men were scattered on chairs or standing in groups on the dance floor, talking and smoking. The perpetual human emblem of Sardinia and, I would learn later, of all southern Italy: men waiting for the women to arrive.

Carnival had started that week, like a band of trumpeters trying to play all the notes at once. Once a year normal restraints apparently gave way to a gaiety that asserted itself in voices and music all the more strident because of the oppressive shroud of Lent, which would shortly descend. Later there'd be more relaxation with the coming of summer, when the beaches would provide escape, but now a conscious determination to have a good time was blared from every street. Yet for all this the restraints were still there, for carnival was presided over by tradition and, outwardly at least, the Catholic Church. It was rather like a children's party, where they were allowed to play games, eat more, and make more noise than usual, but there was always some adult presence that forbade them to go outside the living room.

A sudden tremor of interest. The first few masks had appeared, and the men looked to test their judgement as to what was underneath the comically strutting figures—for these were masks that covered the whole body. Many were identical: black outer garments and pointed hoods with a slit for the eyes, decorated by red or white patches, like a number of dark-phased ghostly birds waiting for an invitation from the land of the living.

"Look at the hands and feet," Gavino warned. I realized that they were old women, all of them, taking advantage of being disguised.

But shortly afterward a new group arrived.

"Come on, Mr. Arthur, they are good!"

"How do you know?"

"I know!" Gavino looked at me full of mischief, trying out an Italian obscenity: "You can smell their figs from here! Continentals."

I danced with a girl in a black domino with blue dress and cape. She turned out to be Roman, and I flirted lightly, listening fascinated to the clipped elegance of her speech. Soon, though, I had lost her. When dancing, I never knew whether to hang on to a pleasant girl and risk boring her by my timidity and lack of small talk, or let her go and try to find her later—with the risk that one of the young wolves might already have devoured her. Gavino, too, had soon deposited his partner with her friends and was lighting a cigarette, looking bored.

Then an extraordinary thing happened. I found myself seized by a masked woman, taller than myself, and whirled onto the floor.

My excitement didn't last. "Enjoying yourself?" said a distinctly American voice.

"Good God! Isabelle!"

She swung me round in a terrifying manner. "That's right. I guess you didn't recognize me." It was small wonder. Her mask consisted of three or four layers of plum-coloured material wound about her, with a hood of mauve flowers on yellow.

"You haven't said if you're enjoying yourself," she went on, pushing me furiously around the floor out of time with the music so that we kept crashing into other couples. I wished I were wearing a mask too. "I'll be damned if I am! Do you know that louse Cesare has stood me up? If I get my hands on him I'll just about murder him. He's a stinking little swine if ever I met one." Part of her disguise came unfixed, and she threw it back across her shoulder in a gesture of defiance. "I'm used to being dated by gentlemen!"

The band changed from its vague rumba rhythm to a cha-cha, and Isabelle immediately started to do a Charleston instead, effectively clearing a floor space. In a few minutes I found myself at the centre of a mob of cheering spectators.

As soon as it ended I pretended to see Gavino and quickly made my escape. "So long!" I heard from Isabelle, forlornly, behind me.

Now the ball was in full swing, but already there were no more partners available. The men who'd been unlucky clustered at the bar in the foyer getting drunk, and a few danced together. Others were wrestling and hurling streamers into the crowd or throwing confetti, without which no dance or party in Sardinia was complete. The few girls who were free all refused me when I asked them to dance.

I found Gavino sitting in the gallery. "We have given up the pretence, yes? Of trying to find a woman?"

I nodded reluctantly but was surprised to see that Gavino was enjoying himself, listening enthusiastically to the band. "You like music?"

"Jazz. Modern. Classics too. You must listen to my records sometime."

Exciting rhythms, Italian pop songs, noisy chatter all around. The night spun on in happy abandon for those who had partners. Balloons cascaded from the roof, while a singer crooned to an endless, hypnotic cha-cha.

The slower dances, though, were painfully static. Men and women clutched together tightly, moving no more than a couple of inches at a time in their one rare opportunity for physical contact. "*Il ballo della matonella*, we call it," Gavino commented scornfully. "In Rome it's just the antipasto to other things. Here, it is the whole fucking meal." I looked at the gallery, where couples were sitting sedately, hardly touching each other, and I thought how hard they had to struggle, so unnecessarily, for the simplest of pleasures.

Later, when the girls had finally changed out of their masks, Gavino and I again descended to the floor, standing with the other men at the side.

I was aware of a conversation close by. "Anyway, I was all ready to shove in my prick"—I recognized a word I'd learnt from Carlo—"when I couldn't get the safe unrolled. So she grabs me and says, 'What do you need that for, lover? Hurry up, you've only got fifteen minutes.' Only now I was starting to go limp again."

I grinned, turned to find Gavino, and then saw that he was dancing—cheek to cheek, obviously with another of his friends. He hugged her close, whispering to her. But when they moved around

I could see that each had an expression of resignation that the other couldn't see.

"I see Maria's doing her stuff again," my neighbour was continuing.

Gavino reappeared not long afterward. "God, that was dreadful. Let's go, shall we? We'll get a bottle of cognac and take it back to my place."

We walked back through the deserted streets of Sassari, Gavino suddenly starting to sing Verdi at the top of his voice, while I joined in the choruses. Passing a truck drawn up against the curb, he stopped and relieved himself against the wheel. "Come on, Mister Arthur, have a good pee. It will make you feel better."

He took my arm as we walked on further.

"It's good to have a friend like you," he said when we sat down exhausted in his living room. "You're so different. You know how to live!"

It wasn't really true, I thought, looking at the richly woven carpet covering the stone tiles. "You're a good friend, too, Gavino."

"Really?" His face flushed as, without getting up, he fumbled in a cupboard for glasses and then poured the cognac. "Mr. Arthur, to our friendship!"

"To us!"

"And to all the English girls!"

"And to the Italians!" We began drinking toasts to the girls of all the nationalities we could think of, our speech getting more slurred with each one.

Gavino curled up in his chair in happiness. "And finally to our beautiful Sard girls," he said, waving his glass in the air. "There are good ones among them, timid though they are. And to their beautiful little figs, just waiting to be sucked. As long as they're young, beautiful, and you don't have to pay. Oh, Mr. Arthur, you like the girls, yes?"

Later, I was uneasy about the heartfelt mutual confessions that followed during that drunken night, for I was afraid of a Gavino within me too, timid and often awkward, whom I'd longed to get rid of.

I arrived back in Alghero just after nine, by train, having failed to get the key of the car into the ignition. The port looked bleak and cold, and I meandered back to the hotel recalling how I'd talked on the train in Sard with a couple of peasants, which was strange because I didn't think I could speak Sard, but they didn't seem to speak it very well either and hadn't understood what I was saying.

I found my way in through the hotel's revolving door with some difficulty. And then I was accosted by an apparition. Two fantastically pointing breasts. Covered, of course—it was before the bra-less age.

"Oh, excuse me, Mr. Fraser." They belonged to one of the attractive tourists. The rest was pleasant too: a youngish girl—twenty?—in tight trousers and a sweater. Her parents wanted their breakfast in bed. How did one order it?

I went to the desk to jot down a note for the porter. The girl followed calmly, swinging her hips.

"What's the name?" It came out wearily and I smiled broadly to make up for it.

"Mr. and Mrs. Pearson, room thirty-two." She spoke in a smooth, controlled voice, exciting. She leaned over the desk, wiggling her bosom on the edge of it, then said slowly, peevishly, "I don't know why they had to put me so far away from them."

I looked at the tight vibrating sweater—or was that because I was still drunk?—and at the eyes looking steadily into my own. "Breakfast in bed for you too?"

"If you like. Room forty-six anyway." She laid her head on her elbows on the desk, then said innocently, "You're a bit under the weather, aren't you?"

Room forty-six, I copied down. She raised herself up, stretched slowly, then turned to walk away. Her behind was wiggling as well. It was one of those occasions—rare, alas—when I knew without question that I'd soon be getting similar views without the clothes.

"Oh, Miss Pearson," I said, making an effort to speak coherently. "What's your first name?"

She turned and stared at me for a minute. "Jenny," she said with a little laugh in the middle. She stretched up so that her breasts were thrust forward provocatively, then turned and disappeared slowly up the stairs.

"Jenny," I repeated, half wanting to follow her, but then with a sudden feeling of giddiness I collapsed forward onto the desk. When I woke up I was still dressed, but someone had placed me on my bed.

I found my dictionary to check the Italian for contraceptives, which I'd have to ask for, embarrassingly, in a pharmacy.

* * *

Why do I never seem to meet the Jennies nowadays? I still think of her in my moods of sexual nostalgia: of her pointed breasts with their prominent nipples, her gorgeous wetness, and the sucking sound from her vagina as I slithered in and out of her. She worked in an office and for two glorious weeks a year would pretend to sophistication. She would find someone to sleep with, aspire to "modern ideas" unrealizable in the normal home atmosphere, and then would probably dream of her holiday for the rest of the year, masturbating when the memories got too exciting. The lot, no doubt, of much of humanity, tied to a particular brand of convention—a thought that repels and terrifies me, the more so since I, too, would later become tied to a convention that I loathe. Rather the beer-swilling debauchees every time (even if, alas, I'm too fastidious to be one myself) than the coercive, terrible respectability of ordinary people, who assure you that maturity and conformity are identical and confuse religion with being "nice, good people like us."

Jenny at least didn't have to pretend she was in love to enjoy getting laid. Nor did she lose her head over the inevitable Italian flattery that surrounded her in one of the tourist bars on her first evening with me. We danced lazily, interested only in the preliminary reconnaissance of each other, kissing deeply and pressing furtively with our hands, rubbing sexual organs between impatient thighs. Back at the hotel I invited her to my room on the conventional pretext of a cigarette, but we didn't even bother with this before getting into bed. The taste of Jenny's nipples in my mouth was indeed delightful, and she whimpered when I entered her.

Even afterward she didn't spoil it with sentimentality. I took her out on a number of occasions, and generally it was just fun being together. We went in Pimple to the Grotto beyond Fertilia, to some of the nuraghi around Macomer, to inland villages almost untouched by civilization. Once, in the most unlikely of places, we actually came upon Isabelle going into a cornfield with a terrified-looking Italian soldier. For a while I even forgot about Teresa.

I liked Jenny, but then I've never made love to a girl I didn't like. Sex, I find, always leads to a greater, not lesser, respect for the person. She was to leave on the Saturday of that week, and by the time Friday was over I was so exhausted that I overslept, struggling up just in time to see her onto the airport coach, with her unsuspecting parents full of thanks for all I'd done for them and their lovely, pointed-breasted, moist-vagina'd daughter.

Carnival wasn't yet over but continued with parties in private houses, where the only prerequisite was a record player. Carlo invited me to one where people intrigued just to meet an Englishman gave me a great reception. I found a girl to dance with and paid her little compliments to make her laugh at me, while others kept interrupting to bring me liqueurs in a harmless attempt to get me drunk. Then the confetti-throwing started, with giggles and protestations from the women.

A short little man with glasses, about my age, came up to me. "My name's Pinna, Enrico Pinna. Mister Arthur, isn't it? Tell me something about England."

I started on the well-worn ritual of saying what things were different from Sardinia, particularly in people's attitudes.

Enrico nodded, fascinated but not really understanding. "Oh, but we're so much more advanced than the south of Italy." He clapped me on the shoulder and started asking me about all my personal impressions and how I was being treated. He was full of determined liveliness and good will, and was something of a bore.

"I'm a teacher," he explained, then he screwed up his face and laughed. "I teach English, can you believe it?"

"You've been to England then?"

"Oh, no. I've never been to the continent." He invited me to visit him and watch television the next evening.

I was ready to dance again, but it was already time for the girls to leave. My former partner insistently refused my offer to take her home and disappeared to the next room to help remove confetti from one of her friends. "Her brother will beat her if he finds out she's been at a party," she explained.

It was ten past nine. Quickly the girls had gone.

Parties like this were so promising, yet so empty. I recall another one, with Gavino and some of Marcella's friends, where one girl enjoyed a few hidden caresses while we clutched together publicly, but reacted scornfully when I attempted to get her outside alone, and the others were quite shocked. Except for Marcella, who made fun of me. Hug and hold tightly in a dance, but be satisfied with this brief, despairing feel of another body, for it's all you're going to get unless you pay a prostitute for more: southern Italy in a nutshell. Yet Sardinia was a land of promise, which I loved even if it remained unfulfilled.

As we walked home, Gavino was in one of his sullen moods, resenting the fact that my behaviour at the party had been commented on. "On the continent it would have been nothing, nothing! Yet one hears of normal people here, too, only one never seems to meet them."

"I met Marcella," Jim pointed out. "I know, though. Let's give our own party. We'll show them a thing or two."

Gavino, suddenly enthusiastic at the idea, offered to take us all for a drink and to have some polenta, a kind of cake made of maize and eaten with pepper. But when it turned out that there was none left, he became angry and seemed to think they hadn't wanted to serve him. After some shouting with the owner of the bar, he sat and sulked. Finally he went off by himself without a word.

Five

At the air terminal the coach had already arrived, and Maurice Winter was standing on the pavement waiting for his case. A few years older than myself, he looked like an overgrown schoolboy, with glasses and a protruding chin. He stepped forward to shake hands with Jim, laughing and immediately recalling the last time they'd seen each other. "Under the same table, wasn't it?"

He turned to me, too, squinting slightly. "Pleased to meet you. Sorry about the short notice. How's your love life?"

Immediately I relaxed. When Maurice's telegram had come, my main concern had been that he was to arrive on the day planned for our party, so I'd hastily invited a few tourists to make it seem it was for their entertainment too. He wanted me to return with him to Rome for a week, and I wondered why.

"I've heard a lot about you," he went on. He screwed up his nose and blinked, looking around him with interest. "Mostly of a scabrous nature. Still, what's tourism for if not for having a good time? Blimey, though, I'm just about starving. Have you two chaps had lunch yet? No? Good, then come along with me. I think the expense account will stand it. Where's a good place to eat? It's a while since I was here."

He treated us to an excellent meal—antipasto, pasta, and dessert in addition to the meat course—and in a few minutes had established a back-slapping relationship with the proprietor and a bottom-slapping relationship with the waitress. He refused to talk business at all. It seemed a good time to mention the party.

"Oh, dear, that's unfortunate."

Jim was surprised. "What's the matter with it?"

"Oh, nothing the matter, no. I was thinking it's unfortunate it should be tonight, when I've only just recovered from one hangover. Two parties on the trot tend to be a bit exhausting. Never mind, I'll survive. None of our tourists coming, I hope?"

34

Maurice came back with us to help with the preparations, insisting we should get our hangovers out of the way before discussing work. It was just a medium-sized dining room provided by Jim's hotel, with a few chairs around the walls and tables pushed to the side. The decorating took longer than expected because Jim kept wasting time on useless ideas—"But it has to be done in style," he kept saying— and it was largely Maurice's energy and organizing ability that got us through in time.

In the middle of it Isabelle swept in with an enormous box of chocolates from a boyfriend of hers whom she'd successfully managed to keep away. "It's Alberto who's coming tonight," she announced, as though he were a visiting VIP. "I have to be careful about Giovanni, though, because of the car. But he's not coming now. I told him we'd appreciate the chocolates more." She made her usual rushed departure with a "See you later!" which stayed reverberating around the room as she disappeared down the stairs.

We'd just sat down when Gavino's quiet doctor friend whom I'd met in Sassari arrived with a bottle of cognac. "To wish you luck. And to say I'm sorry I can't come. I've been called to the hospital this evening."

Jim commented on the famous Sard generosity.

The doctor placed two more bottles on the table. "And these are from Gavino. He'll be along later." He shook hands politely and departed.

I read the labels. "'Sardinian Gold.' And 'Sardinian Silver.' Sounds good."

Jim took them in his hands. "They *are* good. Sardinian Gold's a magnificent wine. Full and rich, almost like a liqueur. A little sweet, perhaps, but not unpleasantly so. Like the true glory of a Sardinian summer, warm and delightful."

"Like Marcella?" Maurice suggested.

"Yes, like Marcella, if you like. It leaves you with quite a head in the morning, though."

"Like Marcella," Maurice repeated, then he lowered his long jaw, let out a laugh, and winked.

Jim was eager to finish. "Sardinian Silver's good too. It's less sweet, just slightly sad after the other one. More like a fleeting memory of something beautiful."

"God, how poetic he is," Maurice cackled. "Just listen to him! True enough, though, they're both delightful wines."

One of the tables was now laden with bottles; another held a variety of Sardinian cheeses and a huge circle of polenta. Paper streamers and tourist posters, advertising the delights of the continent, completed the décor.

Enrico Pinna was the first to arrive, full of enthusiasm as he recalled what the two of us had watched on television some days before. "Carnival's really over now," he said when he was introduced to Jim and Maurice. "We're not used to having parties in Lent. But I think they'll all be coming—just one more thing to confess before the next mass."

Soon a crowd of tourists arrived and Enrico, overwhelmed at the sight of so many English girls, asked one to dance in his stuttering English, then stood tongue-tied as Jim casually sorted through a pile of records, deciding which to put on first. A Yorkshireman whom Jim had invited by mistake tried the inevitable pun about meeting the sardines and laughed at his own joke. The rest stood talking in loud, incongruous voices—for the English were the only ones on time. But the Sards, habitually late, had been told the party was to begin an hour earlier, so it wasn't long before there came shouting from below, raucous voices gradually ascending the stairs.

About a dozen of Enrico's friends burst in. "*Eh, Arturo, come stai?*" Shaking hands, telling me what a good fellow I was, producing more bottles. Suddenly, where there'd been only polite conversation to compete with the record player, there was noise—noise jostling to make itself heard, noise disappearing to take off coats, noise returning in force to dance and throw confetti.

An immediate realization, though, that the girls were the usual children in their behaviour. I danced, aware that I'd expected more. One girl, preferably Sard, for whom my role in this party would be special. Oh, dear, how much time and energy was spent on this so often fruitless pursuit of sex? Of love too. Had I, in Sardinia, no other thoughts? Of course I had. I had a love for literature and art, for the mystery of life, for the wonder of the universe glimpsed on any starry night above. But the torment of desire outweighed—and still outweighs—all this. Hasn't the erotic always been a sultry-sweet urge of mankind, worthy of glorification alongside our so-called higher instincts? In Sardinia the sexual urge was expressed only indirectly, but it was there, unrelenting.

A thunderous "Hello, everybody!" from the doorway and Isabelle appeared, wearing an indescribable outfit and dragging a short man behind her. "Art! Art, meet Alberto." She decided to come over herself, swimming her way through the dancers and leaving Alberto to follow in her wake.

They arrived, breathless. "This is Alberto," she repeated.

Alberto had more hair on his hands than on his head, and his grasp was moist as I shook it.

"He has some obscure position on the local council, haven't you, *amore*? I can't figure out what it is. But he's an angel, aren't you, my *angelo*? Come and meet the others."

Away again to introduce Alberto to Jim and Maurice, by which time—her voice still thundering over the room—Isabelle had promoted him to assistant mayor.

More guests from the hotel had been coming in. "How many do you make it?" I asked the Yorkshireman, who'd been counting.

"Thirty-nine. Not a bad show at all."

Enrico had gone to the doorway and gestured urgently for me to come over. "Mister Arturo, I'd like you to meet another friend of mine, Maria. She's at the university in Sassari."

A dark girl stepped forward, wrinkling up her nose as she smiled. She had one of those faces common in Italian women—too heavy-featured to be pretty, but whose interested expression made one immediately feel at home.

"Pleased to meet you." As I took her hand I heard Jim also calling to me, so without letting go I led Maria over to him as well. She smiled, acquiescing.

"This is Carmen," Jim said casually, indicating a short blond girl who'd come in with Marcella. "From Bologna."

Carmen moved close to me, brushing my jacket with her tightly restrained breasts. I let go of Maria's hand to take hold of hers. From the *continent*, it dawned on me, the wicked, immoral, enticing continent. I introduced myself, since Jim had forgotten to.

Carmen giggled. She had an air of flirtatiousness, of self-awareness, reassuring after the tomboy roughness of some of the Sard girls. I was aware of a heavy perfume. Maria was looking at her with disapproval, yet there was a shyness too, a certain awe of someone from the mainland.

Carmen's impudent eyes wouldn't release me. She told me she was a secretary in Cagliari. "You know, looking after rich old men in the investment business." Raising her voice as though asking a question, she was deliberately, if rather stupidly, provocative.

"She's visiting me for the weekend." Marcella didn't seem pleased about it and pulled Jim away to dance with her.

Maria gave a puzzled smile. "These continentals, Mister Arthur, one just doesn't know how to take them. Their ways are so different from ours."

Carmen brushed against me again. "They all consider us dreadful creatures, just because we like to enjoy ourselves. Instead of being interned after nine o'clock until marriage and interned the whole day after it!"

Maria's dark eyes shone humiliation. "But we Sards enjoy ourselves too! It's true we're not as free as you on the continent, but it wouldn't do for things to change too quickly. We enjoy the simple things. Sards love having a good time."

"Oh, we enjoy the simple things." Carmen sighed, pouting. "But aren't you going to ask me to dance?"

If only, I thought, I could meet a Sard girl who had some of the sophistication of the continental. Not a Carmen, who was too consciously sexy and without mystery—what I would sometimes desire in my dreams but not in reality—but a Sard who could stand apart a little from her own society.

I was about to dance with Carmen, but just then Gavino arrived with the girl he'd been with in Alghero.

"Oh, Mr. Arthur, what a party! Where did they all come from?"

Carmen was snatched up into the crowd.

"You know Claudia already, of course."

She gave me a challenging smile as we shook hands, then her eyes coolly dropped to my feet and rose slowly, examining me. A little pout of the lips, sudden, indefinable. Gavino's woman was attractive. But, alas, Gavino's.

"Thank you for the wine," I said, blushing.

"It was nothing. Nothing at all. Come, Claudia, let's dance."

I helped myself to some cheese and a glass of wine and watched the dancers. Gavino pressed tightly against Claudia, who smiled lazily as she caught my eye. Maria danced stiffly with one of the English tourists. Carmen giggled with one of the Sards. Enrico seemed to be enjoying it most, bouncing about ecstatically, his laughter as though spreading from his face to his glasses as he consciously tried to be pleasant to everyone. Jim danced only with Marcella, in an intense, desperate hug, while Maurice was doing an enthusiastic cha-cha as others applauded. Then suddenly he dashed across to the door to receive a bottle from a new arrival, carrying it high in the air to the makeshift bar with a wild cry of joy. Soon he started demonstrating a trick he knew to persuade others they were drunk.

The Yorkshireman cannoned into me and gave a long bray of laughter. "I'm drunk, I'm drunk!"

"One glass of Vernaccia and a mineral water!" Maurice shouted in triumph.

"Here, d'you know, there are forty-six here now."

"Get away with you! You're counting double." I pushed the Yorkshireman away and saw him begin to count again.

A crowd had gathered on the other side of the room, where Isabelle was leading Alberto flamboyantly around the floor and talking at the top of her voice about some scandalous Hollywood divorce case.

"I think she is a little mad, yes?" Gavino whispered to me.

Enrico had a different opinion. He came over shaking his head and gesticulating with his hands. "What a woman! She's very fine."

"What is it you like about her?"

"Her confidence, her ... her self-possession. You must admit that she's a very attractive woman. Are they all like that in America?"

"Probably. I've never been there."

"Of course, she's not the type that we can approve of here in Sardinia. But then, we're all humans, aren't we? One can't help admiring ... And that's why we have confession, after all. Do you think ... ?"

"Oh, go and dance with her and see what she says. Alberto looks as if he wants a rest."

I saw that Carmen was free and headed over to her, but Alberto, released from Isabelle by Enrico, got to her first.

"Forty-nine," the Yorkshireman said to me loudly.

Gavino appeared at my side. "Mr. Arthur, she's escaped you. All these lost chances in life."

Carmen had fallen into Alberto's arms and he carried her away, whispering something into her ear.

Not long after, a furious Isabelle accosted me. "What do you think of that! Alberto came to this party with me, not that young bitch in heat over there."

"He's only dancing."

"Oh, yeah. Well, he needn't think he's going to dance with me afterward. I'm finished with him!"

Alberto had now sat down with a giggling Carmen in one corner, his hairy hands crawling across her knees.

Isabelle jerked her head away from them. "Now who else could I try?"

"How did you like Enrico?"

"Oh, come on! He does nothing but talk of Catholicism. And his morals are terrible! Too strict by a long chalk."

She found a disreputable-looking Italian and soon was using various terms of endearment to him, causing bewilderment among the Sards, who were not used to hearing "loves," "treasures," "darlings"—almost Isabelle's entire Italian vocabulary—floating across the room. When Alberto finally approached her again, she brushed him aside and finally left altogether with her new partner.

"*Porca miseria!*" I heard Alberto exclaim. About to leave, too, he evidently changed his mind and later was dancing again, cheek to cheek, with Carmen.

"Only forty-one now," said the Yorkshireman, jogging absurdly past.

I sat down. Gavino, too, was alone, sipping at a glass of wine. There was no sign of his partner, Claudia.

"What do you think of our country, Mister Arthur?" The inevitable question, asked with genuine interest by Maria, who wrinkled up her face and smiled as she sat down beside me.

She nodded when I told her how oppressive I found the restrictions imposed on the women. "It's difficult for us," she said, "particularly the educated ones. But I honestly don't know how much I'd want to change things. There's still a lot to be said for our simple lives. I think we're happier, even if one sometimes wants the freedom they have on the continent. Don't human beings, after all, need restrictions on their desires? So many of our desires just lead us into trouble."

"But life *is* trouble. That's a quotation from a favourite book of mine."

Enrico had sat down beside us to listen. "So life's trouble," he repeated. "We sin, you see. But then we confess and it's all right again."

"Sin? What opportunity is there to sin in this place?"

Maria smiled. "Sin there is."

"Oh-ho-ho, Mr. Arthur, we sin! You remember that girl at the party the other evening? She let me touch her breasts for a few seconds when we were in the corridor."

"Did you confess afterward?"

"No time, no time, Mr. Arthur. But at next confession … "

"But what's wrong with it? It's natural."

"Natural, yes, but it's still sin. Or where would it stop?"

"Where would you want it to?"

"Oh, Mr. Arthur, after, well, you know, boom-boom." Enrico slapped the palm of one hand against the other.

Maria was getting uncomfortable and slipped away.

Enrico shook his head. "No, Mr. Arthur, better to leave it as wrong and confess afterward."

"But isn't that just too easy?"

"Of course. That's the good of it. Have a firm set of rules—as the Catholic Church gives—which you can break and then confess. It's simple; you can be happy. Your way you have constantly to think whether it's right or wrong, yes?"

I managed to get away from him and looked again for Maria. She was talking to Gavino—still no sign of Claudia—and had just accepted his invitation to dance when I got there. "*Pazienza*," she said to me with a note of teasing in her voice as they moved away. Gavino didn't look very happy.

I went to get another drink, but by the time I'd found a bottle of Sardinian Silver that wasn't empty, there was a general appearance of coats as the girls were starting to go. It was nearly half past nine.

"All leaving now, then," the Yorkshireman said, shaking my hand. "Nice to see so many here."

Jim returned from seeing Marcella off. "Well, that went pretty well." Thoughtfully, he wetted his handkerchief and wiped some lipstick from the side of his mouth. "Plenty of leftovers, I hope?"

"I've got a couple stacked away," Maurice assured him.

I drank gloomily. "Maurice, how come you're not married? You're older than I am, aren't you?"

"Quite a bit, my lad. But shall we say I've got home interests? Only provisional at the moment, mind you. I've never been much of a one for foreign affairs."

Jim grinned at me. "You seemed to be having quite a time of it. Every time I looked you were with a different woman."

"You know your problem, my boy?" Maurice leaned back on his chair and raised his glass in my direction. "I see it in a lot of the reps. They get one idea in their heads. Too many damn women in your life."

"Too many scattered around the edge, you mean, and not enough bloody women in the middle!"

"Anyway, you'll grow out of it in a year or so." Maurice let down his long jaw and then closed it again as he swallowed the wine on his tongue. "And become an enlightened bachelor like myself."

"I've no objection to leading a bachelor's life, as long as it's enjoyable." It wasn't, though, and I wasn't sure what being an "enlightened" bachelor meant.

Jim poured himself another glass. "That friend of yours, Gavino, is a queer chap. You remember how he came with that girl again? It caused some comment, incidentally. Well, she walked out on him halfway through, didn't you notice? And he seems so nervous with women generally. It's unusual for an Italian."

At that moment there was suddenly a rattle of small stones on the window. I walked over to look out.

"Eh, Mr. Arturo!" Gavino and Enrico stood down below, waving some more bottles they'd got from somewhere. "Let us back in. The door's locked."

By midnight the five of us were swearing lifelong friendship to one another, and we all drank a solemn toast in Sardinian Silver to bachelorhood.

Six

Maurice wanted me to go with him to Rome so I could be in on the discussions with the new rep who would be coming out to Olbia.

"We'll be leaving tomorrow evening. On the boat, I'm sorry to say. Couldn't fiddle air travel for more than one. At least it'll give us a chance to go over to Olbia during the day for you to see the place. You haven't been there yet, I take it?"

"No."

Olbia was on the east coast, from where the ship to Civitavecchia, the port for Rome, departed. That ship to the east, one to Genoa in the north, and another from Cagliari to Palermo in Sicily: such were the nightly links from Sardinia to the continent.

"Is Olbia important?"

"It's the closest town to all the best beaches. The Costa Smeralda's where the future is in tourism, believe me. Anyway, you'll like Margaret. She's quite a character in her way, very reliable."

"Young?"

"Twenty-five. I shouldn't think she's the type for a dreadful fellow like you, though. Technically, you'll be in charge of her, but she'll probably be fairly independent. She worked for us in Rome some years ago, and she's been to Sardinia once before."

I welcomed the opportunity for a break, secure in the knowledge that there was a Sardinia to return to.

The hotel staff was dismayed at the thought that I might be leaving them. That night Teresa pretended tears and again did her body demonstration to show me she was as sexy as any Roman girl. Convincing them all that I'd be returning gave me a great deal of pleasure.

The next morning Maurice and I set off on the train, travelling inland into the northern part of the mountains through bare, rocky country and past villages almost empty of people. "The wild, wicked fairyland of Sardinia," Maurice commented.

Olbia was a pleasant, white town at the head of a large gulf of shimmering blue, into which projected a long stone pier. Moored to it was the ship that would take us that evening to the continent. In the afternoon one of the hotel keepers drove us on an inspection of some of the beaches, and we returned in time for the *passeggio*, which here took place in the main street, closed to traffic for the purpose.

The ship left at ten. We travelled tourist class, and I soon found myself relaxing in the serenity that always comes to me on a vehicle in motion. Unlike the trip from Genoa, I could now rejoice in the extraordinary familiarity of it all. I was on the Tyrrhenian Sea, on my way to a city I hadn't yet been to. The self-contained world of a ship— better even than a plane or a train, mere rows of seats hurtling through space—gives surely, even on an overnight trip, a foretaste of the rich expectancy of eternity.

We docked at Civitavecchia at six the next morning and were in Rome in time for breakfast.

Margaret was tall, with long brown hair that constantly drifted over her face. Pretty, and typically English in a way I couldn't define. Over lunch in Maurice's hotel he explained that her main job in Olbia until the tourists started coming would be to make contacts with the various hotels and local coach firm, and keep me informed.

She sat calmly, looking efficient. "So for routine matters I'll get my instructions from Arthur here? Send him all my accounts and so on rather than to you in Rome?"

Very precise, I thought. But once business was over she immediately forgot about it, attacking her lunch with appetite and ordering the next course as though she were quite at home in Italy.

The business seemed already finished, and I wondered why I had to stay in Rome until the end of the week.

Maurice laughed at me. "Don't you want to see the place? I don't want my reps doing their job badly because they've lost all contact with civilization. Besides which, you can keep Margaret company for a week. It'll be a while before she comes out to Sardinia—the usual Italian bureaucracy—and I've got too much work to look after her. After all, I can't have her seduced by the first handsome Roman who comes along before she even starts work."

She smiled at Maurice coyly. "I've been here before, you know. I'm well able to look after myself." Her face had changed. Her eyes seemed to mist over and then shine through the mist, producing a beauty the more attractive for being momentary.

"You'll have to look after yourself even more with Arthur. He's worse than any Roman I've met."

The same smile was directed at me. Nonchalantly, she said, "I'll have to handle him firmly, then."

"Handle me however you like. What about you? How do you like to be handled?"

"Preferably with gloves."

In the afternoon she took me on a sightseeing tour of the modern Rome. She wandered around serenely, looking in the shops almost lazily; yet underneath there was an interest that wasn't immediately obvious. Her attitude was one of contentment, taking everything as it came without going out of her way for anything. Walking more slowly than I usually did, she was intelligently aware of what was around her, like an interested outsider in an art gallery.

We had tea on the Via Nazionale. "Christ!" she said when she saw the bill. "They believe in making you pay in this damn place!"

For the evening she'd arranged to meet some old friends and suggested I should go along with her. The four young men, about the same age as herself, paid her the usual compliments, while she played up to them, using her eyes in the same way as earlier.

She turned to one of them, who'd scarcely said anything but just looked at her adoringly. "And you, Mario, are you still chasing the women as much as ever?"

"Miss Margaret, how could I chase other women when I am only thinking of you?"

She put her head to one side and laughed graciously. "Oh, thank you."

She turned out to be oddly, ironically flirtatious—and would occasionally wink at me as though sharing a secret, while her friends delighted in being gallant and obviously held her in the highest respect. When we had to go, the four Romans accompanied us as far as the door of the hotel, made the usual leave-taking speech, and all kissed her hand in turn—which she dangled out for them, looking at me as if to say, "I wish they'd hurry up and get on with it."

"They're a nice crowd," she said. "It makes you feel good to be with a group like that after the stuffiness of England. They're a wonderful lot, the Italians."

"Once you've put them in their place."

She looked at me and said nothing.

It wasn't until the following lunchtime that I saw her again. Maurice and I had already started our meal when she came in carrying a number of packages.

"What have you bought yourself?" I said aggressively.

"Nothing I can show you." She sat down. "Christ, I'm hungry."

"Frilly or plain? I'll look forward to seeing them."

She turned to Maurice. "How am I going to manage with him as my boss?"

In the unusual exhilaration she produced in me, I continued teasing her for most of the meal, while she made a show of bashfulness. This was the kind of schoolchildren's banter we adopted from the beginning. Stupid perhaps—it's embarrassing to put such nonsense down. In the afternoon we went out together again, and again I found she enjoyed my laughingly suggestive comments while pretending to be shocked.

We had serious conversations as well. Particularly about the Italians, whom Margaret regarded with amused admiration. For most of the time she appeared to be a perfect English lady, until she'd let herself down by a burst of laughter, a sudden obscenity, or a coarse joke.

In the evening the three of us met for a drink in the hotel bar and, with Maurice as audience, Margaret and I decided to enact a violent passion for each other, getting odd looks from the other people there, which made us laugh even more. Maurice looked on in amusement. I was a little drunk perhaps. But Margaret was a person I could joke with, who made me happy. It was that simple.

It seemed she had heard about Isabelle. "She wasn't there last year as well, was she?"

"Sure was!"

"The one who was had up for bathing in the nude near Fertilia at midnight? Tallish, blond hair—probably not very natural nowadays—age about forty-two?"

Maurice gave a cackle. "That's her all right. What happened?"

"I don't know the full story. I think someone dared her to do it, only a peasant woman saw her and complained. She got off with a warning, I think. One of her boyfriends had influence with the police."

Alone with Maurice in our room, I threw myself happily onto the bed. "Hell, I'm enjoying this trip!"

He grinned as he took off his glasses and examined them carefully. "I must say, Margaret's got more to her than I gave her credit for."

"She's not usually like that?"

"She's always full of fun. Doubtless you bring out the cruder side in her."

"I haven't met such a nice English girl for a long time." I lay thinking about her. "You know, she reminds me of another friend of mine, about the only platonic girlfriend I've got. It's odd. We're the best of friends and yet we could never fall for each other in a thousand years."

"You couldn't fall for Margaret either?"

"You don't fall for people you can flirt with too easily. It's too much fun. You need a certain tension to be able to fall for someone." For a moment, though, I was uncertain.

It was an extraordinary week. Even then I felt I would never recapture that relaxed happiness. With most people, I'm more serious, my shirt stuffed with my consciousness of desperately wanting a meaning for life. My relationship with Margaret was from the first one of sarcastic passion, consisting of flippant exchanges of suggestive inanities.

We all met again the next morning, and I greeted her as boyishly as before, while she responded in the same aggressive manner. My mood continued for the rest of the day, and walking around the Roman antiquities—this time Maurice accompanied us—I kept reverting to my act of enamoured admirer, jealous husband, or contrite lover, with incongruous remarks thrown in to destroy the illusion. All ridiculously harmless.

During the week she always preserved her ironic attitude toward life. Once, a more than usually persistent Italian tried to get into conversation with her. "Oh, go away," she said. "You haven't shaved for a week." For a few moments he tried to treat it as a joke, but his dignity had been wounded and he left. "Christ! He really has gone too!"

But the week was not without its sadness, particularly in the bar where we all went dancing on the last evening. I was depressed at the sight of so many young lovers, and suddenly I wanted to be one of them. I danced with Margaret, half wishing our relationship could be more than a verbal flirtation. It was ludicrous, though: even dancing with her was difficult because she was taller.

By habit I continued fooling, but my heart wasn't in it. When I sat down and Margaret went off to dance with Maurice, I started wondering what was wrong. Not that I wasn't enjoying myself: for this very reason I'd chosen to be a tourist representative. But at times, in unexpected moments of doubt, I felt almost like an exile, rejected by people who felt I was on a perpetual holiday. I was afraid to face up to the routine existence that is the lot of all serious people, both wishing for it and appalled by it.

"What do you think of the tourist business?" I asked Maurice when he and Margaret returned. "As a way of life, I mean."

"It's a makeshift existence really, isn't it? I've been lucky, of course, or I'd never have stayed in it. I still feel dissatisfied at times. You can enjoy yourself, but does that get you anywhere? I'll have to think very carefully if it comes to the point of my wanting to get married."

"You think you might? The girl at home?"

"I'd like to. I'm not sure how keen she is, though."

At Civitavecchia the next day I stood on the quayside beside the ship—the *Arborea*, I noticed—saying the last, oddly formal, goodbyes. I no longer wanted to return immediately to Sardinia. The next week, I thought, would be intolerably dull.

A short, blond girl with an exciting figure went aboard, and I tried to joke lightly. "Pity the cabins are strictly allotted according to sexes." Then I forgot her as one does with strangers who have only momentarily attracted one's attention.

"You're betraying me already!" Margaret objected. "Now I shan't have a moment's rest while you're away from me!"

I went aboard, not bothering to find my cabin straightaway, but stayed on deck watching the complicated procedure of departure until the ship was underway. I waved goodbye to Maurice and Margaret, suddenly alone. I wanted Margaret still to be there with me, to cheer me up in her casual way. I've always been a person of moods.

Wanting love, I picked up my case and started looking for my cabin.

Seven

The journey had started badly, with the type of mistake that never failed to infuriate me: a muddle over my ticket that, despite my protests, meant I had to pay extra and travel second class instead of tourist. As I washed in my cabin—the other bunk was unoccupied—I angrily rehearsed to myself my letter of complaint. Then I went up on deck, vainly searching for signs of the extra luxury for which I had been forced to pay. I stopped by the barrier separating second from tourist class and leaned over the rail, venting my bad temper on the greying sea beneath. If I looked back I could still see the coast I was leaving. Civilization, I thought, compared with the barbarity of Sardinia.

Then I noticed the girl I'd commented on to Maurice standing on the other side of the barrier and gazing like myself out to sea. I glanced at her casually, admiring her full figure under a woollen jumper. About twenty, I thought, and attractive despite her lack of height. Her blond hair was short and untidy, and her roundish face was a little sullen. Then she turned and looked at me, too, with a hesitant smile, so that with my usual initial embarrassment I turned away. When I looked the next time she smiled more. Now her eyes lit up, making her irresistibly mischievous and friendly. Mischievous: that was one of the traits that fascinated me most about Anna. For now I just noted that she seemed pleasant, and when she smiled once more I asked, "You going to Sardinia, then?"

She answered in good English, but with an accent. "But of course. You also?"

We both laughed at the stupidity of our questions.

"Yes, I work there."

"An Englishman working in Sardinia. It's very unusual."

"How did you know I was English?" My Italian still wasn't perfect, but I was enough of a linguist not to betray my origin.

"I heard you and your friends talking on the ... on the kwayside, is that it?"

I smiled, correcting her pronunciation. "Quayside."

"Oh, yes. You were cuddling up to a man and a girl. She is your girlfriend? Oh, I suppose I shouldn't ask such things." Her eyes waited to see if I minded her lack of tact.

"No, she isn't."

"And you work in Sardinia?"

I hesitated, preferring to speak Italian. Who was it that said talking to women in foreign languages gives one a greater sense of freedom, of irresponsibility? So in Italian I told her of how I worked for a tourist company in Alghero.

She explained that she worked for a cosmetics shop in Rome. "It has a branch in Sassari. I go there every few months. But my parents live in Tempio. I'm Sard, you see." Her Italian was neat, precise, almost refined after the hard Sard tones I was used to.

"You don't sound like a Sard."

Deliberately, she exaggerated her cultured north-Italian vowels, which she'd obviously taken the trouble to learn. "I don't want to. I visit my parents when I go there, but I don't like it in Sardinia. People are so backward. Be like everyone else, behave in the same eternal way, marry someone your parents approve of, and serve him like a slave for the rest of your life. That's not my idea of how to live."

I was reminded of Gavino.

Together we watched the sun sinking in a cloudy haze over the sea.

I talked casually of my work, told her some of my more ridiculous stories about the tourists to make her laugh—not forgetting the Yorkshireman at the party—constantly anxious that she might get bored with me. She said she'd once worked in England with a family and asked me to speak English again. For a while we both spoke English, and then the conversation continued sometimes in one language, sometimes in the other.

She told me she was twenty-two.

"Not married?"

"No." She looked sullen again and stared grimly at the sea. "I couldn't care less. *Me ne frego.*" Again, the tight, northern vowels. "Anyway, what does it matter? *Il matrimonio è la tomba dell'amore*—marriage is the grave of love. Don't you think so? If I loved someone, I wouldn't insist on marrying him, you understand? I'd give everything.

Love is all or nothing. I'd want either the complete thing or nothing at all. Perhaps I'm wrong. I don't know. It doesn't matter."

I was puzzled by her sudden, unasked-for confessions and the weariness that went with them.

"I don't quite understand."

"I'm sorry. It's only me. I'm not so very happy really, I suppose. I think too much, that's all."

The water was a pink and steel-blue colour now, from the dying sun ahead of the ship. I asked her name.

"Anna Lorcas. It's Spanish, of course. A lot of Sards are of Spanish descent."

"Yes, I know. Mine's Arthur Fraser. That's a Scottish name for you."

"Oh, very beautiful! Scotland, I mean, not the name!"

She looked at me impishly once more, and I wondered again— as inevitably I had from the moment we'd started to talk—whether something more might develop. I found myself liking her and excited by her presence and the soft breasts that, as she'd drawn closer, had momentarily brushed against me. Yet I was nervous, as always when I started to like and want someone. I glanced down at her in the darkness that had suddenly descended, thinking how an attractive body like hers would be wasted in Sardinia. Used for huddling up to in close dances, pawed by frustrated males, and finally surrendered after marriage, only to be buried under defensive layers of possessiveness. She saw me examining her and gave another of her smiles, about to say something when a sudden blast on the horn startled both of us.

"Surely a girl like you shouldn't be unhappy?" My question was banal, of course, as though happiness had anything to do with being attractive.

"Things just seem to go wrong. At home everything's so ordinary. I can't bear what other people consider important. And the way they live. Going to work, coming home and doing nothing, subscribing to a lot of out-of-date principles that they don't really feel. Everybody knows my father has a ... how do you say it in English? You know, he goes to bed with another woman."

"Mistress?"

"Mistress. And a woman has a ... ?"

"Lover."

"Oh, yes. Everyone knows he has a mistress, but they all pretend not to notice. And because I try to be sincere, to say what I mean, I'm not accepted. I've got very few real friends. But I don't believe in compromise. So often it's just hypocrisy. I try to be truthful in everything. That's what I meant when I spoke about love. Love, I think, is the most important, perhaps the only worthwhile thing in life. So it has to be all or nothing."

In a way I agreed with her, and of course there was nothing particularly original in what she was saying. But I still felt that she was exaggerating love's importance in life.

We continued our conversation over dinner, for which I had to go through to the ship's inferior class as Anna was travelling tourist, in dormitory accommodation. A girl I'd commented on to Maurice, an attractive stranger, and here I was sitting in the restaurant with her, late at night, in an unreal, undulating, boat atmosphere. Oh, some might say it was nothing extraordinary, but the world wasn't blasé about travel then, or even about romance. The girl I'd found vaguely sexy, a desirable female, was now a breathing, vulnerable human being like myself, and if anything her sexuality and desirability had become greater. There was an immediate attraction between us that, even now as we sat opposite each other, caused us accidentally to brush fingertips, wrists, and hands together.

Anna was serious and lighthearted in turn. She spoke of her disappointment with life, then joked maliciously about some of the other passengers. "Imagine what it would be like to be married to him. You'd be squashed, no?" or "Do you think those two nuns over there are really vir … how do you say it in English?"

After dinner we strolled around the ship together, then stopped to talk, looking out on the black, moonless Tyrrhenian Sea. Then we were silent, not knowing what to say to each other.

"I have to get something out of my luggage."

Suddenly she left me standing by myself. I waited, wondering whether she was going to come back. And then she seemed to have been gone too long to return. Had I been wrong about her, lost my opportunity? "It can't finish just like that," I said aloud. "It mustn't finish now. Don't let it end just like that." Looking into the black water beneath, I remembered how earlier I'd been annoyed that everything had gone wrong and thought that the entire trip had been spoilt.

When she came back she was nervous. "Would you help me, stay with me for a while? Some men started to follow me. I don't like them. And now they won't leave me alone."

"You could come to my cabin. There's no one else in it."

"Oh, so you think … you, too, would like to seduce me? Of course I don't mind—that you want it, that is. But I won't let you."

I put my arm around her protectively, and we started toward my cabin. But soon Anna's pursuers found us: three youths who immediately fixed upon her with their eyes, strolling toward her, making what I assumed were lecherous comments—I didn't understand their dialect—and taking no notice of me at all.

"Southerners," Anna said, betraying something of the northerner's contempt she must have assimilated in Rome. "Sicilians, I think. We just speak in English, yes?"

Before we'd reached the barrier to go into second class, two of the men had overtaken us and blocked our way. Then they stood in a semicircle leering at Anna. One approached me and whispered in my ear, asking how much he ought to offer her. Another tried stroking her cheek admiringly.

"How dare you," she said, frightened and moving aside. "*Ma come si permette!*" She pushed past him and angrily opened the barrier.

I could almost feel them breathing down my neck as the pursuit continued in second class as well.

"They're jealous of you. They think you've won, that you've—what do you say?—got there first. How ignorant they are! If *one* can, anyone can, that's the attitude."

I finally found one of the ship's officers who, after my brief explanation, went up to the Sicilians, demanded to see their tickets, and promptly escorted them back to the tourist side of the barrier.

"Just as well he didn't ask to see *my* ticket," Anna laughed. "What would I have done without you?" She gave me a little hug, then drew back and said, "Ooh, *scusa*." It was half past twelve. We went down to my cabin.

She sat on the lower bunk while I perched on a chair opposite, looking at her in the shadows. Neither of us turned on the light. I was nervous now, afraid of trying to kiss her straightaway, of seeming presumptuous. I took her hand. "Tired?"

"Not now. I will be later."

Silence, except for the steady hum of the ship's engines and the whirr of the fan in the cabin. The floor was rocking only very slightly, just enough to remind us that the sea was beneath. The dark cabin seemed remote, cut off from the outside world.

"You know," she said, "it's strange. This is the sort of thing that doesn't happen often. The atmosphere, on a ship at one in the morning, with the light coming in through the porthole creating all these shadows. Perhaps it's just me being silly, but it's ... rather romantic."

I moved to sit on the bunk next to her.

"Oh, I'm a stupid girl," she said just before I kissed her. Then she put her arms out to draw me to her, to kiss me again, lightly. She stared into my eyes.

"Perhaps I'm stupid as well."

We clung together, kissing deeply, feeling each other's warmth. Relieved, since we both wanted it. When I think of it now, it was oddly innocent—for we were young and naive, and despite everything Anna was Italian, Sard. And then, it was a long time ago, when not all girls were aggressively liberated. I, too, was, well, not inexperienced, but forever surprised that girls could be made love to, except for the tourists, where everything—within limits—was routinely easy. Anna and I grasped passionately at each other, pressing together and then pausing after a while, rather in awe of ourselves.

"How crazy we are," she repeated.

Incredibly, I was content not to press for more; satisfied with what, from the point of view of the seducer of women to which in other moods I aspired, was nothing to speak of. Anna caressed me boldly enough, but when I pushed her gently back onto the bunk she resisted, saying "Oh, no, you are very dangerous." She lay there, though, for a minute or two before she struggled to her feet and walked quickly over to the porthole.

"I ought to go back to the dormitory," she said, not very convincingly. She turned around, looking out at the sea.

I went over to her and held my arms across her body, while she leaned back against me and we rocked together. Then she broke away, walked around the cabin smiling happily, and suddenly came running back to be kissed again.

"It's nice to be stupid sometimes." I lifted her in my arms and swung her around. "You're not really going to leave me, are you?"

I put her down and she tapped me teasingly on the nose. "Of course not. *È una stupidaggine, però* ... You are—how do you say?— one of my follies."

I kissed her again, sliding my hand down over her jumper to feel the shape of her breast underneath.

"Wicked!" she said, slapping my hand gently and moving it away. "And you make me feel the same."

We again sat on the bunk together, our arms around each other. A few minutes later my hand returned to her breasts, and she no longer prevented me from feeling their firmness under their protective covering of wool. Then we lay back, resting, content just to feel our bodies moving gently beside each other. Looking up at the other bunk above us and the dim forms of the cabin we talked of all kinds of things—much inevitably containing sexual innuendoes, and we even spent some time translating sexual terms, like a couple of adolescents.

"You know," she said, "one of the loveliest things about this is that it's so out of the ordinary, temporary. Something that will finish tomorrow. Tomorrow—today, I mean. Something that can't last is always beautiful, don't you agree?"

"I don't want it to end today."

"Who knows these things?"

She became merry again, talking once more of her *stupidaggini*. We laughed all the more when we realized the date was April 1. "I think we are both *pesci d'aprile*—April … ?"

"April fools."

The night continued, in quick bursts of eagerness for each other but longer periods of rest, in a spirit of fun that made my vague memory of Jenny's frenzied sexuality seem remote. Finally Anna allowed me to put my hand under her jumper, to press my palm against the protection of her bra and run my fingertips gently along the top over the rising contours of flesh, but she would give me no more than this.

"You know," she said, holding my hand to restrain it from plunging lower, "it's funny. I don't feel in the least ashamed doing this with you." Despite what she'd said about love, she still had her inhibitions.

"Arturo, my dear," she said later, almost sarcastically, "do you realize we'll soon have known each other for a whole night?"

"It seems almost like a month. We seem to know each other so well." Ironic words in retrospect, for we knew each other not at all. "Of course, we could know each other a lot better yet."

She pulled my hair, then giggled. "That doesn't come until next month. I've told you, I won't let you … fuck, is that right? … me. I'm enjoying this month too much."

Eventually we decided to sleep for a while and I left Anna for the bunk above. I must have dozed for about half an hour when I woke to find her standing on the ladder looking over at me. When she saw I was awake she impulsively leaned over and kissed me, then climbed up and snuggled beside me.

It was nearly five o'clock, and with the ship arriving in another hour it was necessary for Anna to leave. She got up unwillingly, bent down and kissed me once more and climbed slowly down the steps. "*Tu sei un tesoro*," she whispered.

We both went out and had coffee at the bar, blinking in the morning light. Then came her silent departure to get her things, the quayside of Olbia, and the slightly faded familiarity of Sardinia.

There was still the train journey. As it rattled through the dreary countryside, we sat together, holding hands, tired for the lack of sleep. Anna, in her own way, was as enthusiastic and loving as she'd been during the night. "If the light would only go out in the next tunnel I would kiss you," she said impishly. Then, when the couple opposite fell asleep, she took the opportunity just the same, and we continued kissing gently, looking around every so often to see if anyone else was watching. Childish, schoolboyish—and, in Sardinia, indecent.

"You know," she said seriously, looking out of the window, "I could love you. It's not often like that, but somehow … "

I was flattered, but caution asserted itself. "Don't," I said gently. I asked for her address. "If you'll be here for some days, we might be able to see each other?"

"Tomorrow, could you phone?"

"Of course."

Later, on the platform in Sassari, we formally shook hands. "*Ciao*, my little April fool," I said to her.

Eight

"And so we went to the cabin to stretch out on separate bunks and get some sleep, only somehow it happened that we kept to the same bunk and didn't get any sleep at all."

"Good for you," Jim said. "I rather envy you. Better not mention that to Marcella, of course."

"Just think: if it hadn't been for the mistake over my ticket, if it hadn't been for those blasted Sicilians even … You know, it's things like this which restore my faith in some kind of divinity putting in a kind word now and then."

In the hotel I'd been welcomed home enthusiastically. Teresa, with a sixth sense, was at her most outrageously provocative. The others obviously noticed something too.

"Leave him alone. Can't you see he's in love?" the old lady said with a little grin.

"Oh, he's in love!" Eagerly they demanded more information.

"It's just a Roman girl I met," I couldn't resist saying. When pressed further, I told them her name was Anna and that she was really a Sard, which brought forth howls of approval.

I phoned Anna as arranged. For the first two days she was busy, but she'd have a free afternoon on the Wednesday. "You will come to see me, yes?"

"Of course." Jim would look after my tourists for me.

On Wednesday I arrived in Sassari long before one o'clock, when Anna finished work. The shop was elegant, and she was in a back room, busy with some books. When finally she was ready, my shyness reasserted itself, so I gave her only a quick kiss.

"How modest you are, my dear," she teased me.

In the car, she kissed me herself, her tongue darting against mine, before I drove away.

"Where do you want to go?" I asked.

"Take me to the sea. There's a beach near Porto Torres. Let me just look at you for a while."

"You want to go swimming?"

"No, it's not hot enough yet." Unexpectedly she giggled. "Besides, I haven't got a swimsuit. If it were only you … Have you got one? No? Oh, what fun! But I don't want to provide an exhibition for all the boys from Porto Torres."

"I'm sure they'd appreciate it."

"You think so? In that case, you'd have to stand on the beach and collect the money." She leaned over and kissed me on the ear, apologizing as the car swerved.

During the drive we didn't say a great deal. For some of the time she was sad and explained that she was thinking how short a time this was to last, that in another week she'd already be back in Rome. "But here with you I'm happy."

We arrived in Porto Torres and found the beach, a small stretch of sand framed by rocks and low cliffs, intimate and happily deserted. For a while we kissed and hugged together, eagerly, timidly.

"You know," she said, "my only really happy days in my youth were when I was swimming. We used to go to Isola Rossa, on the northern coast, not that far away. We must go there together someday. It's a wonderful place. So wild and lonely, and the sea's so passionate."

I laughed at her description.

"Normal existence is so dull. Only love, perhaps … But look at that marvellous blue sea, the red rocks. Life itself is so petty. It's only people who can't think who are content with it."

At that moment we became aware of whistling and shouting, obscene comments. A group of youths had appeared on the reddish cliffs above and immediately started jeering at the sight of a man and a woman alone.

Anna was sullen. "I don't like Italian men! They're so rough, so lacking in feeling." Suddenly she was kissing me, passionately, pulling me from the rock we were sitting on and pressing me into the sand, her body stretched out on mine, in defiance of the youths looking down on us.

The shouting got louder, and we looked up to see the men facing toward us and urinating.

"Let's go," she said in disgust.

"Sards!"

"Oh, no! Sards would never behave like that. Sards can be shocked, it's true. They can be jealous of their own women, protective. But they have an inborn courtesy. Those are certainly strangers—Sicilians or Calabrians, they seem to be everywhere—not Sards. You mustn't think that badly of us."

We crossed the beach and went up a path to the top of the cliffs, leaving the men behind. Playfully, we picked flowers and sang. Yet underneath Anna was still serious. "In a week or so's time you'll have forgotten me. You'll have found someone else here in Sardinia while I'm in Rome."

"Perhaps you'll find someone in Rome."

"Perhaps."

We had a drink at a bar on the coast nearby, holding hands.

"These people think I'm your mistress, yes?"

We drove back to Sassari and went to the cinema, a sentimental love story that fit our mood. Afterward, we had a meal in one of the less expensive restaurants. It was now well past the time when all good Sard girls should be safely at home, which made it all the more exciting.

"I've got something to tell you, Arthur. I didn't want to before. I have to go home to Tempio for a couple of days. I won't be able to see you again before Saturday. Our time together's going to be so short."

I drove the car out of the town and found a spot off the road, where we both moved into the darkness of the back seat, pressing together in a breathless kiss. I was almost afraid because of my urgent emotional involvement, not considering that it simply could have been an urge for sex. It was that time of life when sexual desire is so intense that it is itself an emotion, but I wasn't yet experienced enough to understand this. I felt almost ill with its demands, while constantly asking myself if such passion could last. This time Anna no longer tried to stop me, so that inevitably I undid her clothes and my hands explored her body: her gorgeous young breasts springing out toward me as I removed her bra, sweet-smelling as I took them in my mouth and ran my tongue around her large, stiff nipples. She gave a start as I slipped my hand under her skirt and panties and felt how soft and moist she was, but she didn't stop me.

"I'm so stupid," she repeated as I slipped my finger inside her. "I feel so confused. I don't know what's happening to me." She pulled my head to her breasts again. I felt drawn to her almost against my will. I'd been in love before; now I told myself—with all the wisdom of immaturity—that I didn't want to fall in love again.

"Anna," I said nevertheless, "I don't know what I feel. I don't know whether it will last—it probably won't—but just in this moment, just for tonight, even if I should feel different tomorrow, let me say now that I love you."

"I too," she answered. "*Anch'io.*"

I don't know why we drew back from making love completely. The car was small, but that was perhaps no more than an excuse. Perhaps both of us were too much in awe of ourselves; perhaps there was an unconscious superstition that to make love then would have been to reach the end of our relationship. But I was still incredibly naive, and so, perhaps, was Anna. It was one of the things that made her so attractive.

Finally, I took her back to where she was staying, repeating that I loved her as I said goodnight.

"Yes," she said. "Yes."

I drove back to Alghero not understanding how, normally so cautious, I could have committed myself to words. "April fool," I chuckled to myself. But I was uneasy, wanting to rest from the emotion of unsatisfied desire—or perhaps I wanted to keep it unsatisfied and prolong it.

There were two days to live through before I could see Anna again. On one of them I went to a concert with Enrico, and on the way home I told him of my meeting with her.

Enrico showed his enthusiasm. "Oh, Mister Arturo, what's she like? *È buona?*"

"*Buona.*" There was nothing offensive in his enthusiasm for a woman with whom one might enjoy physical pleasure.

"You'll be getting married soon, then?" he went on, spoiling it.

"No, I shan't marry her. Anna's not your conventional Sard."

Enrico looked disapproving. "Well, in that case … Eh, Mister Arturo, I shall pray that your sins be forgiven you. May you have plenty to be forgiven! And do me a favour. Give her to me afterward. I haven't had a *buona ragazza* for a long time, *capisci?*"

On the Saturday morning a letter arrived from Jenny, and I stuffed it into my pocket for a later occasion. Shortly after midday I was driving over to Sassari once more to collect Anna and bring her to Alghero.

She was strangely silent in the car and then said suddenly, "Arthur, I'm leaving tomorrow."

Was there relief mixed with my disappointment? A feeling of complying with the inevitable?

"So this will be the last time," she went on, "unless you could come back to Rome with me."

"I wish I could."

Silence.

"Anna," I went on, keeping my eyes on the road ahead. "What I said the other night—I still mean it, you know."

"Don't say things that aren't true," she said, trying to be sarcastic and not succeeding. She was in a strange mood, as though hurt by the fact that we had to part and angry with me for it. But then she rested her head on my shoulder with a sigh of resignation.

In Alghero we walked by the sea, then had a drink at one of my usual bars, where somehow we got involved in a long conversation with the proprietor. Anna kept looking at me, eager to be alone with me, yet I purposely delayed, not wanting to spoil our moment of coming together by rushing things. We returned to the hotel to go up to my room, and without saying anything lay down on the bed together.

For the first few minutes we pressed painfully close, then separated again while I undressed her. I took her, naked, in my hands once more, kissing her body tenderly and deliberately showing my excited admiration. Now I was prepared for us finally to make love, and yet there was a sense of disappointment, too, as though it would be reducing our relationship to the same level as it had been with Jenny, whose letter remained in my pocket. But now it was Anna who said no, preventing disappointment by stopping me, when I was half undressed, from removing my trousers.

"No, my dear," she said in her deep, mock sarcastic voice. "You could do anything if I were absolutely sure, you know that, but I still don't know exactly what I feel."

Perhaps I was relieved, afraid of making love to her and more carefree without that necessity. It was still like being in a world consisting, despite my trousers, of our bodies and emotions alone: an intimacy the more complete, paradoxically, for being partial. And inevitably the limits were relaxed as our desire grew stronger, our hands explored further, our caresses became wilder and deeper, and our aching for each other more intense—until we grasped desperately at a mutual, manual climax, and then suddenly there was calm and we rested warmly together.

Finally I removed my trousers; they were wet and uncomfortable, and Anna couldn't resist a giggling obscene comment. Then as she caught sight of our naked bodies in the mirror, she suddenly became embarrassed. "Oh, look how naked I am! Oh, no, hide me!" and she gave a little squeak trying to cover her body with her arms. She threw herself against me to use me as a shield, so she should appear decent once more.

We got dressed in time for the *passeggio*, so I could parade her through the streets of Alghero and show her to my friends. We met Jim and Marcella. We met Enrico, who joked with us and told Anna how for the last few days I'd been talking of nothing but her. And then we met Gavino, here in Alghero with yet another glossy woman looking unashamedly bored with his company. He invited us for a drink, and I introduced Anna simply as a friend of mine. He was hardly in one of his better moods and appeared almost not to notice her, even though he seemed honoured to be introduced.

"What an odd person," she commented after we'd left. "He seemed to be afraid of me. And the woman he was with, she was a … ?"

"I don't know."

As we drove back to Sassari in the dark, she sang Italian and American pop songs to herself in a pleasant, expressive voice. She was mysterious, intriguing, as the lights from other cars flickered across her face. "*La Belle Dame sans Merci* hath thee in thrall," I thought. The quotation from Keats seemed appropriate.

"Arthur, come back with me to Rome, just for a day or so."

Why did I refuse? I could have gone, had another day with her before returning. Perhaps it was a sense of the pointlessness of it, a feeling of not wanting to spoil what had already passed. She was to return to Sardinia in three months' time, or I might be going to Rome earlier. I'd see her again. Better to just see what happened, I reasoned.

She was disappointed.

"I could see you tomorrow, before you leave."

She shook her head. "I'm going on the day boat—they put on an extra one before Easter."

I'd forgotten it was nearly Easter.

We reached Sassari and drove to the small *pensione* that her company provided for her. We kissed a little in the car, but there was no point in further intimacies. I said good night, repeating what I felt about her. She went in, turning to wave before disappearing behind a dull, brown door.

I drove away feeling weary. Emptiness lay ahead, and I remembered with a shock how I'd felt the same when I'd left Rome.

The next day an unexpected excuse cropped up to go to Olbia, but too late for me to see Anna onto the ship. When the business there was over, I wandered around the white streets thinking of how a week ago the two of us had arrived here after our night together; of how this morning, even, it was from here, from the end of the long stone pier, that she'd left for Rome. The evening ship was already in, but not *our* ship. I sent her a postcard.

In the late afternoon, walking along by the harbour, I came across the letter I'd received the previous morning. Jenny wrote that she was contriving to come back in August. I read it twice, screwed it up, and tossed it into the sea.

Nine

My letter to Anna was a long outpouring of uncontrolled emotion. In my enthusiasms I rarely paused to think or use artifice; in love, tormented as I was by doubts, I always spurned caution. Yet I wasn't prepared to abandon my job and go to Anna in Rome. We may complain that our lives are boring, yet conscience, even inappropriate conscience, really does make cowards of us all.

Easter was approaching, and in Sardinia the preparations for another festa came as a sudden release from the grey monotony of Lent. As soon as Holy Week arrived the processions started, gathering from all over the town and involving every street in the sorrow of Christ's passion, to finish, invariably, at the cathedral. Banners and images were followed by people either in mourning or in strange costumes with long-peaked caps, which gave them the appearance of walking birds. A monotonous chanting, beautiful despite the droning of the town band marching in front, accompanied the processions. I was impressed by the seriousness of the onlookers: some stood silently, some kneeled in adoration, while the police stiffly saluted the figure of the Madonna, itself escorted by two pious *carabinieri*.

On the Wednesday of Holy Week the first letter arrived from Anna, who, not knowing of my enthusiasms, hadn't expected to hear from me. She wrote that she was happy thinking of me but confused, unable to say exactly what she felt, only that "she might have loved me." I spent a long time composing my next letter.

In the meantime more tourists were arriving, and a minor scandal created by Isabelle added to my work. Despite a reconciliation, her friend Alberto had finally decided she was making life too hot for him and had ditched her. So Isabelle got drunk, went to his house at two in the morning, and insisted on seeing him—until, after being turned away, she cried for a couple of hours in the middle of the street. This, with other things, led to her being turned out of her hotel, and I was forced to help her find somewhere else to stay.

Then at the hotel that same evening I found a more than usually vicious row taking place in the kitchen between Signora Anna-Maria and Teresa, who was shouting loudly that she was a maid of all work and wasn't adequately paid. Her body quivered with anger as she lashed out at anyone who ventured to say a word. The old lady also was upset, appealing to the others in a high-pitched wailing to confirm that she was right. Then suddenly it finished and Teresa went away to her room to cry.

The next day she left without a word to anyone, but on the Easter Monday she was back again, cheerful as though nothing had happened. Franco said it was an excuse to spend Easter at home.

I met Maria again, the Sard student. I certainly wouldn't have bothered with her if Anna had been there, but, attracted by her seriousness and intelligence, I wondered whether I shouldn't still try inviting her out somewhere. Unlike Anna, of course, she was truly Sard, but Jim, in his phlegmatic way, was encouraging. "She'd probably be flattered. After all, she's about our age—quite old in Sardinia not to be at least engaged. Have an affair with Maria, and it can finish conveniently when you see Anna again."

"I should tell Anna afterward, though."

"What on earth for? Do you think it'd do any good?"

"She believes in sincerity," I replied, with the arrogant oversimplification of youth. "We both do."

Maria lived in Fertilia, and it wasn't until over a week later that an outing to a nearby beach could be arranged so that she and her friends, chaperoning one another, could meet me and mine. I decided to invite Gavino, too, phoning him on one of his better days, and he accepted willingly.

When the day came, he arrived in Alghero with Claudia, the elegant, bored-looking companion I'd first seen him with. He was in a mischievous mood. "Oh, you will see what beautiful girls we have on the Sardinian beaches! I'm not saying they're as good as the English girls, of course. But Mr. Arthur, how is your friend Anna? Have you heard from her?"

Her second letter had come that morning.

Jim nudged Gavino and said, "Only I shouldn't mention Anna this afternoon."

"Yes, you said we were to meet Maria." He spoke to Jim in a loud whisper. "I think Arturo is very lecherous!"

We reached Fertilia by noon and picnicked among the tufts of grass growing out of the white sand. I lay on my elbow staring at the emerald-blue monotony of the sea. Beaches bored me, and a day that should have resulted in a justifiable feeling of guilt toward Anna had already turned into an anticlimax. Since Maria and her friends weren't coming until later, there was nothing for me to do but join with Gavino in admiring the other girls on the beach and making the customary obscene comments. Marcella lay with her head in Jim's lap while Claudia went to stretch out provocatively on the sand. Gavino seemed hardly to notice her. I wondered why: she was eminently worthy of a few pleasant obscenities.

It wasn't until late afternoon that Maria arrived with two girlfriends, dressed as though it were still winter. The proper thing to do, it seemed, was to take a formal walk along the beach. Maria's friends, once they had been introduced to Claudia, hardly stopped giggling.

Maria tried to excuse them. "I'm sorry, Mister Arthur. You must forgive us Sards. We are easily amused. It must seem impolite." In her home environment she seemed as Sard as they were, and for all the afternoon neither of them left her.

"You remember Carmen?" she asked as we turned to walk back. "The girl who came to the party? I have a friend in Cagliari. It seems she's making quite a name for herself there. Everyone regards her as an 'immoral continental'—she's always out with different men." She was serious, trying to understand. "Life is perhaps old-fashioned here, but I can't see it's any better on the continent. What do you think, Mister Arthur?"

With the three of them so typically proper, consciously accepting the repression of their society—knowing that any sexual situation such as a man walking with a woman had to be neutralized by the presence of others—it seemed futile to argue.

I thought of Anna's letter in my pocket. "Life will change here eventually. I have a friend who's a Sard but lives in Rome now, and you'd be surprised at the difference between her and those who've never been out of the island."

"What's her name?"

"Anna Lorcas."

Maria nodded. "I know her. Used to go to school in Sassari? Her home's in Tempio." She frowned slightly and changed the subject. Her two friends were giggling again.

So much for my attempt to take out a Sard girl. Maria and her friends soon left us.

"What did you expect?" Gavino asked. "But look, Mr. Arthur, why don't you come back with me to Sassari for the evening?"

"What about Claudia?"

He wrinkled up his nose in disgust. "She has her period. She wants to go home early. Come on over when you've dropped Jim and Marcella, right?"

*　　*　　*

When I arrived, Gavino had just finished speaking on the telephone. "Mr. Arthur! Imagine it! I've got to go to Rome again. I'll be leaving in two days' time."

I grasped Gavino's hand, smiling at the ecstasy that had spread over his face. "Why, that's wonderful. How long for?"

"I don't even know! It's a complicated legal matter. It could last for months." He related all the details, got up to telephone again and book his flight, then sat down but kept slapping his hands on his knees in excitement.

I had an idea. "Look, will you do me a favour? Take Anna a present from me, as a surprise."

"But I don't know her address," he said weakly.

"I'll give it to you."

He tried to find another excuse, but I brushed it aside.

I'd been thinking of buying Anna a record of a song I liked. "I'll be back later, all right?"

I found the record easily enough and returned to Gavino's to listen to it: "Tying you to a grain of sand … tied to a ray of the sun … but you will flee and become lost in the night."

Gavino sat looking at the floor, as though impatient at the sentimentality of the words, then fetched some paper in which to wrap the record.

His exultant mood returned, his face lighting up in his naive enthusiasm. "Just imagine: Rome! After this! Oh, Mr. Arthur, I'm going to have a good time in Rome! Do the things I can't do here—the lot! The theatre, music, restaurants, high-class whores, everything. So I can have something to remember when I come back to this cesspool."

Driving back to Alghero I sang to myself, elated at the thought of Anna's pleasure.

The next evening my mood was changed for me again. I'd been to a concert with Enrico. Walking back, he took my arm: "Your friend Anna's gone back to Rome, then?"

I nodded.

Enrico stopped, moving one hand in front of him, trying to find the words. "Mister Arthur, I shouldn't become too involved with her if I were you. She's not ... well, she doesn't behave the way good girls behave."

I took my arm away. Everything suddenly seemed stupid. "You've changed your opinion since the last time, haven't you? I don't expect I'll be seeing very much of her anyway."

"It's just that a lot of people here won't have anything to do with her. You know what I mean."

"I know. The perpetual bloody Sard morality."

I went into my hotel angry and upset. Of course, Enrico, with his local narrow-mindedness, wasn't important, for Anna was bound to offend other Sards. Why, then, my sudden depression? Was it because, in spite of everything, I remained emotionally with the middle class I detested intellectually—knowing, too, that Anna wouldn't find easy acceptance in my own family? I started imagining having arguments about her with my parents.

Jim was reassuringly sensible when I told him the next morning what Enrico had said. "What difference does it make? You're not thinking of marrying her, are you? You know what the Sards are like. Take Marcella, for example. She gets into awful rows with her parents sometimes, because of me, and they'd be far worse if they knew some of the things we get up to. It's no use complaining. All you're doing is wishing people were different from how they are."

*   *   *

"It was such a surprise! I thought you'd forget me, and here we are, writing regularly, and you sending me presents. Did you know that the song was one of my favourites?

"Your friend Gavino was terribly awkward when he brought it! He wanted to leave immediately, before I could even ask him about you. He seemed to think I would eat him. But then, yesterday, he phoned and asked me to go out for a drink with him. I felt rather funny about it, but finally I went. He's much pleasanter than I imagined, and once he started he talked a lot. I've decided I quite like him—as a friend only, of course. I couldn't imagine him ever being like you in other ways! Oh, when I just think of your hands and lips upon me ... "

A moment of unease, an awareness of being half jealous because Gavino could see her while I couldn't—dispelled by what Anna wrote next, recalling our time of intimacy together.

"Yet I'm still not sure of myself. You suggested in your last letter that we might go for a holiday together at the end of the season. Give me time to think, my dear. It's not that I don't want you; physically, I want you too much, but I'm not sure it would be wise to go away together. Do you understand? I doubt it, since I hardly understand myself."

I wrote back, trying to persuade her. It wasn't only that I wanted to sleep with her. In Sardinia, everywhere, surrounded by tourists as I was, I so much wanted union, complete, with another person. Anna, idealistic, had talked about all or nothing. Wasn't it this that I wanted, too, in the whole of life, not just in love? Oddly, that night I thought also of Margaret, her calmness, her enjoyment of flirtations. Reliable, someone to relax and be happy with, someone my parents would certainly approve of. But it was Anna I was imagining as I fell asleep—lying beside me, her breast in my hand, as she whispered how much she wanted me.

By this time it was already the beginning of May, more than a month since I'd first met her.

*   *   *

"So you've come to me at last!"

"I've been waiting for you with bated breath!" I held Margaret's hand to my heart. "I can't tell you the joy it was when I got Maurice's telegram to say you were arriving! It came at the same time as a letter from a client saying the drains smell bad."

"Idiot." She took her hand away to carry on with her unpacking. "Thanks for coming to Olbia to welcome me. Maurice is arriving tomorrow morning, he told me to say. He wanted a couple of days off, but he couldn't make it today."

I relaxed into her one comfortable chair. Margaret's room was smaller than the one I'd booked into, and the sun shone brightly on the bare plaster walls.

"You can help me get one or two things straight," she went on, "and introduce me to all the important people."

"The handsome men with cars, you mean? Let's talk about it over lunch."

She gave a coy smile. "That's right. Hold on a minute. If you'll just give me time to put my hair straight, I'm all yours."

"All?"

"Of course! All or nothing, you know."

A flicker of pleasurable anguish as I recalled how Anna had said the same. After all, I thought, here in Olbia she was only a night's crossing away.

We had lunch under the red parasols of an open-air restaurant looking out over the shimmering Tyrrhenian Sea.

As we ate, I became aware of an elderly couple at another table. The man constantly touched his wife's hand and sometimes tried to kiss her on the cheek when he thought no one was looking.

Over coffee Margaret nudged me and nodded toward them. "They remind me of my parents. They're over sixty—I was a late arrival—but you'd think they were still teenagers. They hold hands and touch each other so much it's embarrassing!" She spoke sarcastically, but her eyes had misted over, and for a moment I was tempted to touch her hand too. "Can you imagine two sixty-year-olds, married for over forty years, sitting in the back row of the cinema so they can still neck in the dark? That's my parents for you!"

She took a cigarette from her handbag, then had difficulty lighting it in a sudden breeze that came from the water. The older couple had produced a portable radio, which now started pouring out the song about the grain of sand—producing in me an irrational guilt as I again remembered Anna somewhere over the horizon.

"Perhaps it's because of them I'm not married," Margaret went on. "If they thought I was even the slightest bit unhappy they'd be terribly upset. Yet I'd hate to disappoint them by not marrying."

"I'll marry you, Margaret!" I tried to respond, but after a few moments of aggressive flirtation we fell silent. The fairy-tale ending on a beautiful day like this would be for me to propose to Margaret, for her to accept, and the two of us to return to the joyful blessing of her parents. I looked at her with a sentimental affection—realizing, though, that when we weren't joking I never quite knew what to say to her.

The next day I slept late, and going up to Margaret's room I found Maurice already sitting there.

"Arrived by the early-morning boat." Maurice vigorously shook my hand, opening his mouth in one of his huge grins.

"All in my nothings, I was, and no one to protect me!"

Metaphorically I sprang forward. "I'd have protected you, my love!"

"Oh, bliss, I am saved!"

Maurice peered at us over his glasses. "From the frying pan into the fire, from what I can see of it. Strike me, can't you two ever behave normally?"

We decided to return to Alghero, all rather crowded in Pimple. In the evening, after I'd found them a room each in my hotel, we went dancing in a bar full of English and German girls on holiday, for whom the Italians were competing. Margaret, too, was in demand, but when the locals became too insistent, we resumed our flirtation to get rid of them, cuddling up together in an exaggerated manner.

"*Siete fidanzati?*" one Italian asked.

"*Sì, siamo fidanzati,*" Margaret replied firmly, and she laughed with me over the pretence.

"What's this I hear?" Maurice chortled as he returned from a rather dubious tango with a tall Scandinavian girl. "One of the Italians just told me you're engaged."

"Engaged for the next dance is what he meant." Margaret got to her feet. "Come on!"

I felt the attraction of her stability, her Englishness, which, however, was combined with an understanding and love of other countries. If I ever had to choose, I thought, between Margaret—who despite her sense of fun was basically reliable and normal—and Anna, representing the insecure and irrational, which would it be? The perpetual human dilemma.

"I'll try to get over again for the *Cavalcata,*" Maurice said on the station platform the next day. "That's only two and a half weeks away." He turned to Margaret. "You'll go over to Sassari too?"

"Of course. I can't miss the biggest day of the year."

I was looking forward to it too. For months everyone had asked me, "You'll be here for the *Cavalcata,* Mister Arturo?" with enthusiastic descriptions of the dancing, horseback riding, and folk art I'd see when representatives of every village in the island would assemble in Sassari in their traditional costumes.

"It's only an excuse to see Arthur again, of course," Margaret added, flinging her arms around me dramatically. We made our customary mock-amorous comments about the tragedy of our parting, promising that we'd spend every minute thinking of each other.

When Margaret left, my depression returned, together with thoughts of Anna almost unbearable in the sudden emptiness of that week. I was already waiting for her next letter.

*   *   *

Some evenings later I was sitting in the hotel kitchen when Enrico called on me unexpectedly. "Finish your meal," he insisted. "I can talk while you're eating. I … you see, Mister Arturo … that is … "

Enrico had a problem of the type he'd thought I had with Anna: he was afraid of falling in love with a girl who wasn't suitable for him. "You're different, Mister Arturo. I thought you might understand."

I couldn't help laughing at his seriousness. Teresa, too, had heard, and started to make fun of Enrico. "Oh, we have another one in love," she cackled. "What does it matter what kind of girl she is? If two people like each other … " She joined her fingers together and laughed excitedly.

One of the quieter maids, Francesca, started laughing as well and stayed to listen after Enrico had angrily chased Teresa out of the room.

He sat down again. "Oh, dear, life is so difficult! We're just here to do what little we can to make it better. More spiritual. If only people realized it, life could be so very beautiful."

I let him talk, my impatience growing. I perhaps agreed with his words, but Enrico's maudlin piety reminded me of so much I loathed in his type of religion.

"You know, Mister Arturo, it's true. Material things are very sordid, really. The more I think about it, the more I'm convinced that all my finest moments have been spiritual moments. Don't you agree?"

"No, I don't." I took a deep breath. "If you want to know, my finest moments have been in bed with a woman."

There was a sudden giggle from Francesca. "In bed with a woman," she repeated, delighted.

Enrico laughed uneasily. I was taking an extreme position, of course. I well knew what he was talking about and would never deny not only the beauty but also the reality of spiritual moments. But Enrico had chosen one pole of the duality of life, which was made up, thank God, of opposites. I was forced to spring to the defence of the material, the sensual, for Enrico needed no convincing of the other side.

He shook his head sadly. "But I just can't understand … "

"I don't mean with *any* woman. A woman you can share something with. In bed you can both find the deepest happiness and satisfaction, which goes far beyond the merely sexual."

Enrico waved his arms as he became more excited. "Yes, but even admitting that may be true, however beautiful it may be, it's surely only something temporary that doesn't last. Whereas those moments when you perceive something of life beyond—"

"Don't last either."

"But it's the reality behind that lasts." He got up and started pacing up and down the kitchen.

"True. But the reality is behind both the spiritual and the physical. And the deepest eroticism is often followed by the deepest spirituality."

Enrico suddenly surprised me, lifting both his hands to eye level and slamming them down to emphasize his point. "Yes, I agree with you! And that is provided for in the sacrament of marriage!"

Sacrament—the mystery word sanctifying something so you can no longer argue about it. "Yes, marriage is the logical result, a making permanent of the relationship—which often turns out to be disastrous. Or destroys all eroticism, at the very least. Granted, there are other advantages. But it certainly doesn't follow that a less permanent relationship shouldn't also be valid!"

"But ideally ... " Enrico began, sweating a little.

"Oh, yes, ideally nobody's supposed to do anything, until you're thrown together in one tremendous release. Unless you're like Signora Anna-Maria in there, who spent her first night locked in the bathroom, she told me. We're not ideal, and I don't want to be ideal. It's human imperfections which make man's glory."

Enrico shook his head. "But in England you allow divorce," he argued illogically.

"Because of human imperfections."

"But marriage is a sacrament of the church! If a person makes a mistake, he should have the spiritual courage to live by it." His body was in full motion now. "You can't go against God's law! Our way is more honest, at least."

More honest—the eternal answer. *Honest, courageous, ideal, spiritual, pure*—not bad words in themselves, but attached as mere labels to concepts that people don't want questioned. Words that, in the mouth of a bigot, however well-meaning, are worse than the foulest of obscenities. There was no convincing Enrico, and my Italian wasn't sufficient to stem a native enjoying the national pursuit of argument by the sheer volume of words.

*   *   *

For a while I still tried to see Maria, but every time I asked her anywhere there was something that prevented her from coming. "*Pazienza*, Mister Arthur," she said simply, after I'd tried my best to persuade her. By the next weekend I was tired of the difficulties and decided it wasn't worth the trouble.

In the meantime Anna's letter was late in arriving. I was uneasy. Her first ones had been so regular. I got into the habit of being in the hotel when the postman called, which only made each day start badly when he brought nothing from her. Something was wrong. I was bored with Alghero, with my tourists, and with pointless arguments like the one with Enrico.

Two, three, four days. Another weekend with the knowledge that nothing could come on Sunday. It was the end of May, and the *Cavalcata* was only four days away. It had been three weeks since I had received a letter. There was nothing on Monday either. Tuesday morning brought a letter from my parents, the afternoon nothing, Wednesday morning nothing.

Ten

"Can we still be friends? Can you perhaps help me, or am I asking too much?" The last line before Anna's rounded signature caught my eye as I tore open the letter.

I didn't read it in detail, skimming through to know everything all at once. Tears, anger, resentment tugged against one another, creating a hollow inside me that grew and grew; until finally it had to explode, and I banged my hand down on the table with a half-whispered "damn!"

My immediate reaction was to fight back, impelled, I think, by sheer obstinacy, for it's always in desperate situations that I dig in my heels. In love I'm like the soldier who suddenly finds himself at Dunkirk, not having made the right stand earlier, and now remains to fight on the beaches when it's already too late. But I told myself something different: that Gavino was a friend, was probably feeling badly, too, and perhaps needed Anna more than I did. I tried vainly to convince myself to be generous, but at the same time I was angry and confused, recognizing the similarities between Gavino and myself that I wanted to deny. Something in me needed to see him as less successful—and, if he really needed Anna more, for that very reason she should love me and not him.

Why had I given him the record to deliver? The words of the song "you will flee and become lost in the night" now struck me with ironical force. Had she actually got into bed with him? She didn't say. I remained sitting in the hallway of the hotel, where I'd received the letter by the afternoon post. I saw the revolving door where I'd come in with Anna, the stairs we'd taken up to my room. I remembered her with me on my bed, our anguished caresses. And now her words struck hammer blows as I read them.

"Arthur, I feel dreadful saying this, but I must tell you. I mentioned that Gavino asked me out for a drink. Well, we saw each other once or twice after that, just as good friends. Then we saw each other again, only this time it was no longer as 'just friends.' I don't really know how it happened."

I swore to myself, more strongly but more consciously, taking care that Carlo, still working at his desk as he'd been doing before the world had fallen in, shouldn't hear.

"What my feelings are toward you I no longer really know. I still admire you as a friend, am fond of you, but something's changed. I'm in such a muddle. I need you to understand and help me."

"Is anything the matter, Mister Arturo?"

"No, nothing."

I read the letter more carefully, grasping at those few sentences that still gave hope. Futile, for in spite of Anna's confusion, her feelings were clear.

"I'm not certain of anything, but I think I'm in love. I *think* I am. I don't know. Perhaps it's because Gavino needs me so much. He's so terribly unhappy underneath. He told me how he often hates himself, how alone he is. And I'll be miserable unless I can help him in some way. For the short time he's in Rome, I must do what I can to give him some happiness or we'll both be even more unhappy.

"As I say, I don't know I'm in love. It may not last and tomorrow I may regret having written this. I kept putting it off—and I realize all this isn't exactly pleasant for you. I'm sorry. Perhaps it's just that I'm too generous. Always I seem to give my love to the wrong person. But I can't help it! What does it matter, though? It will come to an end, sooner or later. It always does. My whole life's been unhappy. Gavino's too, it seems."

And mine too. I glanced at Carlo behind his desk, where, I recalled, Jenny had once wiggled her bosom for me. Perhaps I should continue to fuck the Jennies and leave the complicated, interesting women alone. Jenny was coming back. But it wasn't Jenny I wanted.

Later, Jim had the usual coffee, while I had a brandy. "Here, look at this."

He read the letter through while I watched him anxiously, then he gave it back without saying anything.

"Extraordinary how fatalistic these Italian girls are," he pronounced eventually. "Marcella's always talking as though things were preordained. I'm sorry. What else can I say? It mightn't be serious, of course. She was lonely because you weren't there, wasn't she?" He went on, sucking at his pipe. "And it's the *Cavalcata* tomorrow, after all. That should cheer you up."

I returned to the hotel to write to Anna. In my muddled letter I tried to impress her with my fair-mindedness, saying almost the opposite of what I felt so she should admire me more and start to love me again. I slept badly.

*   *   *

At eight in the morning I strolled along the Via Roma past the assembling procession, camera in hand but with impatient detachment, glancing perfunctorily at each new group of costumes so I could feel I'd done my duty toward them. Jim had agreed to look after the fleet of coaches for the tourists while I drove over to Sassari in Pimple, so we could have it for the evening. Sassari was all excitement. Packed streets, strange music, *carabinieri* marching; dark southern women in multicoloured costumes; men in less spectacular ones of black, white, and red—some on horseback, some already dancing, some posing for photographs. All gathered to form the procession from the Piazza d'Italia to the football stadium, where the parade was to take place. *La Cavalcata Sarda*—something I'd probably never see again in my life, and I was as interested as I'd have been in the hospital carnival at home. The locals, of course, were making as much noise as the occasion demanded. Men sold balloons, children waved flags, and the bars swarmed with sweaty Italian life. Already there was a throng of people moving toward the stadium, and my coat got smeared with ice cream from a five-year-old waving her arms in the air.

At the stadium I met Jim, busy photographing nothing at all.

"Maurice and Margaret might be coming," I remembered to tell him, "if Maurice can find an excuse to come over on expenses."

I left him and found my place in one of the stands, where I was squeezed into a jostling, intimate group of overlapping elbows and knees used as backrests. My neighbours had neat, folded triangles of newspaper over their heads, and I was conscious of other people's breath fouling the air around my neck. All around the field was a vast, noisy crowd, its anonymity sometimes broken by individuals who caught the eye: someone running onto the field here, a wave there, a shout—"Mario!"—an argument with a couple of policemen, two drunks dancing with each other.

After some hesitant but growing applause, the parade began. I convinced myself to be enthusiastic. Village contingents trooped in, circled the field—often stopping to do a figure from a dance—then took up positions in an enclosure in the middle. The costumes were magnificent, some ornamented with silver or other expensive decorations. The sun shone on the *Cavalcata Sarda*—and it shone on me as well, so that very soon I began to feel damp patches of sweat around my ears.

Rome, I thought with sudden despair. Was it as hot there? I forced my attention back to the spectacle. Some of the Sard girls parading in front of me were prettier than Anna, giggling virgins though they were, protected by reams of coloured material designed to hide their more feminine features.

A loudspeaker continued to drone out its muffled, indistinguishable commentary. After an hour and a half I was cramped and exhausted, but more and more villages poured into the arena. Two hours later still, after an exuberant gallop of horses and riders around the field (the actual meaning of *Cavalcata*), the day's official entertainment was over.

People leaving, trampling horse manure underfoot to get back into the town. With a sudden stab of hope I thought I saw Gavino. But no, Gavino was still in Rome, and a sigh of emptiness within told me of the falsity of all this gaiety, a human device for forgetting the realities of individual lives. Costumed figures strolled about the streets in this, their one day of glory—one out of 365. Oh, well, they had a few more days, too, probably. But even out of that one day, how much time was spent in total happiness?

Like the first time I ever kissed a girl, I recalled, as I gazed at the oil and vinegar bottles in the restaurant where I stopped for lunch. I was young and wanted to kiss someone; it didn't matter whom. There was a group of us on a hike somewhere, and I spent the first few hours changing partners and trying to decide. And then finally I kissed one girl when we said goodbye. It was over, and I never saw her again. Oh, she responded, willingly, and she probably spent the next week as I did going over it in her mind. Now, eating my meal, I tried to work it out. The kiss itself had lasted no more than five seconds, but had been anticipated for about eight hours. A week followed in which that kiss was the only important thing in, say, eighty-seven hours of my waking life. Three hundred and forty-two thousand seconds as opposed to five: the dream exceeded the reality by a ratio of 68,400 to one. Wasn't most of life the same?

In the afternoon I wandered around the streets, less busy now, thinking of Anna. I returned at five o'clock to the piazza, where the crowds had grown again to see the costumed figures dancing. It was dreary in the extreme, a slow jigging of various village teams to a wailing accompaniment. I was weary, but now there was nowhere to sit down. Lads from all over the island were behaving as though they were still in the country, fooling around and shouting coarse remarks at the girls, who responded with giggles or turned backs—like a rough agricultural fête. For the want of anything better to do, I followed a couple of beauties from Tempio in their handsome, billowing gowns of black and white. Did Anna ever wear her local costume? The bodice could be pulled down to reveal those breasts with large pink nipples, exciting amid the black and white disorder of her dress.

I lost the girls in the crowds on the piazza, where now everyone was beginning to make the customary *passeggio*. I wondered where Jim had got to and tried vainly to find him. Finally, I walked to the public gardens and sat reading a paper on a bench, tired of wandering to no purpose. Alone, I was painfully aware of the letter in my shirt pocket weighing on my heart like a sentence of execution.

It was getting dark by now. I sat until it was nearly time to go back and see my own and Jim's neglected tourists onto the coaches. At the parking lot, at last, Maurice and Margaret turned up, in the unexpected company of Isabelle.

I became more cheerful. "You made it then? I thought you couldn't have come after all."

Margaret flung her arms around me dramatically. "You don't think I would miss an opportunity to see you!"

"We've been looking for you all day," Maurice said. "A bit hopeless in this crowd."

I grinned at him over Margaret's shoulder. "How do you manage it? You seem to be over here in Sardinia more often than in Rome."

Margaret released me, and I left with Isabelle to count heads and send the tourists home. All was in order, and I waved in relief at the departing coaches.

Isabelle came over quite satisfied that only five of her Americans were missing. "Hell, let the driver see to it all."

The evening had become more worthwhile. We went for a meal, and Maurice explained that he and Margaret had tried to find me after the parade but had been swept away by a couple of Italian friends of Margaret's who'd brought them from Olbia. Margaret, in the meantime, was listening to some hilarious account from Isabelle about her personal life.

"His whole trouble," Isabelle was saying, "is that he doesn't have any psychological background!"

Maurice burst out laughing. "What on earth does that mean? No 'psychological background'? What's your psychological background like?"

Margaret favoured me with one of her smiles. "I'm hearing all about this sex-starved German she met up with on a fishing expedition."

The story continued for twenty minutes, by which time no one could remember how it started.

"Why don't you and Margaret stay overnight?" I suggested to Maurice.

"Can't, more's the pity. We've got to get back to Olbia so I can see to a spot of business there tomorrow before leaving again for Rome." He gave a sly grin. "There's always a reason for me to come, you see."

We returned to the piazza. At half past nine the celebrations were already over and we found ourselves alone on the darkened, empty square. We sat on the stone benches around Victor Emmanuel feeling cheated, and if Jim hadn't turned up with Enrico and some friends, the evening might have ended, for just then Margaret's friends with the car arrived, too, wanting to leave. But they were persuaded to be patient, and the whole group of us moved to the bar on the corner of the square.

And this was the most successful part of the day: sitting outside, drinking and talking in the silence of so remote a part of the world as a small town in the north of Sardinia. Such atmospheres could still appeal to me. I flirted with Margaret all the more because of my deeper depression, ostentatiously holding her hand and acting so well that Enrico became convinced that I'd forgotten Anna (no, Enrico, not for a single moment) and was now in love with Margaret. The other Italians, who didn't understand what Margaret and I were saying, thought it was serious too.

Enrico made jokes all round, while Jim, who'd obviously been drinking earlier, started on a chorus of "The Red Flag."

"Oh, yes, workers of the world, unite!" Margaret proclaimed, waving her glass in the air. "And all that rot!"

Jim struggled to his feet. "*Evviva la rivoluzione*! Let's drink to the revolution!"

"Speech, speech!" from Maurice.

"Comrades!" he began, enjoying making a fool of himself, "in Italy we see the pitiful spectacle of the proletariat … "

Margaret kept handing him more to drink, so that soon he was giving an impassioned tirade against the evils of capitalism. When the bar closed we all returned to the middle of the square.

"Here, Lenin, get up on the seat," Margaret encouraged him, "under Victor Emmanuel." She clambered onto it with him and gave a rival speech at the same time.

"I never knew he had it in him," Maurice whispered.

"He expresses these views from time to time, even if he's too complacent ever to be a political activist. But I haven't seen him as drunk as this before. Perhaps he's had a row with Marcella."

"On the contrary, it's the result of pure exuberance, mark my words. I happen to know he and Marcella took the opportunity of being away from home for the day to book into a hotel, for daytime use."

Again a stab of pain …

Jim was still declaiming, with Margaret arguing back at him. Then she saw the policeman approaching. "Christ!" she muttered, jumping off the seat.

Jim became louder, flailing all over the place, and then started arguing as well with the policeman, who got angry despite the urgent attempts of the Italians to calm him. He was taken off singing "The Red Flag" once more.

We remained silent, ashamed, until nervous giggles turned into laughter.

"They'll let him out tomorrow," Maurice said lightly.

Margaret, exhilarated by her own escape, soon became gayer than ever and flirted madly with everyone. When finally her friends insisted on leaving, I enacted a passionate departure scene with her, chasing after the car and holding her hand through the window—all pleasantly crazy.

I drove Enrico and Isabelle back to Alghero. Enrico was serious, talking first about Jim. "You think they'll let him out tomorrow, Mister Arturo, yes?" Then he spoke of Margaret. "My heartiest congratulations! Eh, Mister Arturo! No more worries about Anna Lorcas, eh?"

After we'd left Isabelle at her hotel, Enrico spoke just as enthusiastically about her. "She would be one of your beauties in England, no? And Miss Margaret would be a typical … how do you say … English rose?"

In bed I at first smiled over my memories of the evening. But in the end less pleasant thoughts prevailed. Again I didn't sleep. I found myself thinking about Anna, imagining her there with me. But Gavino was there as well—and then suddenly I'd jerk to my senses, realizing it was only a confused dream. In the semi-darkness of my imagination everything became muddled: bodies making love, discussions, letter phrases repeated over and over again; an empty longing for a dream figure who receded into the more substantial forms of pillows and bedclothes in turmoil. Then I would wake to find myself surrounded only by the hostile shapes of a bedroom in darkness, except for a glimmer from a street lamp falling on one of the angels on the ceiling, who gazed down in derision.

Eleven

The next day Jim was released, and the two of us decided to forget work and go to Cagliari for the weekend.

Here, at any rate, was Italian civilization. Trams and trolley buses careered through broad streets with fine shops, intersected by narrow, steep, cobbled ones. There was noise, life, and the difficulty of driving through the city and finding a place to park. Houses, cafés, and offices towering all around were solid and reassuring. The majesty of ships in the port proclaimed that the continent hadn't forgotten Sardinia after all, with the dreamlike pale-blue Mediterranean beyond, and hazy mountains almost enclosing it. It was as though we'd left the overgrown fishing village of Alghero and the mock urbanity of Sassari for the world at large, for an elegant southern city that at least had the semblance of belonging to the continent.

After lunch and a short siesta at our hotel, we went to explore, inevitably ending up on the Via Roma, with its long colonnades on the one side and the activity of the port on the other. We walked to its end, to the gardens and fountains, behind which was hidden the grandiose façade of the central station. We'd thought of going in the afternoon to the ancient city of Nora, one of the best-preserved Roman settlements on the island, but it was too hot; and after innumerable nuraghi on the journey south, we were tired of antiquities.

We went instead to the beach, some way from the town centre and colonized by treble rows of huts and casual open-air bars with jukeboxes. A few other people were there, but the beginning of June was still early for most Italians to go bathing, although one could imagine the laughing, careless crowds that would gather once the season had begun. We paid our hundred lire to change in cubicles at the back of one of the bars and went out into a powder-like sand that burned our feet. We stretched out on towels to feel the sun eating into us. A group of boys were playing football, and from further away came the shrieks of a family chasing around in the sand.

This was the kind of place I'd like to have brought Anna to. We would go swimming, lie on the sand, and then go into one of the beach huts to take off our bathing suits and make love, still wet and covered with salt from the sea. Jim, in the circumstances, was a poor substitute. "Oh, it's a pity you don't like men," I could imagine Anna saying in that mischievous voice of hers.

Yet today I was calmer. It was to an atmosphere like this that Anna belonged: the romantic side of Italy, to which people escaped during the summer. The world of the jukebox and sentimental songs, beautiful because they tried, impossibly, to eternalize the transitory. The world of love and sensuality, where those authoritative voices that spoke of preserving life by measuring it out in controlled, cautious doses were quieted by others saying one should gulp down its heady draft without regret. I persuaded myself that I really did want Anna more than physically, that for me she was a symbol of everyday normality seeking to break out into the freedom of the carnival, longed for by all and yet so much feared at the same time. After two days of anguished questioning, I at last felt justified in trying to win Anna back.

"Would you marry her?" Jim asked.

Cautiously, I replied, "Who?"

"Anna, of course. You've been talking of nothing else all afternoon."

Would the compromise be necessary even here? If I took her away from Gavino, would I feel compelled to justify my actions by marrying her? "Perhaps."

We sat at a table in the open air under a wickerwork shelter, listening to pop songs on the jukebox. The outdoor, lazy Italian summer: elemental, savage at times in its simplicity. One day I would return with her here, would tell her, laughing, how unhappy I'd been. Now I wanted to write to her again.

Toward evening we walked up to the old part of the city, set high above on a pinnacle of rock. Climbing a stately flight of steps, we came to a wide, stone-paved terrace shaded by trees. Cagliari was at the head of a bay, and we looked down directly at the port with the sea beyond and the mountains beyond that, where the sun was descending. To our left, after a short, tree-covered promontory, was the broad curve of sand where we'd bathed, and further still were mountains stretching around to meet the sea. The little square gave an impression of stillness: one of those places that had a perfection of its own and lacked only the right person to share it with.

From nowhere the town band appeared. After taking their places solemnly on a platform, they embarked on a concert of light classical music and some modern pieces. We sat listening, watching the sun go down and the shadows creep over the town and port below. As some lights flickered over the sea, I was reminded for some reason of once being at a firework display where, after ten minutes of politely applauded pieces, a spark had fallen into the box holding the rest, igniting them. I was only a boy and had thrilled to the display that suddenly outshone everything that had gone before. Regret soon followed, because it was so quickly over. To eke out a long succession of petty moments, or to burn up a lifetime in a sudden blaze like that of stars exploding? I'd long been aware of this as a basic human problem. But Anna and I hadn't had the chance to burn ourselves out.

I decided I'd like to spend my honeymoon in Cagliari.

Jim and I eventually left the square and walked on higher to the cathedral, which presented a different kind of peace in its devout splendour. Here, for a second, I wanted to kneel down and worship, and probably would have done so if Jim hadn't been there.

We walked back a different way to the bustle of the city, the Via Roma and its bright lights contrasting with the now darkened sea. I bought a postcard to send to Anna, a view of sea and mountains that expressed my mood of the day. Wrote casually, "Greetings from Cagliari," and then went back to buy some notepaper. But that evening Jim was in a talkative mood, so my intended letter was postponed. Instead, we discussed the deep concerns of life until the early morning.

The next afternoon we returned to the beach and sat at the same bar after swimming. And here I began my letter, trying to describe to Anna the thoughts that Cagliari had inspired. Then Jim wanted to return to the terrace again to try some photographs of the sunset, so the previous day, in all its sad loveliness, was repeated.

I was thankful that these two days had brought peace instead of turmoil, an uncertain hope instead of despair. It was difficult to imagine a city anywhere more beautiful than Cagliari.

That night in the hotel I continued my letter, telling Anna how much I still wanted and needed her. I suggested that her emotions over Gavino were only the result of a sympathy arising between two people who were unhappy, ignoring what a powerful force that can be. I didn't finish, although I wrote well into the night, occasionally trying to picture her asleep in Rome.

The next morning we departed, and because of the vague promise this city had seemed to offer, I determined to keep a souvenir, an absurd little thing: the ticket for the cubicle where I'd changed into my bathing suit—something I could look at afterward, once Anna was mine again, to remind me of the atmosphere that day.

During the next week in Alghero I found sufficient reasons as to why I should be in love with her. With awakening intuition, I had begun to understand that many of the dark, masculine secrets that were normally hidden from women could be revealed to Anna without shame, and she would accept them. Such things were hardly talked about then, so that Anna was reassuring, like a woman telling a child ashamed of being afraid of the dark that most other children were afraid too. At twenty-four, I was still a child.

That week there was an upset at the hotel when Teresa was caught attempting to smuggle a so-called fiancé out of her room at five in the morning—she then tried to convince everyone that she was soon getting married. It seemed absurd now that I'd once taken her seriously. And I saw Maria again, but managed only to exchange a few polite words with her.

In any case, by then I'd decided that as soon as Gavino returned to Sardinia I'd go to Rome in spite of my job and win Anna back again. "He and I will only have a few more weeks together before he leaves," she'd written in her reply to my hastily concluded letter. "Then it will all be over." She assured me she still loved him, but my feelings of sympathy for him had by now been undermined by anger that he'd taken from me something to which he had no right.

I heard more rumours about Anna's reputation in Sassari. I discounted them but they upset me, and thoughts of her continued to torment me. Yet when Enrico called to invite me to go on an excursion with the senior classes of his school—to Isola Rossa, an island on the northern coast—I couldn't at first remember where I'd heard the name. Then I remembered how Anna had referred to it as the one place in her youth where she'd been happy. So I went there telling myself heroically that it would be a kind of pilgrimage before I left for Rome.

* * *

At seven o'clock they were all assembled in front of the school: hordes of young men and women carrying bundles of food and bottles of wine, as though trying to see who could make the most noise. When the coach departed it was like a jungle of animals going on a joy ride, the girls if anything behaving more aggressively than the men, asserting the emancipation that was theirs for the day. I found myself on the back seat with a group of boys intent on out-shouting those at the front. Every few minutes one curly-haired youth would jump to his feet, arms in the air, exhorting the others to enjoy themselves. We stopped in Sassari to pick up someone's record player and transistor radio, and then the singing started, with the back half of the coach in competition with the front. From my vociferous neighbour I learned a number of indecent songs, to which none of the girls seemed to object.

Enrico was sitting at the front with another teacher, a rather plain, stern-looking girl. Eventually he came back to ensure that I was enjoying myself. "Everything fine, Mister Arturo?" He smiled happily, staying to joke with his students and trying to make himself one of them.

As the coach bounced over the barren plains of the northern part of the island, through tiny villages with little trace of civilization, the countryside gradually became wilder, the roads poorer and whiter. Occasionally I glimpsed a nuraghe, reminding me of a civilization that had once existed. After an hour or so we were travelling along the coast, where a blue sea shimmered against deserted stretches of pale yellow sand or battered against huge outcrops of rock. Further away, I reflected, were the unseen shores of the Corsican coast, northern Italy and the French Riviera. And soon, I myself would be going to Rome. Soon, I thought, I would be crossing that sea.

The road became higher, skirting large knolls of rock; below, the shores were wilder still, the rocks a more reddish colour. Suddenly we were descending over a cart track toward a stretch of beach flanked by a promontory with a stone tower at its tip, standing like a solitary phallus. From the sea there arose a small island of sharp pinnacles, the colour of congealed blood but polished by the sun and shining as a ruby. Isola Rossa.

"We must go there together," I recalled Anna saying. "It's a wonderful place. So wild and lonely, and the sea's so passionate."

The wild was about to be assaulted, the lonely overpowered. We all burst out of the coach at a tiny café below the promontory, taking the radio, record player, and records—shouting over the rocks, defying the deep crevices where the sea had thrust itself in. The whole purpose of the outing was to take this area by storm, to plunder and rape, assert the tribal rite of conquest.

"We could be alone. I used to swim naked there, you know?"

The sea came beating its way up a narrow inlet, angrily demanding a sacrifice. Everywhere was this reddish stone, now being trampled underfoot by these schoolboy invaders.

A sudden shout. The tower, too, had to be made our own. All turned obediently to race across a short field and burst our way inside. Up a rickety ladder within an encircling wall of stone, emerging suddenly into daylight, and dispersing over the coarse rocks and grass at the top.

"It's only the people who aren't able to think about it who are content with such a life."

The record player was set up on the low rampart at the edge, and we danced crowded together and tripping over the stones. The girls somehow were more vitally alive than in town, and I watched one in particular, with dark eyes, slender legs, and all the attractiveness of youth, for she couldn't have been more than sixteen. She'd been the first to the ladder, and I'd watched from below as her tight little behind wobbled seductively upward. Now her movements were the most vibrantly expressive. I was angry with her—for being young, extroverted, sexy, and unattainable.

We returned to the café for lunch and then to change into bathing suits, by which time a fishing boat had been chartered to take us across to the island. We departed piled together like the fish it usually carried and whose smell surrounded us. A sudden confusion ensued when we arrived, as men and women dived off the boat while those not bathing scrambled up the rocks.

I went to join Enrico. Of the men, he was the only one who couldn't swim and was sitting pathetically on top of a large boulder, his white body contrasting with the colourful towels he was carrying for the others.

"I've been meaning to ask you, Mister Arturo. How's your friend Gavino getting on in Rome?"

"All right." I winced as I accidentally put my bare foot on a sharp point of rock.

"He's coming back on July 19th, eh?"

I stared at him. "How do you know?"

"I met that doctor friend of his. I think that's what he said."

July19. That was the date, then, when I would leave for Rome. I tried to work it out while Enrico was talking: four and a half weeks.

Enrico loved discussing other people. "He's such a strange chap. I can't understand how he goes out with the girls he does. Why doesn't he find a proper girl and stick to her instead of all those … " He trailed away. "He seems so tongue-tied with women. Perhaps that's the reason."

"He's too sensitive," I said grudgingly. "He should be doing something artistic instead of working in that lawyer's office."

There was a sudden interruption, with everyone shouting and pointing at something in the water, followed by a barrage of splashes as half a dozen young men dived in. A hairy, muscular youth emerged from under the water triumphant, holding up his knife in one hand and something long and wriggling in the other.

"Ooh-ah, he's got an octopus," Enrico said in excitement. "Bring it here!"

Proud manhood, the whole group of them, ran it laughingly up to us, a slithery yet awesome, primitive creature, with flailing tentacles about fifteen inches long. Its vanquisher dealt the deathblow, turning its bulbous head through its mouth and biting directly into its brain. The tentacles were cut up and passed around to be eaten.

I wanted Anna, wanted her unbearably. Wanted to take her here, naked, on this island, even watched by the others. Wanted to press my own manhood upon her. She could be passed around, too, afterward, if the others needed her. To my surprise I was physically excited at the thought of seeing her shared. I saw the attractive girl examining me with wide eyes and I blushed and turned away with an irresistible stirring within. Feeling her eyes on my bathing suit, I wanted to strip it off, stand outrageously hard and naked before her, and say, "There!" For a moment I wished I were in Sassari so I could go with trembling determination to the prostitutes in their sordid monastery home.

Frustrated, I made the journey back with the others to the mainland, sensitive to the warm bodies pressed tightly around me and the even stronger smell of fish. Back at the café there was more dancing. The youths seemed inexhaustible, intoxicated by their perpetual motion, and now my head began to ache from the pulsing of the arteries around my eyes. The same boisterous exhibitionism went on until late afternoon. Knowing nothing of the confiding intimacy of love, these youngsters chose instead either an animal-like parading of their physical prowess or a close hugging together when they danced. One day they would be plunged into a physical love devoid of tenderness in the sudden assaults of marriage.

I remembered to ask Enrico how his unsuitable love affair was going.

"All over, Mister Arturo. She wasn't really, you know … Just a temptation, and I'm better off resisting."

I turned away and looked at the girls, imagining what it would be like to enter them one by one. But the violent demands I'd felt on the island had given way to weariness. My mood became more subdued, softened by the glow of the late-afternoon sun in what was, after all, a romantic setting. For once I longed for England, with its gradual initiation into sex at tender exploratory parties. I thought of Anna's unashamed awareness and these people trying to hide the explosive and violent demands of their youth behind dark clouds of ignorance and fear.

A sudden call to return to the coach punctured my thoughts, for next on the program was a visit to a well-known spa nearby. Many of the men, including my neighbour on the back seat, were drunk by now and the shouting was more confused.

The spa, Castel Doria, was at the head of a narrow valley on a river smoking mysteriously from the hot waters that poured into it. There was a hotel, the woods, and the river, in an odd way reminiscent of English river scenes; and the sun was going down in jagged, steaming reflections on the water. On a terrace over the river the record player was again produced, and some started dancing once more while others descended to the mud onto which the boiling water from the springs was pouring.

I wandered off by myself, wanting to be alone where the shouts of the crowd, heard from a distance, could become a part of the atmosphere instead of competing with it. Standing among the trees— imagining Anna with legs spread apart in front of me, holding those fleshy lips wide open for me to enter—I hastily, meanly, found physical relief, forcing myself into my cupped hands until suddenly they were wet and sticky with my fluid. But then followed a feeling of anguished despair because the sensation hadn't been intense enough, and Anna was in any case a chimera, unreal. Doing myself up, I wondered if I was even sure who she was.

Guiltily, I returned to the others.

"Will you dance with me?"

It was the young, attractive girl. Dark eyes looked at me timidly, with none of the loud ebullience I'd first noticed.

We danced slowly across the bare wooden boards of the terrace. She talked shyly, showing a naive interest and a typical Sard sense of wonder at the outside world. Holding her close, I could sense her excitement. She told me her name was Caterina. But she was too young.

Enrico called me. "Mister Arturo, you haven't met Elena yet."

I broke away from Caterina, who followed as I went to sit down with Enrico and the other teacher.

"Elena's from Orgosolo, the village famous for its bandits." Enrico tried to joke: "She's not dangerous, though. Quite normal in fact. She teaches history."

Elena formed her hand into a pistol and went "pow" at me before giving it to me to shake. Then she chuckled. Her hard features relaxed.

Caterina shuddered apprehensively, but her eyes were all excitement.

"You must have seen the film about Orgosolo, didn't you, Mister Arturo?"

I hadn't, although since I'd been in Sardinia I'd heard Orgosolo mentioned several times, and hushed silences had always followed.

Elena's voice was gruff but reassuring. "It's not so bad there now. Though we still get bandits hiding there. Ten years ago the police used to be stationed all around the village to prevent people from going in, it was so dangerous."

Enrico was eager to explain: "Now they have so many police in the area that it's difficult for anyone to commit a crime."

"But every so often there's a murder up in the mountains," Elena continued. "They're very high, and we're so remote. It's perfect bandit country. Even the main road to Nuoro, the nearest town, is hardly more than a track. We're all secretly afraid of knives in the dark."

Caterina interrupted to ask breathlessly if there were bandits in England too. Elena was rather mannish, but there was something about the idea of knives waiting for a person—and connected with a woman—which was again stirring my excitement.

Elena had realized my interest. "Look, we're going home for a while on Tuesday—I live in Alghero with my brother—and life will be terribly dull there. Why don't you come and visit us? What about next weekend?"

Enrico showed a sudden enthusiasm. "Why not, Mister Arturo? Get Jim and Marcella to come along as well. And Miss Margaret too. I've never been to Orgosolo."

"Well, if they can."

"Decide during the week, and Enrico can phone me," Elena suggested.

It was dark by now. The four of us remained chatting. Caterina, I noticed, was listening carefully to every word I said.

In the coach going back, my noisy neighbour had at last been disposed of by alcohol. Caterina, quite devoted, had contrived to get the seat in front of me. A younger Anna, I thought, but she would probably remain on the island, chained to a life from which Anna had escaped. Caterina would remain moral. I was disturbed by her simplicity, her naivety, and by the fact that she was, as I learned, just fifteen and a half.

The coach rattled on through the darkness. At home in England couples would be kissing after a day of shared happiness, but here the conclusion was lacking. There was less noise because everyone was tired, but no tenderness, perhaps because of fear of what others might say. Instead, some of the men expressed themselves in deliberate insults to the girls.

Caterina still smiled and tried to talk over the back of her seat. Determined not to be too repressed by Sard morality, I managed to touch her fingertips, which were grasping the headrest. She responded. After looking round cautiously in case anyone should see, she let her fingers rest on mine, and for all the journey back I lightly caressed her hands, the tips of her fingers, the joints, even daringly running my finger up to the point where her two fingers met below the knuckle. And she would give a little giggle because she was being so sinful and look round again hastily. My desire for sex was nearly unbearable, and the most I could do was caress a girl's fingertips. Just once, for about five seconds, she allowed me to stroke her cheek. For a moment I even managed to laugh at myself. But that, I thought, was that.

* * *

I set about planning my departure. July 19 was a Thursday, so I decided I might as well finish that week and leave for Rome on the Sunday evening—which made five weeks to wait. There'd be a problem with my tourists, so again I would have to rely on Jim.

And by now there were plenty of them. Attractive girls, too, but I made no effort to take any of them out. Teresa commented on my lethargy, teasing me about being in love so that I no longer noticed anyone—prancing around the kitchen, showing off her body, making coarse gestures, and asking how Anna compared. I'd only laugh and pretend to a gaiety I didn't feel. Few people noticed my depression, and one guest even complimented me on finding a way to enjoy life so much.

A few days later, Margaret came on another surprise visit with Filippo, the man who'd brought her and Maurice to the *Cavalcata*, and a friend of his. Filippo was a big, good-natured Italian, pleasantly spineless.

"A real pain in the neck," she said. Not understanding Margaret when she was speaking English, he gave her a sheepish grin. She smiled at him sweetly. "He's real keen, although all he gets from me is my company in his car whenever I want to go somewhere. Last time on the way back I fell asleep on his shoulder and now he talks of nothing else. His friend's a local poet." She made a face. "He started spouting on the way—it seems it's a Sard tradition to improvise—in honour of me and Filippo, as far as I could understand. It sounded like a funeral dirge."

Filippo and his friend left to see to their business, and I spent a pleasant afternoon with Margaret doing nothing. When I suggested going to Orgosolo at the weekend, she said she'd always wanted to see a bandit. "Phone Maurice too. I'm sure he'd love to come."

Late in the afternoon we met up with Jim and Marcella, who were enthusiastic too. We all went for a stroll along the beach before returning at half past seven to meet Filippo.

"We ought to be going, Margaret," Filippo said, looking at her adoringly.

"Oh, it's too early yet!" She added privately to me, "He's always like this. Try to drag it out as long as possible."

We continued strolling up and down the piazza. Only half intentionally we started our flirtation again.

"Margaret, my love, please don't leave me!"

"You know I'll never leave you!"

Marcella giggled at Jim, while Filippo made a sarcastic comment about the two lovebirds.

Margaret was scornful. "He doesn't know whether to be jealous or not." She turned to him to try out the story of the two of us being engaged.

Filippo smiled broadly as he tried to hide his embarrassment, unbelieving. Jim formally shook my hand, and Marcella kissed me on the cheek in congratulation. The poet friend asked eagerly when the wedding would be. "You must allow me to make you a poem for the occasion."

"Christ! I couldn't face another of his poems."

Perhaps Filippo sensed that Margaret was making a fool of him, but his pride didn't permit him to show it. She made the poet buy drinks for everyone, then had them all looking in the shops for wedding presents. Filippo again suggested leaving, but she persuaded him we should go for a pizza first. When we finally got back to the car, she was still in a mood for fun. "No, I've decided to stay here and spend the night with Arthur."

Only a joke, of course. Filippo, by now used to our performance, drove slowly around the square to let us make the most of it.

"I've a good mind really to stay the night here. Why shouldn't I, after all? You could find a hotel for me?"

The car returned and stopped. Margaret strolled up to it, where Filippo was hanging out of the window waiting. "No, I told you, I'm spending the night with my fiancé."

He laughed disbelievingly, drove on another twenty yards, and stopped again. When Margaret reached him, she shook his hand politely, thanking him for having brought her. Finally he pulled away, and the car disappeared down the road.

Margaret shrugged her shoulders. "That's another boyfriend I've lost."

We went dancing and afterward, somewhat regretfully, I left her at another hotel in the town. It occurred to me how little I knew of her. She never mentioned her personal feelings, her thoughts on life, or whether she'd ever been in love. Certainly I was attracted to her … but then, it was now June 19, exactly a month before Gavino was coming back.

*   *   *

Enrico phoned Orgosolo, and Elena confirmed that a grand welcome in the usual Sard style was being prepared. "That means they're killing a piglet for us," he explained. "These villages might be poor, but they do well for themselves by way of food up there in the mountains."

The trip to Orgosolo, I realized, might be the last chance for an outing with friends before I left Sardinia again—perhaps for good. I was rather enjoying the feeling of putting a woman before everything, as I'd done only once before, in my even younger years. I was sure I could win Anna back, for secretly I was proud of my lovemaking, my tenderness, of the way I could show my worship of a girl I loved— when all my longing for sexual conquest, so desperate in loneliness, would give way to the peace of just being together. Even in bed I'd always had a tendency to put a woman on a pedestal; yet oddly, once past that terrifying hurdle of initial conversations, I'd never been shy in my caresses. It was always in intimacy that I could truly relax.

I couldn't conceive of Gavino treating a woman in the same way.

Twelve

I was, of course, eager to rush over the next few weeks, to make my trip to Rome and get on with what seemed to be the urgent business. But during this period came a day that jarred my consciousness—one that, I now know, was the happiest of my life. Perhaps this isn't very logical, since, if I set my mind to it, I could probably find other days with greater amounts of happiness in them. But for those I have to think and analyze, it's a struggle to remember them.

Orgosolo stands alone. For that reason the name will always sound bubbling and delightful to me—to be pronounced carefully, rolling the *r* and stressing the second syllable, with each *o* tense and rounded throughout, and the *s* sounding like a *z*: "Or-gó-zo-lo."

Even on the day itself I knew it was the happiest, although I mentally added, "so far." And in a way it involved Anna, too, since I still longed for her desperately. It was a combination of things: the deep joy of companionship, for normally I'm a lonely person; Margaret; and a sense of—what shall I call it?—*dislocation*, the realization of the insubstantiality of normal, everyday life.

* * *

An odd quietness surrounded us as the car ran downhill without the engine, with low, intermittent groans each time I put my foot on the brake.

Enrico was delighted. "Eh, Mister Arturo, we'll save a lot of fuel this way. It all helps with the cost."

Towers stood darkly on low hills in the shadow of higher ones: an army of nuraghi waiting to see if we were hostile.

Jim's voice came from the back. "As though we're entering a forgotten civilization, peopled by the ghosts of ancient warriors."

"Oh, how poetic!" But even Marcella, who'd been in a tight hug with Jim since we'd left Alghero, spoke with awe. "Macomer's famous for its nuraghi."

Already the countryside was trembling under the warmth of the sun, the shimmering currents of air giving the road ahead an elusive, insecure quality. As we rolled around a final corner onto a flat stretch, I jerked the car into gear again so that it pulled forward with a reassuring roar. Tall trees—chestnuts and a type of oak—lined the road, which soon was taking us into a winding valley with broad fields and surprisingly green vegetation.

"Oh-ho, we're going to Orgosolo, Mister Arturo." Enrico could hardly contain his excitement.

I'd awoken disoriented that morning. I'd been dreaming of a woman trying to kill me, but the shot turned out to be the sudden burst of my alarm, which I must have turned off as I stretched out my hand to protect myself. In the half light, the angels on their blue background above me could have been actual ones.

The four of us had set off at six. Now the sun was higher, more intense. Gradually the road was rising again, constructed to form broad curves that had been cut into the edge of the mountains, then crossing saddles of connecting ridges. Every so often we went through a village, following large blue signs indicating the road to Nuoro, the capital of the eastern mountainlands. Finally, we descended toward a large town in a narrow valley, from where we'd strike off into a region remote from even the modern Sard civilization.

We were expected in Orgosolo at eleven, but Enrico insisted on a detour. "Mister Arthur, Mister Jim, Marcella! We must go and see the *Redentore*. It's what Nuoro's famous for."

So now we stood leaning against a low stone wall with a shaky handrail, where the roofs of the town lay spread out below us. Picnic tables stood in sandy earth in the sparse woods behind us, but above them was majesty in austere isolation: an enormous statue of Christ the Redeemer raising mighty arms in benediction over the valley below. It was cold, for there was a wind blowing. Mountains and valleys stretched into the distance, with caps of snow, clouds in strange shapes—a country as endless as a scene reflected between two mirrors. Looking into the haze it was just possible to make out thin strips of white roads, lacking in confidence, leading toward villages huddled in the shadows.

Jim and Marcella wanted to climb up onto the statue to have their photographs taken. They writhed their way with difficulty around its projecting limbs, clutching hold of a stone toe or fold of clothing to support themselves. It seemed irreverent, but the Redeemer continued, unconcerned, to give his blessing to the valley, no matter what liberties others, even the religious Enrico, might take with him.

For a moment I wanted to be alone and experience in silent worship the permanence of what the statue represented. But I responded to Jim's call to come up and join them, clutching hold of a foot as large as a sprawling lion to help me. I almost expected it to wriggle in irritation, but it remained firm and reliable. Looking down on the lands spread out before me as Christ must have done when tempted by the devil, I thought of Anna, who seemed no more than a distant, insignificant image enslaving me. Here in the mountains there was freedom.

But Orgosolo was waiting. Enrico had managed to identify it out of the other mountain villages, a cluster of anonymous houses, some twenty kilometres away.

Spiralling silently down the mountain again, past the same views, we came to the shouting, peasant-filled streets of Nuoro below. We decided to take the direct but most primitive road, a cart track that sloped deeply into a wild, barren valley: dusty, bumpy, abandoned, going into the wilderness.

It was unbearably hot. A quarter to twelve. Five minutes passed, ten minutes more, and then suddenly the village was there before us, a mass of squalid, dilapidated houses, a solid square church standing out in grim isolation. We drove past a few outlying shacks, then the usual blue board saying prosaically, "Orgosolo."

We stopped at the only bar to ask for Elena's house. Suspicious hostility surrounded us, giving way to hesitant smiles as a handsome, dark-eyed man pushed his way forward. "I will show you," he said. "I'm a friend of Alberto's."

"Who's Alberto?" Marcella asked dubiously.

"Elena's brother."

The man squeezed into the back seat beside her and she wrinkled up her nose, hastily pulling her dress away so he shouldn't sit on it.

We descended through narrow, treacherously steep alleyways—a stone maze through which it was barely possible for a car to manoeuvre, courtyards of houses all cramped together in improbable confusion.

Concentrating on the driving, I couldn't immediately say what I found odd about the place.

Jim whispered to me in English, "Look how the shutters are closed. They're watching us from behind them. Like a hostile army."

We reached the yard of the house, and I edged the car in carefully so as not to hit any of the chickens squawking in front. Getting out, I was aware of an old woman looking down with unveiled malice from one of the windows. From the same house or a neighbouring one? I didn't know.

We entered a cool, darkened room—shutters closed here too—of a house that at first impression seemed endlessly large.

"Meet my brother Alberto," Elena said in her pleasant, gruff voice.

An older, serious man stepped forward to shake hands. "Welcome."

Everybody spoke at once. Cold water was brought in stone pitchers. Children clamoured around, demanding attention. Confused, excited conversation followed, while Elena and Alberto disappeared into the labyrinth of rooms to make some kind of arrangements.

I was greeted by younger brothers and sisters, by different people in turn. Alberto's friend Mario started asking me about my life in England, so I had to talk about mundane things when I'd have preferred time to absorb it all, to experience a life which suddenly was impossible to take for granted. It occurred to me that Alberto's and Elena's parents were missing. Did they live somewhere else, or was it one of those situations which everyone knew about but never mentioned in Orgosolo?

Escaping the conversation to go to the bathroom—how proud they were of having one—I was aware of how the house stretched on menacingly, how many dark corners there were even by day. There was a cellar too. Returning, I was startled by Alberto's head emerging from a hole in the floor of the stone passage.

I wandered into another empty room and sat down on a surprisingly comfortable couch.

The house remained cool, I realized, because of those closed shutters. As I sat staring toward the window I must have dozed, and then somehow I was in a dream. I had the arthritic body of an old woman, and there was a strange car arriving in my courtyard. I stretched out hands with aching fingers to push the shutters a fraction wider open. I tried to muster up enough saliva to project it down on the newcomers, but I hadn't the strength and could only drool a little onto the old, dry skin, which was pulled over my face like a tightly fitting mask. Interfering strangers.

I edged forward on my chair, gripping the windowsill. That young upstart Mario Cossu was with them. Then a girl, indecent, with a light dress, shoulders and legs all visible, pretty enough. That will soon change, you no-good hussy. Going into the Monagheddus' house, naturally. That's what comes of going away from home, thinking they know better than others because they've been to some kind of school at an age when they should be working. Their mother was no good, too, corrupting her husband, trying to lead him away from the life we've known for centuries. But we'd shown her. Now there were always interfering foreigners here. Said we had to change. Why? I'd like to know. What business was it of theirs? Someday we'll show them too. And Elena Monagheddu, with her so-called modern ways, not knowing her place. There she is now, with a whole crowd of them, shouting with excitement. What is there to shout about? Into the house with all of them.

People coming into the house—and I started awake, uncertain where I was. More clamorous introductions, and I could hear Maurice and Margaret's voices among the others. I sat for a few moments longer, shaking off my drowsiness, then made an effort and returned to the main room.

Margaret, talking to Elena, didn't at first see me. She seemed quieter than usual, overwhelmed. Maurice was in his usual wildly exuberant mood, joking with everyone.

He finally came over to me. "We had to come by coach. None of Margaret's friends would bring us. All keen on going out in their cars somewhere until we mentioned Orgosolo, when they suddenly remembered they were busy. As for the coach from Nuoro, we had an escort of police on motorbikes about ten strong. I've never seen a place so swarming with *carabinieri*."

We moved toward the door. Covered baskets were being loaded into Pimple and another, larger car, and I realized we were going out somewhere for a picnic.

"What are those?" Maurice asked, pointing at two large bundles.

"Those'll be the piglets," Enrico answered, rushing by with something. "It looks as if they've killed two in honour of the occasion."

We were ready to go, but Maurice needed to buy a film. It was decided that he and Margaret would come with me in Pimple, with Alberto's friend to guide us, while the rest would follow in the other car.

As we strained in low gear back through the alleyways, I was again aware of people watching us from behind the windows. The few women I saw in the narrow streets wore sackcloth masks over their faces and peculiar little four-cornered caps on their heads, reminiscent of the costumes I'd seen at the *Cavalcata* but drab and uncivilized, without their brilliance.

While Maurice and Mario were buying the film, I went with Margaret to stand by a wall at the side of the road, from where we could look down at the roofs of the houses on the next level below.

She gave a shiver. "Can you believe all this is real? I've never been to a place even remotely like this before. Just think, all this—and nothing else—is their daily life."

I watched two youths strolling casually past the car about ten yards away and wondered whether I should have locked it. But they satisfied themselves with spitting through its open window and moving on.

The other car arrived. Maurice and Mario returned and we set off, in a cloud of dust, along another white road, leading up the mountain. Rising hills, with patches of trees merging gradually into forests, which became denser as we climbed. Finally we arrived at a wide, open space in the woods where there was a *casa cantoniera*, a house for the road workers, next to a local garrison of *carabinieri*.

Alberto came over to the car. "They use it as a hunting lodge. You can leave the car open here. This is one place we'll be quite safe."

The man and woman who kept the house came out to meet us and we went into a room—dark stone again—bare except for a table, a couple of benches, and numerous pouches for the cartridges used in hunting wild boar. Alberto and his friend set about unloading the food: the two plump piglets, two hams almost as large, cheeses, masses of the local unleavened bread, and bottle after bottle of wine. Elena started sorting it out, while a younger sister got the record player out of the car and wound it up on a stone bench under the fir trees. That song again, about a grain of sand …

Now everyone was bustling around doing jobs, collecting firewood, carrying pots—I had to go and get water from a pump. Jim and Marcella had wandered off somewhere, and I thought it rather unsociable of them. I tried to imagine Anna being there, perhaps making her demands on me as Marcella did on Jim. And a doubt crossed my mind: wrapped up in herself, would she be out of place here as well, unappreciative of an atmosphere that somehow spoke to my deepest longings?

The fire was lit in an enormous hearth in the one bare room, and the two piglets were covered with fat and placed on spits above it. I stood with Margaret watching the ceremony. Alberto started cutting slices from one of the hams, and others came in to drink wine.

"They know how to be hospitable to guests in this part of the world," Enrico said. "Orgosolo might have a terrible reputation, but when you're friends, you're friends." He hurried away again to see if there were any other chores to be done.

"You're quite safe at the moment," Elena assured us. "All the bandits have gone away. The last one left five days ago."

This preoccupation with being safe …

Margaret gave a giggle. "Oh, dear, I was so hoping we'd see a bandit."

"You should be thankful. You never know what might happen."

I followed Margaret outside, where Maurice was cha-cha-ing with Elena's sister. We made our way around the clearing, past the *carabinieri* in their compound, to a spot where the forests were thinner, giving us a view over the valley.

"Did you know Elena's mother was murdered?" Margaret said. "And it seems the father's in prison. It's this vendetta business. She was saying there's not a single person in the village without some near relative who's been murdered at some time."

"So there's often no alternative but to become an outlaw."

"Even now many of the villagers go in fear of their lives. You wouldn't believe it was still possible in Europe, would you?"

We fell silent, listening to the sounds of the forest. We stood away from the others, looking down over a wire fence onto thick woods and scrublands below. On a day like this the violence seemed impossible, and the knowledge of its constant presence gave the beauty around us an inexpressible sadness. Yet such was the reality, the tragedy not only of Orgosolo but of the island as a whole, ashamed of this hidden secret of the mountainlands. Somehow the close awareness of death gave everything here a greater vitality, a sense that one must hasten to grasp life before it suddenly ended.

I watched Margaret while she stared thoughtfully into the distance. It was a day to experience in its fullness, rejoicing in life, in the sun, in love. "Ah, love, let us be true to one another, for the world, which seems to lie before us like a land of dreams, so various, so beautiful, so new, hath really neither joy, nor love, nor certitude, nor peace, nor help for pain"—a Matthew Arnold poem I'd learnt long before.

But now I frowned, for amid all the pain I still sensed joy and love and light, even certitude. I wanted to touch Margaret, take hold of her, tenderly; to take refuge in the normal, forgetting the frenzy with which Anna and I had struggled together. Was I right to be planning to leave, crazily, in a few weeks? Why pursue something illusory, when here I could be happy with friends as I probably couldn't be with Anna?

"And what's my love thinking about now?"

"A girlfriend. Only things have gone wrong."

"You don't mean you've been unfaithful to me!"

I grinned. "Not recently."

Her eyes rested on me playfully. "Are you in love with her?"

"Yes."

She was smiling, laughing at me, yet for a moment I thought I noticed an expression of sadness. I looked again, and she was as bright as ever, demanding I should tell her about it.

Just a few sentences, treating it as a joke.

"There's always me to fall back on."

She gave a cry of pain as I pretended to take her literally and we almost fell over. I put my arms around her to support myself. But at that moment there was a shout for us to come and eat.

Tables and benches had been carried outside under the trees. Alberto poured more wine, and we helped ourselves to tough little pieces of ham, of a stronger flavour than I was used to. This we ate with unleavened bread, adding liberal sprinklings of pepper. More heady wine followed, and then the almost traditional Italian cigarette between courses.

The piglets were brought out, dripping with grease. Elena fetched a couple of large enamel bowls, and Alberto and his friend started carving, the spits resting on the end of the table. At last the piglets were reduced to square lumps of meat coated with fat, and we again helped ourselves from the bowls.

"Eat slowly," Enrico warned. "It needs to be well digested."

The fullness was satisfying, but painful to the stomach. Another wine, sweeter. By half past three we sprawled, exhausted.

Reality. An atmosphere of happiness. Orgosolo, a place feared by the rest of the island, a country of bandits and suspicious, primitive people. How different from the traffic-packed, steel-and-stone civilization of Rome, where Anna, a remote city dweller, gave herself to love—with Gavino perhaps—and looked down on the barbarity of the south.

It was Margaret I could share this day with. We flirted as always, making the others tease the two of us, which cleared the way for us to go into the house so we could be alone together. I enjoyed letting them think we were going to kiss and be romantic. I wanted indeed to kiss her, when in our exuberant state it would be fun, natural. But she was still too enthralled by the surroundings and wanted to skip about frivolously. And then Jim and Marcella joined us and it was too late.

A shout from outside. "We're going up the mountain!" The jeep was waiting, with two *carabinieri*.

We all scrambled onto its open back. With a sudden lurch it set off along a narrow track through the woods. Soon we were shouting and singing, making turns of over ninety degrees and clutching on as though the sides of the vehicle were the edge of our world, whatever breath remaining from the singing bumped out of us by this crazy drive.

Consciously happy, I held on so as to have my arm around Margaret, feeling her bouncing up and down beside me. We drove through bushy country, still climbing, along narrow tracks, thrown about, bruised but emboldened by singing and alcohol. Still we went up, still I had my arm around her, hanging on to prevent her from being lost over the side.

Only small shrubs lay around us now. Already a wind was blowing, and we could see way down into the valley below. Above us a tall pinnacle of rock stretched up against the sky. With a skid the jeep stopped, and in the same moment the fitter members of the party descended to the ground, eager to set out on the final conquest.

Led by one of the *carabinieri*, strong and healthy in his khaki uniform and thick climbing boots, we started upward, trampling through a prickly gorse, heaving ourselves up over the rocks. My lack of breath made it slow and difficult. I was unsteady from the wine, and it seemed an impossible task to climb to the top of a mountain. Margaret was tired as well, and I found myself helping her, so that both of us lagged behind. "Oh, dear," she kept panting. "I'll never make it. Why the hell do we have to have such violent exercise after a meal like that?"

Long after the others we reached the top: a slab of rock, a wooden post, and a cold wind. But down below, the entire mountainlands of Sardinia stretched out endlessly into a dim, mysterious haze. We saw only mountains and forests, for the villages were too far in the valleys to be seen. A barren land devoid of any kind of civilization, even that of the village of Orgosolo itself—this was the notorious *Sopramonte*, beautiful, but hostile as an animal untamed by humans. Now I could envisage the murders and crimes as a manifestation of that country itself, a beast playing with men between its paws, forcing them to do what it demanded. You could still be happy, forget the monster existed, but it was always there, threatening, magnificent. Nature shouted its praises to God, proclaiming its own existence and demanding the attention to which it had as much right as humans—asserting that beyond these mountains and the echoing winds around them there existed only eternity.

From his mountaintop above Nuoro, I thought, the towering Redeemer surveyed these same lands. He saw with unchanging stone eyes the villages, the men living and dying within them. He saw in Orgosolo an unloved old woman who still muttered imprecations against everyone else. He saw an army of men, spread out through the forests around us, making their way toward some fugitive bandit, unshaven and dirty, with a gun and a bundle over his shoulder. And, if he looked toward us, that same Redeemer could see a young Englishman in baggy trousers and an open-necked shirt, with a tall girl in white blouse and plaid skirt: two tiny figures who had now moved away from the others they were with and sat sheltered from the wind.

Shots vibrated from below. Hunters.

Margaret seemed depressed now, tired. Both of us had become more sober. But there was a bond between us, a friendship that could perhaps have become more. I wondered what she was like at home, with her family. Did she blossom in a family atmosphere? Did she want a family herself? What kind of family would one have with her? Now I regretted having told her about Anna. I wanted to say, "I didn't mean it. I'm not in love with her. I only thought I was."

But even if in that moment I wanted Margaret more, we both knew it was only a strange aberration brought about by this curious day, when my usual values were being challenged. Anna was unimportant and yet all important. Nature was cruel and barren and yet sung praises to God. Margaret and I wanted each other and yet were rejecting each other. So many paradoxes.

We made our way back down the mountain with the others, aware of our sore feet and aching calves. I thought again of the Redeemer, supposedly existing for all of us: for Anna in Rome, for Margaret, for myself. I thought, too, of home, England.

In the jeep I sat next to Maurice, with Margaret opposite. I realized I'd hardly spoken to him all day. "How have things been treating you, then?" I had to shout to compete with the singing, which had begun again.

Maurice gave an unexpectedly broad grin. "You know why I came over this weekend? Because things would have seemed so intolerably dull in Rome after the week I've just had." He paused as the jeep swung round once more and he had to grab Enrico, who almost went over the side. "My girlfriend in England suddenly decided to have a holiday in Rome."

"Good for you! So things are going all right then?"

"Couldn't be much better." Maurice started a laugh, which changed to a hiccup as we went over a bump. "Boy, what a time we had though! But steady on, Winter, you'll be giving too many secrets away."

I felt pleasure for my friend, yet envy, too, remembering my own past week of happiness with Anna.

"You seem to be doing pretty well too!"

A moment of hope. "How do you mean? Have you seen anything of Anna since she's been in Rome?"

"Oh, good God! Sorry, old boy, you meant Anna. I'd forgotten about her. I meant with Margaret there."

"No, we're just good friends!"

"Pity," Maurice said without thinking.

We came upon a stream and everyone had to climb out so the jeep could cross. When we set off again, I was next to Margaret once more. For the rest of the way down, bumping wildly all over the place, we clung together.

I didn't want this to finish. I didn't want to return to Alghero. Nor did I want to leave Sardinia in a few weeks' time.

The track broadened, and there ahead was the *casa cantoniera* and the two cars parked in front of it. The jeep made three wild circles on the yard in front of the barracks, throwing us all into one another's laps until we begged for mercy. I ended up in one big hug with Margaret.

Back to Orgosolo, to collect our things that had been left at the house. I noticed that the old woman wasn't at the window this time.

Alberto was to take Margaret and Maurice to Nuoro to catch the coach to Olbia, and soon our two cars were bumping down the dusty road to the provincial capital.

In Nuoro, Maurice and Margaret departed. We said our goodbyes to Elena, Alberto, and his friend too. I told myself that my next really happy day, even happier than this, would be with Anna in Rome.

"What was Maurice saying 'pity' about?" Jim asked as we drove away.

"He thought it a pity that Margaret and I are just good friends."

"Good friends, good friends," Marcella said, trying scornfully to copy the English sounds. "That means *buoni amici*, right? How can any man and woman be just good friends!"

The road led on toward Macomer, and then back to Alghero.

And from there to Rome. At least, that's what I thought.

Thirteen

"Coming to Sardinia July 8th. Going to my parents first in Tempio. *Ciao*, Anna." Nothing else but the address in Tempio; on the other side of the postcard, a view of Roman ruins.

Carlo had brought me the card as we were all finishing our lunch, but Teresa had grabbed it from me and I was forced to chase her around the room to get hold of it. Even then she danced around, mocking me. "Oh, how serious he is! Still in love." She strutted toward me, thrusting out her breasts and rubbing them with her hands. "I thought this interested you at one time! Why won't you love me, Arturo?"

I managed to escape her for a quiet spot in the vestibule.

I stared angrily at the card as I read it again. Anna was *coming back to Sardinia*? On the *eighth*? Before Gavino arrived on the nineteenth? I sat bewildered, thinking how in the week since Orgosolo I'd been consulting timetables, making sure the boat was leaving on the right day, figuring out how much it would cost. I'd called it "working on the problem" or "making progress"—for how easy it is, while not achieving anything, to console oneself with mere activity. I'd looked forward to Rome as a new battleground, but it had all been for nothing. Now there would be the same old atmosphere, with its daily routine, instead of a romantic departure into the unknown. The thought of seeing Anna so soon—the coming Sunday—gave me no pleasure, since presumably Gavino would still be arriving on the nineteenth, just eleven days afterward. Desperately I searched for a different strategy. I decided I'd wait for a week after her arrival before going to find her in Tempio. Keep her in suspense, I thought.

But by the time the eighth came I'd changed my mind again. The knowledge that she'd arrived that morning left me with a feeling of urgency, and I couldn't bear the thought of delaying. I decided I'd wait only three days and leave for Tempio on the Wednesday. Jim, who'd claimed the car for his day out with Marcella, consented to run me into Sassari in time to catch the 6:15 bus.

"It's quite exciting, when you think of it," he said. "Just think: it might even change your whole life."

It was another beautiful morning, and I felt encouraged until I discovered that the direct bus had left at 6:00 and the 6:15 was the slow one. It took me all around the villages of the northern coast, and the patient beauty of the sea rather than the inland road only irritated me. I'd seen it all before, for it was the same road I'd travelled to Isola Rossa—and I recalled the immature affection of Caterina. Two hours went by before the bus even reached the promontory opposite the island. Then with agonizing slowness, it started to cross the mountains separating Tempio from the sea. High crags rose up in great blocks, sparkling in the sun, demanding admiration. I gave them their due, noting that the journey had now lasted three and a quarter hours. It was a quarter past ten by the time the coach was finally pushing its way through the streets of Tempio.

The driver backed the bus into position, then cut off the engine. The Sard voices became louder. I struggled impatiently with the other passengers, pushing to get out into a small, shaded piazza with the inevitable bar and people standing outside doing nothing. Tempio was like most Sard towns, with two squares, a prominent cathedral, and a small market in a back street. It was difficult to believe that Anna was somewhere in the meandering streets of this rough, provincial capital.

I found her house without difficulty, a crumbling plasterwork edifice indistinguishable from those on either side. A bell push labelled in fading ink with the word *Lorcas*. I pushed it with an expectant stab of recognition before advancing into a dark passage toward a flight of steps. Rumblings from above. A door opened and a sullen shout asked who was there.

"*Scusi, c'è la Signorina Anna?*"

"*No, non c'è.*" The door was about to be closed again.

I hurried up the steps, insistent, and asked the woman in front of me where Anna was and when she'd be back.

She came out of the door and stood on the steps where I could see her more clearly. "Who are you?" she said suspiciously. She was fat, and her hands were covered in oil and bits of green from the herbs she'd been preparing. Her face, although older, wasn't unlike Anna's.

"I'm an English friend."

She made a grudging effort. Anna had been there that morning and would probably call again the next day. She wasn't sure.

"She's not living at home then?"

"No." The woman squeezed around the door again and dragged it shut behind her.

I returned to the main square, depressed at the thought of having to wander around all day just hoping to find her. Several hours of lost time seemed worse than three months of waiting.

"Excuse me, are you German? Or English?" An unshaven, middle-aged man in baggy trousers took me unexpectedly by the arm and led me across the square. "I know of a valuable plot of land for sale on the coast, very cheap. Come and see the plans."

I gave a click of annoyance. "I haven't the money. And if you don't mind I'm in a hurry trying to find someone."

"A foreigner?"

"Yes."

"Arrived a few days ago?" Having failed in one enterprise, the man was equally willing to help in another. "I think I know who you mean. She won't be difficult to find."

He started to shuffle along one of the side streets, with a wave of his arm for me to follow. We entered quite an elegant restaurant, where he started to question the waiter.

"Yes, she's been coming here every lunchtime. She'll probably be here today. Came over from Alghero to get away from things, she said."

There was something wrong. "From *Alghero*?"

"That's right." The waiter evidently found it amusing. "She's American, I think, doesn't speak much Italian. Works with tourists or something."

I remembered something about Isabelle's having a boyfriend in Tempio. Some divinity was playing a joke on me. "She's not the one. I'm sorry, I should have checked who you meant first."

"Who's it you want then?"

"She's Roman. When you said a foreigner … well, really she was born in Tempio, but she lives in Rome."

"Anna Lorcas? She arrived on Sunday. Isn't staying with her family, it seems." My guide was exchanging glances with the waiter. "Never mind. We'll find her."

My companion delighted in this unexpected game. His pursuit, owl-like, was like a bird's courting. Back to the main café, where he asked others. Several of them knew Anna but not where she was living. More steps to other bars, back again to shops. Everyone seemed to recognize her (and didn't want to be associated with her) but could only suggest other places to ask. All tended to assume at first that I was looking for Isabelle.

Soon we'd covered most of the town. It was half past twelve. At last there was more definite information. Anna was friendly with one of the maids from a hotel on the road out of town. The guide strutted ahead proudly as we approached it. More suitable for Anna, modern, with a small but elegant bar that was luxuriously furnished for Sardinia.

We asked for the maid.

"Oh, that'll be Nella," the porter said. "She has a friend who came from Rome recently. Was going out somewhere with her today, I think. It's her day off. I have the friend's address, though."

A smart walk now, back to the town centre, to a dreary apartment house. Panting up seven storeys and drumming on the door.

"Anna Lorcas? She left with a friend twenty minutes ago."

A crestfallen descent into the street below. The man refused the tip I assumed he expected. "No, it was a pleasure to help you. And remember, if you do ever want to buy land … "

I returned for lunch to the restaurant, wondering what to do in Tempio for the rest of the day.

It was as I was finishing my coffee that Anna came in through the door.

* * *

Lying in bed after a night of making love, with the first light filtering through the shuttered window, both of us happy with all problems between us resolved; getting up to a breakfast together and a day spent out of doors, wandering over the mountains with nothing else to do but think of each other—such in my more fanciful moments were my dreams of that first meeting, impossible though they might have been, impossible as reality had shown them to be.

"Oh, and there was a bus strike in Rome."

After half an hour Anna and I were still sitting in this dreary restaurant, talking of trivialities like two strangers. After the initial surprise she'd been glad to see me, and the first ten minutes, when I'd mistaken her welcome for something more, had been happy. The inevitable exchange of unimportant news had followed, and neither of us mentioned Gavino.

I was bored. Sitting talking to the woman I'd wanted for three months, I was aware that it was an anticlimax. I tried to remember the girl I'd known in April, who'd been in love with me; but it wasn't that girl at all, just a twin sister. Oh, she was still the same person, who constantly drew misfortune, who even after arriving in Sardinia had spent only one night at home because her brother-in-law had almost forced himself into bed with her. But between the two of us was a chilled restraint, as though we were lying together but separated by a blanket that both, for different reasons, had to hold in place.

I sat wondering what she was like when she was with Gavino.

"I was unhappy without you for a long time," she said timidly. "Do you know that?"

It didn't matter now. That was as completely finished as the week in April was finished. But as she spoke, sadly, of her first unhappiness in Rome, talking with her soft, genteel, romanized accent, I was aware that I still wanted her. Disappointed because it was a gayer, more capricious Anna whom I remembered, I told myself it was still possible, after all, to love the twin sister. Outside the sun was shining, and a couple of youths were strolling by unconcernedly. What a strange scene, I thought, sitting here in the middle of Sardinia, wanting to say "I love you" to a girl I scarcely knew. She wasn't even beautiful, I realized.

"How I hate coming home," she was saying, her mouth pouted forward. "They criticize me for behaving in a way they consider shocking, and then my brother-in-law dares to treat me like a prostitute because no one outside will know about it." Her indignation reminded me of her attitude toward the Sicilian peasant on the ship: *Ma come si permette!* But then she turned and smiled suddenly, and there was that old mischievous glance. "All the men, they come after me like that, you know!" She snapped her fingers.

She looked down at the table. "I suppose I'd better tell you about Gavino."

I said nothing.

"That's what you've come for, isn't it?" She waited, then went on: "Arthur, *mi dispiace …* "

I'm sorry. Was that all she could say?

She started rattling her spoon in her coffee cup. "I know it seems wrong of me. How shall I explain it? Perhaps this sounds heartless of me, but he was there and you weren't, or it wouldn't have happened, of course. And then it happened without either of us wanting it. You remember I said he'd taken me out to coffee? Well, it was just one of those things without importance, and then he asked me out again, and I went because I felt sorry for him. He seemed so lonely. And he was so kind, so childishly happy, so much in need of help."

She smiled happily as she recalled it, and I felt physically cold.

"He wanted to kiss me and I said, 'No, I'm Arthur's girl. It would be wrong of me.' And then we went out again the next day, and he did kiss me, and well, it wasn't so bad, you know. And it didn't seem very wrong either. So we started ... going out with each other. I think I love him, *e basta*. That's all."

"Does he love you?"

Lost in her memories, she hadn't heard me. "Gavino, when he's not afraid of himself, is one of the most charming persons I've met."

The nagging thought returned: had they, to what extent, made love?

"What about you, Arthur? Why did you come to see me when I've treated you as I have?"

"I wanted to see you."

"And now you're sorry?"

"I came because I was determined to compete with Gavino. I want you too much to let it finish like this. But it seems it's useless."

The two youths still strolled outside, back and forth. A motorbike went by.

"What do you want me to say?" Her elbow was propped on the table, her head resting against her hand. "I ought to tell you there's no point, that I can't give you what you want. I'm sorry. I don't want to make you unhappy. You're too kind and good for that."

I grunted, although, absurdly, I was gratified at being praised.

"I don't want you to love me," she continued. "You once told me not to love you, remember? But then, I *think* I love Gavino, but I'm not sure. I might be able to love you one day, if that helps at all. I just can't say there's no hope. And I'd still like to see you as well. I like you. But at the moment I feel I love Gavino, have a responsibility toward him, more than to you. Do you understand?"

"Yes."

"You're unhappy, but you're stronger than he is. He needs me more."

Again my pride responded to the compliment. I shrugged my shoulders. Ironically, it was my very strength that had made me lose Anna.

"Arthur, I'm in such a muddle. Then I think, what does it matter? This won't last very long, and when it's finished, will it have been worth it? Perhaps not, but I don't care."

Silence. Her solution would be to remain with Gavino as long as it lasted. But I couldn't tell her that. I wanted her for myself. As she continued talking about him, I sat looking out of the window, at the neat, white cloth-covered tables around us, at a calendar of a woman in a provocative bathing suit. "I think I could love you, you know," I remembered her saying before. I'd spent so much time thinking of her, longing for her—invested so much in my feelings that if I walked away there'd be nothing to fill the emptiness.

It was time for action, if only leaving the restaurant and getting into the open air. I stood up, and she followed without question, indifferently gathering her things together, then waited while I paid the bill.

I slammed the door behind us as we went out into the street.

"At times, I feel I don't love anyone," she continued as we walked. "I feel that nothing matters at all. So the thing to do is make the most of everything that comes, enjoy the moment without thinking about the future. When it finishes with Gavino, I'll be unhappy for a while— my whole life's unhappy—and then there'll be someone else perhaps. Or perhaps there won't. Who knows?"

"And then what will happen?"

"What does it matter what happens to me? I'm not particularly important."

"But you can't just go from one man to another!"

"Why can't I? For goodness' sake, don't start on a moral lecture now!" She banged her bag against the side of the houses as she walked along. "Oh, yes, it's not the done thing, I know. But the done thing is usually hypocrisy—what do I care about it? I'm sick of thinking about things, what's right and what's wrong. It doesn't mean anything anyway. There's one thing in life that's worthwhile, what most people call love, and when I find it I'm prepared to sacrifice everything for it, and I couldn't give a damn what people think of me!"

"Oh, yes, that's all very well in theory. In theory I agree with you. Say to hell with others as often as you want, but what's going to happen to you in the meantime? You go from one to the other having as much experience as you like!"—venting my anger on her by condemning her behaviour.

Walking past the main square I was greeted by my guide of the morning. I nodded back, uneasy because Anna and I weren't looking as happy as we should have been. And because of the sermon I was giving her, which even at the time I knew was insincere.

"I don't go with just anyone! I thought I was in love with you, and then I was—am—in love with Gavino. And why should you bother about it? You'll have forgotten me in a little while."

I didn't know what to say to her. So began my constant preaching to her: playacting, all of it. Words just to show my resentment and make an impression on her, which I had difficulty believing myself. Because I resented being the loser, I took refuge in the opinions with which I'd been brought up, sounding no doubt like the guardian of the middle-class morality I detested.

The sun, still eating into the stone of the houses and streets around us, was reflected from one window after another. Tempio, attractive in its siesta, intruded on my thoughts. I started looking at a couple of kids brawling, trying to take an interest in something other than Anna and myself. But there was no pleasure in it, or in Anna's company either.

We reached the hotel where I'd hoped to find her a few hours before, when reconciliation still seemed possible. Mechanically, I ordered two coffees at the bar. We sat down in red and green upholstered chairs, at modern tables, a reminder that there was a civilization outside Sardinia. And none of it had the slightest importance.

I struggled with my words. "All this you say about love being the only thing worthwhile, and giving yourself to it completely—"

"Why not? It's in moments like that that I'm happy. I was happy with you too. Wouldn't you have wanted me to give myself completely to you?"

"Yes." But she hadn't. I'd willingly have argued her views with others, but directed against myself they became a parody of my own ideas.

"Do you and Gavino make love much?" I suddenly asked.

"It depends what you mean by making love. Completely, no."

I quickly changed the subject. That they hadn't made love completely was a consolation worth holding on to.

From the jukebox came a hit tune of the day, the melody of a trumpet dancing and crying to itself. Melancholy words. "*Ti perdevo*"— I was losing you. Anna saw me looking at her and turned away, while the trumpet danced on to the end.

"My mother's miserable too. My father has someone else. I've always hated it at home. I just try to make the most of life when I can. I just don't care anymore, and I'm sick of thinking about it. *Sono stufa di pensare, capisci?*"

I, too, had had enough of thinking. I felt as though I'd been crying the whole afternoon, and the tears in my mind had washed away the pastel image I'd formed of Anna, distorting it into an ugly blur.

There was a shout from the doorway, loud enough to have reached me from a hundred yards away. "My gosh! Now who'd have thought to find you here?"

It was none other than Isabelle, in the company of a tall, rather distinguished-looking man. "Larry, my darling, this is Art Fraser, a friend of mine. Gee, what a surprise!" Isabelle, with her "goshes" and "gees," sounded more like a crude imitation of an American than a real one.

There was no point in pretending we were just leaving. I introduced Anna.

"So this is your ladylove you've been pining for! Well, what are we going to drink? Larry, love, how about a cocktail each?" She flopped into a seat. "Of course, his name's not really Larry," she confided. "It's Renzo. So superbly romantic, don't you think? But apparently that's short for Lorenzo, Lawrence, so I call him Larry, get it?"

Anna looked puzzled.

"But what a day we've had! I just can't tell you." She grabbed hold of us to be sure of her audience. A long story followed, as Isabelle squawked away.

I looked at Anna and smiled. Perhaps our discussion, after all, was better interrupted. With more opportunity to observe her as she sat pretending to listen, her face both sullen and mischievous, I realized how little she'd changed.

A small thing brought us closer together. Larry hardly said anything, sitting uncomfortably as though in anxious awe of Isabelle. But as she finished her story and we all leaned back in relief, there was a sudden silence—bowels evidently relaxed too—and there came one of those unavoidable explosions loud enough to reverberate around the bar.

Isabelle was furious. "Larry, how could you! That's disgusting!"

He protested. "Isabella, *cara*, it was you!"

"What d'you mean? It was *you!*"

They were still arguing about it when they left.

"Arthur," Anna said, hiding a smile. "Can I tell you something? I just couldn't help it."

*   *   *

In the evening, when we were having a meal in the same restaurant as earlier, she started talking about Gavino. "He can be so wonderful at times. His eyes are so tragic. Haven't you ever noticed? But he always says how happy he is with me. I don't think I'll ever forget the weekend we had in Amalfi."

"Amalfi?"

"In June, when there was a feast day and a Sunday together. Some relatives asked him to stay with them, and they invited me to go as well." She remembered who she was talking to and looked at me anxiously. "We ... only had the one night together."

It was the weekend I'd been with Jim in Cagliari. On the jukebox here, too, came the same record we'd heard in the hotel bar, of the trumpet playing.

"Why do I always give my love to the wrong person? I give him everything because I want to, yet he takes it without knowing what it means, doesn't appreciate it. He says he loves me, that it's different with me than with the other girls, and then he's strange, won't talk to me. Doesn't believe me when I tell him I love him. Or just laughs and says I'll be sick of him soon. When I said I was coming back to Sardinia, although he's coming as well, his first words were, 'Oh, good, now you'll be able to see Arturo again and forget about me. Make love to him if you like. There's no reason why you shouldn't. It doesn't matter to me.' He's not even jealous of you, and yet he says he loves me."

In a way we were happy in our unhappiness. We both got a little drunk, which united us against the outside, sober world.

"Can I see you tomorrow?" I asked.

She looked doubtful, but then gave a grateful smile. "I ought to say no. Oh, dear, why is it so difficult? It's up to you whether you want to see me or not."

"I want to."

"In the evening then? I promised to go and see an old friend of the family during the day. Then the day after tomorrow I'm going to Sassari, with Gavino."

"The day after tomorrow? I thought he wasn't coming until the nineteenth?" I'd planned everything around what Enrico had told me.

"No, the fourteenth. I'm going over to Olbia early to meet him off the boat. Oh, but I might have to leave tomorrow if there's not an early bus."

A tactical manoeuvre: "I'll go back to Alghero tomorrow morning and get the car. I can take you to Olbia."

I took her to her apartment and only then realized I had nowhere to stay. All my plans had been for nothing. I walked back to the hotel with the bar, more concerned with Gavino's impending arrival than with getting accommodation. But they had a room.

It was difficult to sleep. The day had been long, full of unpleasant facts that had exhausted my mind and left it like a ransacked room. In my imagination it was like going around trying to tidy things again, in a chaos where I didn't know where to begin. All night, in the midst of my confusion, Anna was lying there on the bed with Gavino, giving herself to him. But why not completely?

In what must have been a dream I merged with Gavino—enjoying Anna, who was holding back because of this other man Arthur. Anna, I want you. Why hold back? I need you more than Arthur. Why should Arthur resent me? He's from the outside world, has more chances. Go back to him, though, if you want. Why should I bother with it? Oh, your kisses …

But there was something wrong. Anna had now disappeared, and there were only lumpy pillows and tangled sheets.

I woke up. Something Anna had said about Gavino's not believing in her love, not being jealous of me. Why, then, if he was too insecure to accept that love, shouldn't I take her from him?

I lapsed into sleep again.

Fourteen

I must have woken late. I lay for a while looking at the bedside lamps, the clean stone floor, the walnut wardrobe beyond the white glaze of the washbasin. For a moment, at least, I could enjoy the feeling of freedom, although there was a lingering knowledge of muddled dreams in the night. I pushed back the sheets and started to get up.

I had to get the car. I booked a phone call to Alghero and had a leisurely coffee while waiting for it to come through. Then I spoke briefly to Jim and was just in time to catch a coach to Sassari by the direct route.

It took me down through a valley surrounded by mountains that reminded me of Switzerland, then onto lower hills whose monotony was broken only by occasional villages, all looking the same. After two hours we came to Osilo standing isolated on its hilltop. As we approached Sassari, the earth, flecked with white from the chalk, sparkled in the sun. My body felt loose and relaxed from the heat, and with sweaty peasants intimately close, I was aware of my strong physical urge to make love.

I pictured Anna's body, the moist nakedness I'd known but which, it seemed, I'd have so long to wait for again. Now there was only this bouncing coach with its few, handsome, perspiring girls—whom it might have been fun to strip bare and penetrate in this wilderness of nature, but they were Sard, impenetrable. Like Caterina, I thought.

Another coach to Alghero.

"Oh, here you are," Jim said casually as I walked into his room. "I was just going to lunch with Marcella. Want to come along too?"

Both were eager to know what had happened. I told them about it while we were eating.

"So the chase is on, is it? I suppose I'd better say goodbye to Pimple for the next few weeks."

Marcella pretended indignation. "What a nasty man he is, taking our car away from us."

"Perhaps you wouldn't mind helping out with the tourists."

"Of course." Jim pushed his plate away and thoughtfully lit his pipe. "So things are going badly then?"

"Oh, she still thinks she's in love with Gavino. She's ... been to bed with him."

Marcella gave a giggle, then stopped because Jim was looking serious.

"Never mind. It doesn't always mean much."

It did, though. These things mean a great deal when one's young and tormented by ideas of supposed fidelity. The human vice of jealousy is, after all, the one major stumbling block to sexual freedom.

Immediately after lunch I left again in the car, along the same hot road to Tempio.

"*Ciao*," Anna said as I walked in. "I was hoping you might come sooner. I got back earlier than I expected."

"You wanted me to come, then, after all?"

She bounced across the room—she was wearing slacks, which made her look plump—to a suitcase she was packing. "You know what I said last night. I enjoy your company."

"Nothing more?"

"I don't know. You make me feel very guilty."

"It wasn't your fault."

"Because of Gavino too." Quickly she bundled the rest of her things into the case. "Arthur, dear, I've been thinking. If you've got the car, let's go over to Olbia straightaway. I can stay with some friends of mine."

I nodded. "Have you told your parents you're leaving?"

"No. Why should I? They don't care what I do as long as I don't make a scandal for them."

The drive was a happy one. Both of us tried not to dwell on the things that were separating us, so for a while Gavino was excluded.

"Arthur, I'm glad you've come. I oughtn't to see you like this, but there's no harm in it, is there? If only you didn't think you love me— that's what makes it so dreadful."

As we drove into Olbia the sun was low over the mountains; beyond were the darkening waters of the gulf. The road ahead was closed to traffic, while the crowds surged over it in their daily *passeggio*. While Anna went to her friends, I walked to the hotel near the port, remembering the day I'd spent in Olbia after she'd left for Rome. I felt a sad affection for this town, which had been part of my nostalgia. I still wanted her.

At the hotel there was no room, nor was there at three others I tried. I called on Margaret, who now had a flat of her own, but she wasn't in. I wrote a note asking her to phone the first hotel and leave a message if she could put me up and went away to find Anna again. She was more worried about my not finding a room than I was, and it was oddly satisfying to tell her I'd sleep in the car if necessary.

"Arthur, what's happened to you? You seem to have gone quite crazy since I've been away."

"Perhaps I have," I said heroically, realizing I was actually enjoying the thought of abandoning my normally cautious behaviour.

We decided to go and watch the ship leave. We strolled along in the half-light, holding hands, with the sea slapping gently against the stone wall a few feet away. A little further, mysterious in their dark, spiky forms, were the frameworks of the wooden posts where a kind of rockfish was cultivated. Two figures in a faded landscape, I thought. I put my arm around Anna, and she giggled and did the same.

She was sarcastic. "Oh, how romantic it is. They must all think we're in love. It's funny, isn't it? If only they knew."

The train rumbled slowly past us on the other side of the pier, taking passengers out to the ship. People were getting cases down from racks, meaningless forms who nonetheless had lives of their own. We stopped to watch it pass, and I thought of how earlier I'd expected to be on that train myself, on my way to this girl who was now beside me. Instead, it was probably this very train that would take her to Sassari, with Gavino, the next morning.

Suddenly Anna broke free from me and started to skip along the quayside. "I'm happy with you, you know," she said when I'd caught up. "Happier than I am with … " She didn't say his name. She ran up to me, stood on tiptoe, and kissed me on the side of my face. "There, you deserve that. You're so nice, and I like you so much."

We were approaching the pier head, where the ship, close in against the side, towered above, with the name *Arborea* in large letters on its bow.

"Have you seen which ship it is?" Anna asked sadly. "I shall remember that, you know."

We watched the people going aboard. The walls of the ship, up against us, were solid and immobile. In some unknown place within them we'd first kissed and lain down together.

"There'll be another ship arriving tomorrow morning," I said. "With Gavino. He'll be getting onto it now in Civitavecchia."

"It's strange. I feel almost afraid of seeing him again. I shan't know what to say to him. Yet I want to see him so much."

At just after ten there was a loud blast on the siren and the walls began to move, edging their way out from the quayside, while the passengers looked over them and waved. A few minutes and the ship was turning, slowly swinging its bows away until, after a wide arc, only the stern was visible. Then with a surge of water it pushed its way toward the gap in the mountains, steaming more quickly. Very gradually its lights became smaller. For a long time it was there, still a part of Olbia, and then it was too small to be significant any more. Another ship, at the same time, had put out from Civitavecchia.

We walked back quickly to the shore, for it was cold now, and went to the hotel for a drink. There was no message from Margaret. We sat listening to the pianist, watching other foreign couples.

"They probably take us for lovers here as well. Arthur, I hope you don't have to spend the night in the car. You know, it's nice to have someone do stupid things for me."

When we left there was a message at the desk. Margaret had phoned to say I could stay there if I didn't mind a camp bed.

I took Anna to her friends' house. "Enjoy yourself tomorrow. You'll have a good time forgetting me."

"Don't you think we'll be talking about you most of the day? Gavino will talk a lot of nonsense about my not needing him any longer. We'll probably spend most of the time quarrelling. I'll hardly be able to forget you."

I kissed her on the cheek. "I'll see you in Sassari, then."

"Perhaps it would be better if you didn't."

My obstinacy asserted itself. "I'm not going to give up when at last I know what I want."

"If I refuse to see you?"

"I'll come just the same."

"I can't stop you from being stupid."

*   *   *

Margaret let me in, indicating not to make a noise. "If my neighbours know I've been entertaining a man in my flat, my reputation will be lost for good! It's already half gone because of the number of men I go out with."

"I hope you haven't been waiting up for me."

"Only an hour or so. It doesn't matter, though. What on earth are you up to?"

"Anna's arrived. She's staying in Olbia tonight as well."

"So why didn't you bring her along? I could have had the camp bed. My bed's big enough for two."

I was too tired to respond to her gaiety. The bed was already prepared, and after a few more questions Margaret left me. I heard her for some time afterward in her room. No Italian, I thought, would ever believe we'd slept apart, and I felt a moment's regret. But I undressed and turned out the light, crawling into a lonely camp bed, to torment myself for a second night with thoughts of Anna and Gavino.

At just before six I was wakened by the siren of the ship as it came into the harbour. I pictured Anna standing at the end of the pier, waiting for Gavino. I dozed off again and woke half an hour later. Now they'd be on the train, holding hands.

I didn't say much about Anna to Margaret, although she seemed to understand. It turned out that she, too, was having an affair with someone, which vaguely disturbed me.

Over breakfast I remembered to tell her how I'd met Isabelle in Tempio.

She helped herself to some English marmalade. "You know she came here a few weeks ago? That's another scandal I'll have to live down." In her bewilderment Margaret looked oddly pretty. "And then she had the nerve when she left to suggest how I should liven Olbia up a bit for the tourists!"

The day passed slowly, although the heat and the sea made it pleasant to do nothing. I was grateful to Margaret, who was reassuring precisely because toward her I felt little of the sexual desire, almost nauseating in its intensity, which drew me toward Anna. Margaret represented normal, comfortable values I could relax with. Marriage to someone like her, I thought, would probably lead to an easy life. But deep within I longed for the warmths that creep over one's body, the drowsy submission to one's senses—all those burning and pleasurable symptoms of the consumptive illness that was my love for Anna.

At last I set off back to Alghero, prepared to sacrifice myself to this disease. Or was it really that, anymore than the sleeping sickness of everyday life?

Whatever it was, I wasn't yet interested in being cured.

*   *   *

A day or so later Anna and I were at Castelsardo. A northern bastion of Sardinia impressive in its strength, it aggressively defended the feudal lands behind it. Looking toward it from the coast, you saw it as an enormous promontory of rock standing proudly in the sea, wearing its clusters of houses like a cloak flung behind it and falling in careless folds to spread out majestically over the surrounding countryside. For its head, this crouching figure had only a stone fortress looking out blindly toward the northern sea. But if you were standing on the fortress itself, the power and security of the walls were taken for granted; you could relax and look down on the houses of the village, with their patchwork of roofs turned upward in obeisance in a long procession up the road. The view of the blue sea and the tiny harbour to the west created a mood of serenity disturbed only by the wind.

In the heat of a July afternoon, the wind was welcome as the two of us leaned over the wall looking at the dark blue line of the coast below and listening to the waves as they tried to crash their way through the rock.

"I think I'll throw myself over there," Anna joked. "That would be an answer to everyone's problems."

"Don't be silly. Today's too pleasant to commit suicide. Besides, do you think I want to get married to a corpse?"

She giggled. "I suppose not."

She allowed me to stroke her arm, and then she was holding my hand, squeezing it. I leaned closer to her, aware of her pleasure at feeling me beside her. We'd driven out that afternoon from Sassari, where she was staying in the same *pensione*—but not with Gavino. "You crazy?" she'd said. "In Sardinia, well even I haven't the balls for that."

Now I told myself that she was getting used to being with me once more, and from this it would be only a small step until she wanted me again.

"It's weather like this and a scene like this that are the glory of Italy," she went on. "Everything else is horrible—the people are primitive, their behaviour primitive, however nice they may be. But then you get the Italian summer, and all that doesn't matter any more. The sun makes you lazy and contented, too lazy even to think about your own problems. Arthur, let's just be happy. We're friends, aren't we?"

"Of course." There was no reason at the moment for discord. Anna had told me in the car about her meeting with Gavino. They'd quarrelled about me, little else.

Together we walked down the long road through the village to the beach. The inhabitants stared at us disapprovingly because we were holding hands.

"How stupid they are here!" Anna said impatiently. "And to think I might have the same mentality if I'd never been away to Rome."

"You'd never think the same as they do."

"I'd have had to become a whore."

"Who taught you *whore?*"

"You did, of course. Who else? It was one of the first things you taught me."

We came to a stony beach, where a few young men were playing football and others were swimming noisily a little way out from the shore. Watching them from the terrace of a café nearby, talking idly, I reminded myself that I had to be patient. Anna had been cuddling close to me as we walked; already I was beginning to master her spirit, but she'd probably continue for a while to feel awkward about Gavino.

We went for a walk, arm in arm, following the course of a stream that crept into the sea. I was still aware of a restraint between us. I couldn't expect everything to change at once. I had to give her time. But it was better than the long weeks of waiting and doubt.

"Where are you taking me?"

We walked on by the stream, through shrubby fields and over a barren hillside, away from the road. The sun had disappeared over the hills to the right and evening was beginning. She was silent, knowing I was taking her somewhere where we could lie down and kiss; that alone with her in this evening hour I could have no other thought.

But there she was wrong, I told myself. She'd expect it, want it, but I'd make no move toward her—and this would make her want me all the more. She'd be disappointed, thinking I was holding back because of her feelings for Gavino.

We came to a sheltered spot where the stream formed a small pool. She didn't say anything but put her coat down where I suggested. We sat talking, and I soon became aware that I hadn't the will power to carry out my plan. It was no longer a question of not kissing her but of delaying it, letting her *think* I wasn't going to kiss her. She lay back while I sat sucking at a straw, pretending I was resigned to the fact that she belonged to someone else. But her breasts filling out her blouse, her white cardigan around her shoulders emphasizing the softness of her body, the reeds around us in the half-light hiding us from the rest of the world—all this made it impossible to resist for long. And was there any point in resisting? Take the moment as it is, something whispered.

What use was there in endlessly waiting, sacrificing the present for an uncertain future?

I lay back, too, feeling the contact of her arm and the side of her body, tempting me. I still made no move toward her, and she was probably wondering why I was waiting, wanting me to take her in my arms.

I sat up again and looked down at her. She closed her eyes. I waited for some moments longer before kissing her, gently, hesitating. She responded, timidly, then slipping her tongue into my mouth.

As my body pressed down on hers, she put both arms around me, pulling me to her, then kissed me with angry strength, lifting her own body to force it against mine, wanting me.

For a moment I didn't believe it. But then, incredibly, it was true. She was abandoning herself, demanding me. I reacted at once, eager both to dispel my first disbelief and to show my sudden joy. And it was true; it must be true. My desire overcame my doubts, and I felt pain in my sudden happiness like the surge of blood into a limb that has become numb. My plans, it seemed, had worked already. As I kissed her, forcing her to the ground so she could feel my hard penis pressing against her through my trousers, my pride told me that now— whatever might happen in the future—I and not Gavino had won. She was kissing me too fiercely for me to say anything, her tongue seeking mine, her hands rubbing upward over the small of my back. I drew away enough to undo her blouse and slip my hand inside, urgently, and once again her soft breasts were mine. With outstretched fingers I tried to touch the nipples and draw them together so as to have them both under my hand, while they kept slipping apart elusively.

Within myself, paradoxically, I recognized a feeling of anticlimax. I'd expected more of a struggle, and my victory seemed too easy. For an instant I was uncertain whether I really wanted her, like a man who, having made one difficult conquest, is immediately more interested in the next. But I had to love her now. To forget my doubts I started to caress her more violently, wanting her all at once. Rolling her breasts, flattening them, kneading them with my one hand. Pushing the other up under her skirt until I reached her panties; pressing down firmly to feel her pubic hair, rough and moist, underneath the silk-like material; stroking through it her two pouting folds of flesh—she gasped as I did so—preparing gently to slip my fingers underneath to begin the final conquest.

In those few seconds my life had suddenly changed. My physical environment consisted only of this woman's body while all else was obscured by a fabric of exalted emotions surrounding me and soaring to heaven like the over-gilded pillars of a baroque chapel. For a few seconds—for such emotions were too intense to last—there echoed in my ears only the hymn of joy to express my private communion with her.

So it was a sudden shock when the hymn stopped and the walls disintegrated to admit again the bare world of the reeds above me.

"No, that's enough," Anna gasped, struggling to get her mouth free and pushing my hand away.

I paused, not understanding the interruption.

"Enough," she repeated, firmly moving my hand from the moistness around her legs and then trying to ease the other from her breasts. "Please!" She pushed herself up onto her elbow.

I let go and sat up, looking down at her and the disorder of her clothes.

"I'm sorry," she said, starting to put her clothes straight. "I shouldn't have let you do that." She was breathing heavily, frightened. "It's not good for either of us. And then Gavino … It's not fair to him. I can't just—"

"Gavino!"

The world of fact had returned completely, and there was a mocking fanfare from the angels inside the chapel as it finally disappeared with all its gold luxury. I turned away in hatred. Leaning back, I looked up at the twilight above, aware of the sound of the stream still flowing on callously. I moved forward a little, and there on the hillside was a grotesque phallic cactus bending toward me in derision.

"I'm sorry," Anna said. "It was my fault."

It was mine, a total defeat, for trying to take her prematurely. I'd spoilt everything. My sexual urges, hers too, had been too strong, seducing us both from what I'd intended.

"I thought for a minute that you really meant it."

She hesitated. "I'm sorry. Did you really think that … Gavino was as trivial as all that?"

For a while neither of us spoke, then she looked at me and repeated that she was sorry. "Didn't you enjoy it, though? Even if I stopped you before you reached … ?"

I was too angry to give in to her lightheartedness. Instead of accepting, joking, and perhaps beginning again, I had to let my hurt self have its way, dramatizing the whole situation, spoiling it.

"Why the hell did you have to let me pet you at all?"

She was surprised. "Didn't you want to? I thought you did."

"Yes, I wanted to, of course I did! But it happens it was a little more than sex I wanted. Why did you have to be so bloody convincing if you weren't interested?"

She didn't understand. "But you wanted it and so did I. I enjoyed it, didn't you? But I didn't want it to go too far because of Gavino."

I didn't say anything. I insisted on demanding the impossible, angry that it had meant nothing to her, angry at my own physical frustration.

"You're nice to make love to, you know. You've got a wonderful body. But I'm one of the few who doesn't want you to be only a body."

Silence followed as she tried to tidy her hair and only succeeded in releasing some more strands.

"Perhaps I *am* only a body. It seems like that at times." Then she contradicted herself. "No, I'm more than that, you know."

"Are you?"

"*O basta!* Perhaps I'm not, who cares?" She got to her feet and flung her coat around her defiantly. We started walking back down the valley, the same way we'd come. I was still angry, uncomprehending of her attitude, while she couldn't even understand what was wrong.

"Oh, don't be so serious. What have I done that's so dreadful?"

I thought I'd won, and I'd lost, that was all.

She kicked a stone lightly out of the way. "We're friends as before, aren't we? Oh, Arthur, you wanted it and so did I, because I like you. What was so wrong about that? But now it seems you don't like me any more."

I put my arm around her again and started holding her to me. I still wanted to be close to her. Something in my attitude had changed, but I couldn't identify what it was.

"Arthur, what's wrong? I'm sorry if you were disappointed and thought I'd forget Gavino because we … nearly made it together, but I don't see that anything else is changed. I told you before, I do as I feel like. I suppose we're meant to stay apart and not touch each other because of a lot of out-of-date principles."

I should have said, "But why won't you go further with me?" but I didn't, because my own motives weren't clear enough. My very despair, of course, wasn't so much that she didn't love me but that she refused to go far enough with me in pure sexual enjoyment.

We drove back in near silence. Eventually our antagonism became stilled, our bitterness softened into regret that we were fighting each other. Before reaching Sassari, we stopped at a bar for a couple of beers and took them to the car, driving on and stopping again off the road. I suggested we should sit in the back to drink them.

Anna changed places without a word. "Again?" her glance seemed to ask me.

My physical need for her was too strong. She showed no surprise when I started to kiss and caress her once more. She even responded, joking about it, pretending to enjoy it—no, not pretending, for there was a sense in which she always enjoyed it, loved the physical stimulation. But she was remote, too much in control, strangely maternal and aware of her own strength. It was the moment in love when the man is reduced to submission by the woman who's spoiling him, caressing him as though he were a baby in her arms. When he can be conscious only of the comfort of her breasts in which his head is buried, and she can be distracted, think of other things, yet not forget her responsibility. Her eyes watched the lights of passing cars.

"Can I see you tomorrow?"

"No, Arthur. I only came in the back with you because this will be the last time I shall see you."

"I shall come just the same. I've told you."

"I shan't see you. What's the point? You don't love me now."

"I still want you too much to let you go like that."

She sighed. "Come tomorrow if you like, then."

We drove back into Sassari. "When are you seeing Gavino again?"

"I don't know. He said he'd phone. He just leaves me waiting, because he thinks it's pointless our going out too much. Unless there's something special to do we only ... find ourselves thinking of the one thing."

Sassari was empty; there wasn't even anyone coming home from the cinemas.

"I love you," I said, meaning, "I want you desperately."

"It isn't true. You'll see that yourself when you come to your senses."

"I don't want to come to my senses!"

I needed to make her believe it. Instead of stopping at her house I pressed on the accelerator. "Let's go for a drive!" I raced around a couple of streets, came back to the house again, slowed down, then did the same a second time.

"Arthur! How ridiculous you are."

I screeched around the same two corners and back to the street. A third time past the house, and then, instead of turning, I headed out of the town, to the south.

"Let's go down the *Scala di Giocca*. See how long it takes us!"

We passed the road leading off toward Tempio and came to the Madonna at the top of the modern hairpin road descending in a dozen spirals to the valley below. Anna, I noticed, crossed herself as we went by the Madonna. Good, I thought, I'll frighten her. At the first bend I swung the car around it, taking it on the inside, conscious of the proximity of the darkened tree shapes coming to meet us. There was no sign of other cars on the road, so I could afford to take the bends at speed. The second bend was to the right. I came out of it badly, well into the other traffic lane. At the third bend I screeched around the corner, zigzagging the steering wheel.

"Arthur, be careful."

"It's all right." I went faster.

I was safe, only pretending to drive carelessly. It was just a game. More bends, and I was aware of Anna clinging onto her seat beside me.

"Shit!" At the bottom I must have hit something in the road and suddenly I was on the edge of the road, careening toward a tree. I grabbed the wheel more tightly, missed it, and skidded on the gravel along the shoulder before I could manage to brake and come to a halt.

Anna gave a sigh. Then silence.

A little frightened, angry with myself, I drove on and turned the car around by the cement works. Going back up the same road, I had to drive slowly anyway, because it was steep.

I felt foolish. Without intending it, I still jolted the car over the curb when I finally got back to her *pensione*.

"I'm not worth an accident," she said quietly.

No, I thought bitterly, you're not.

I drove back to Alghero.

Fifteen

"Oh, Mister Arturo, *buon giorno.*"

I turned toward the voice that had come from behind me as I unlocked the car. I felt the envelope lodged thickly in my inside pocket, my own rhetoric sealed securely within it. The sentences I'd just written still echoed in my mind, and I put them aside with some reluctance. It was Caterina, the girl I'd flirted with at Isola Rossa.

"*Buon giorno,*" I greeted her politely, amused at the idea of a Sard girl actually coming on to me. "*Come stai?*"

"*Bene. E tu?*"

"I'm fine."

She was embarrassed, not knowing what to say.

"So how's school?"

She looked down at the ground. "We've finished for the summer now."

I made an effort. "Will there be any more excursions?"

"Perhaps."

We managed a minute or so of conversation, and I was aware of her looking at me as I got into the car and drove away. I was still smiling a little as I turned onto the familiar road to Sassari.

My mood, I told myself, was one of unconcerned resignation: like an empty bag blown helplessly toward some destination by the wind. Writing my letter had been exhausting work. As I drove I tried to recall all I'd said, satisfying myself it was as forceful as I'd intended: "Suddenly I realized I was in love with a girl who no longer exists … who had unacceptable ideas … who was sincere … enjoyed physical love because she really felt something, but held herself back because she wasn't sure."

Next I'd said something about longing for that girl again, "foolishly," and asking myself what had happened to her. Then came the first bludgeoning reproach: "But I'm not in love, never shall be, with a girl who makes love violently with one person while claiming to love another, who regards it all as a pleasant occupation to be indulged in whenever the partner is pleasant enough … who says she's more than 'just a body' but encourages people to think of her in just that way. Who gives the impression that she means it and then: 'I'm sorry, it was just a bit of fun.'"

With self-righteous satisfaction, I rehearsed more phrases. The ending, too, was important. Was it conciliatory enough? For I didn't want to force a break with her. "Perhaps I've been unfair. I don't know. I shall probably still come in the evening, because in spite of everything I still want to see you. And then, who knows? My love to the first girl, Arthur."

I drove up to Anna's *pensione*, resisting my desire just to see her and be friends. I left the letter in the box as I'd planned, then departed quickly since it was lunchtime and she might be home from work. Driving away, I was half aware of a figure at a window above. I imagined her coming anxiously to the door, finding the letter, thinking perhaps it was goodbye. Opening it hastily, afraid, skimming through the first few lines without taking them in. Running to her room, flinging herself down on her bed to read all of it, crying. Miserable, lonely, realizing she'd lost the good opinion of the only person who could make her happy.

I drove back to Alghero feeling rather pleased with myself.

After that day in Castelsardo I should have left Anna. But I was a terrible loser, determined still to win by almost any means. And so I said—wrote—some quite odious things that in other circumstances I'd have ridiculed for their hypocrisy. If I now reread that letter (for Anna later returned it to me), it embarrasses me with its reminder of the melodramatics one will stoop to so as to get one's way. I know in advance where I'll find certain sentences, such as, "You take my love, with a '*mi dispiace*, it's Gavino I want,' and then decide to rub dirt all over it by giving me free samples," and others as bad. All for the sake of producing an effect, although I told myself I was honestly expressing what I thought. But the letter did serve a purpose as far as my own attitude was concerned, for it drained away some of the venom within.

I was deliberately late arriving that evening, and Anna met me at the door. "I thought you weren't coming."

"What made you think that?"

"Well, you were so late, and … other things." She took me in. "My landlady says you can come in if you like, but you mustn't stay late. I've got some letters from the business to translate into English. Would you ... like to help me?"

I agreed, without enthusiasm. We went into her room, and I glanced with curiosity at her hastily made bed. She got out a dozen or so folders from a pile of things on a bookcase and pulled up two chairs to a table.

"Your letter was quite a shock to me," she said quietly. "Can you see I've been crying?"

"It doesn't show." Gratification, though. "I'm sorry, Anna."

"It doesn't matter." She took one of the letters from its folder, brightening a little. "Did you hear me this morning when you came? I called out to you. I was at the window."

We started translating. Doing something together, dull, normal, was reassuring after the last two days.

"Thank you, Arthur," she said when we'd finished. "I enjoyed it."

"I too. *Anch'io.*"

"You know, I'm such a stupid girl. I was upset by your letter, and it seemed the best thing all round if you stopped seeing me. And then this evening you didn't come and I was disappointed."

My letter, then, had had the effect I intended. Now I could be conciliatory. "There's still something of that first girl in you, you know."

"Try to understand me. I ... like you so very much, but I still feel the same way over Gavino."

The next evening was less successful. We'd driven to the coast for a meal at the Lido di Sorso, a place noted for producing some of the best snails on the island. Outside was the unseen beach and waves of the northern Mediterranean. There were crowds around us, subdued lights, and a jukebox playing sentimental tunes. To talk to Anna I had to lean across an inexplicably large table, emphasizing our isolation from each other. Not having heard anything further from Gavino, she was worried about him. I felt his unseen presence distracting her attention, drawing her gaze away as though to an unhappy ghost she was seeking, in doorways, windows, at other tables.

We started with scraps of peppered ham similar to the hors-d'oeuvres I'd had at Orgosolo. The meal, at least, served to cover our silences. But each time a man came through the door, Anna would glance hastily toward him before turning back and smiling conscientiously at me again.

The snails brought some relief. Smaller than the French escargots, they were rather tough, with a strong sauce, so that she had difficulty eating them. "How on earth shall I get through all these?"

As she struggled with her piled-up plate, she kept looking at me helplessly, asking what she should do. There was something about that smile; in such moments I felt like Tantalus trying to pluck his grapes, unable to believe his senses when they resisted his grasp.

"It's true, though," her distance from me seemed to be saying. "You're the outsider now, trying to steal Gavino's girl from him."

She left most of the snails. "I'm sorry. I'm not hungry. You finish them if you want."

They were hard, tough, and black, like parrots' tongues.

"Arthur," she said over coffee, "may I show you something?" She took a letter from her handbag. It was addressed to her in Rome, in Gavino's writing.

I hesitated.

"I'd like you to read it." She gave me the first two pages.

There was none of the usual Italian rhetoric for the sake of effect. It was direct, a sincere expression of bewildered feelings, telling Anna of Gavino's difficulties, his lack of confidence.

I paused in my reading. "Surely someone who can write like that doesn't need to have such a low opinion of himself."

"*You* did of him. You said you were surprised that anyone should fall in love with him."

"I know." Something I'd said, carelessly, in that first letter after her explanations.

"He was very upset by it."

"You showed him?"

"I shouldn't have."

It was wrong of her. How could I ever apologize to Gavino for that? What I'd said was unkind and unjustified, written in a moment of anger—but I'd never intended Gavino to see it. I felt ashamed. It had turned into a gratuitous insult, creating an unbridgeable gulf between us, and he'd probably never forgive me.

I read his letter more carefully, contrasting its simple nobility with my own pettiness. Then the last sentence on the page: "I shall never forget that unbelievable joy during that weekend when we were together … "

"And?"

She hesitated, then, with a shrug, handed me the other pages.

Gavino had written a description, as though it were a story, of his feelings when he and Anna had been at his cousin's house in Amalfi. With other people there he'd barely managed to kiss Anna before she went off to bed. After the goodnights he'd been by himself in his room.

"I was alone," I read, "as always. I undressed and got into bed, listening to someone in the living room clearing away the dishes and taking them to the kitchen. Sounds of running water from the bathroom, and then an uncertain silence. Wanting you, Anna, yet not daring to go to you. Better sleep, I thought.

"Then a slight creaking told me I'd woken again. The darkness breathed in a way it hadn't before. I stretched out my hand and touched your leg where you stood. A rustle as your nightdress slipped to the floor. Your hand was groping, too, pulling back the sheets so you could move in beside me. You pressed your lips to mine. Tears sprang from my eyes in disbelief.

"You had nothing on but your panties, and my mouth found your nipples. 'Shh!' you whispered as you took hold of me."

The beauty of Gavino's letter partly mitigated my pain, and I looked at Anna with a loving respect. I knew now that my love was hopeless, unnecessary. But it hurt, just the same.

It should have been a moment of catharsis. But then came the reaction, a determination to suppress any thought of surrender. Self-centred obstinacy overcame my nobler instincts, making me dismiss them in the overbearing imperative of "I want." I started to behave like a jealous child, despising myself, summoning my stubborn will—*calling it up*—to do my bidding.

"Let's go for a walk."

We started walking along the beach, arms around each other, still aware of an attraction making its demands of the moment. Me too! my pride demanded, as though I were one of the Sards. Anna didn't say no when I tried to kiss her, for our sexual urges remained, tempting us with their heady promises.

"Don't you feel anything for me?"

"Of course. I'm a woman. I'm weak too. You excite me. You do just the right things."

I tried to excite her more, but she quickly moved away out of my reach. "No, that's enough."

We walked back to the Lido, then to the car for the return to Sassari, a journey that went on and on in its silences.

Then once more we were in Sassari at night.

"I'll see you tomorrow."

"No, not tomorrow. I usually went out with Gavino on Thursdays. He may phone me."

A number of men were walking home from the pictures.

"Arthur, stop, quickly!"

Surprised, I pulled to the curb.

Her hand was on the door. "That was him! I'm sure it was. With some others turning into the Via Mazzini!" In an instant she'd flung the door open and was gone, running headlong back along the avenue and disappearing into a side street.

Suddenly alone, I leaned over to pull the door closed again. After a moment's reflection I made a clumsy U-turn, then drove back and turned onto the other street.

She was still running, pushing past other men in front of her, her bag bouncing against her side. As I drove alongside she clutched the arm of a tall man with glasses walking with three others.

Then she stood where she was, turning away in sudden misery. The man smiled.

"Oh, but never mind," I heard someone's voice through the car's open window. "Come along with us. We'll give you a good time."

They gathered around her, mockingly inviting, jeering at the sight of a girl out alone at night.

"Don't go with Giovanni here, though. He'll only give you the clap."

"Here, twenty thousand lire. How will that do?"

She tried to push her way through but they wouldn't let her. Her voice came loud and angry through their laughter: "*Canaglia!*"

"Eh, take it easy!"

I got out and elbowed my way to her. She caught hold of me and I led her back to the car.

"I thought it was Gavino," she sobbed.

The men, still laughing, shrugged and walked on.

I drove her back to her *pensione*. She was crying now. "*Buona notte, Gav ... Arturo,*" she said, hardly noticing her slip of the tongue.

*   *   *

"One final question, young man, if you'll excuse the indiscretion. Ha ha ha!"

It hadn't been a good idea to use the day to catch up on my work and see tourists. I sat talking to a man in his early fifties, almost bald but with a wide, bushy moustache.

"What can you tell me about the maid who does my corridor? Teresa, she's called."

Guardedly, I replied, "She can be very lively at times."

"Yes, but you know what I mean. You're a man of the world." He gave a nasty smile. "What about other things?"

Illogically, I resented another Englishman's interest in Teresa, who'd already commented on his attentions. "You can try if you like. I can't say what success you'll have."

I left him and went for a walk. I found guests like this particularly nauseating, with their jocular confidences and hints at the way I must enjoy my work. I strolled down by the port, wondering what Anna and Gavino were doing on their day together. Sitting on a wall and looking at the angular fishing boats, I watched a swirling eddy of water around one of the posts in the harbour. It seemed that Anna and Gavino were driving my mind into revolving circles, and the only thing to do was withdraw from it all. And—I thought again of the man with the moustache—why not find another girl as a consolation? Even now I could return to sleeping with my more attractive tourists. Wouldn't that be more realistic?

It was now, though, that outside events took a hand, imperceptibly. For most of us it's not the earthquakes, the sudden calamities, that change our lives. It's the little things—the car that won't start, the friends who visit at an inopportune time—which can set in motion an apparently arbitrary chain of events that at some point impinge on our major plans or set new ones in motion.

"Arthur!" Maurice's voice came over the phone. "Get over to Cagliari for me tomorrow, will you my lad? We've got to get things sorted out with Ruggiero there straightaway."

Which meant, I thought gloomily, that I wouldn't be able to see Anna that day either.

I dialled her number.

"Gavino?" Her voice had a kind of muted eagerness.

"No, it's Arthur."

A long pause, followed by an "oh" I could hardly hear.

"I've got to go to Cagliari tomorrow. I won't be able to see you after all."

An uninterested silence on the other end of the line.

"It doesn't matter. *Ciao.*"

"Anna?"

Silence.

"What's the matter?"

A mumbled answer I couldn't understand.

"What is it?" I repeated three times into an unresponsive void.

Finally the voice made an effort. "I'm sorry. You phoned at the wrong time. I ... was crying, that's all."

"Gavino?"

"I asked for the day off tomorrow. I'd hoped ... but he doesn't want to see me. I'm not seeing him today either."

"Shall I come over?"

"No, please don't." A long pause, as though tears were dropping into the phone. "He just kept on saying it's useless, that we don't feel anything, that it's just a temporary sexual attraction."

"What will you be doing tomorrow then?"

"I don't know. *Me ne frego.*"

"Why not come with me to Cagliari?"

"No."

"Why not?"

She hadn't the will to argue about it. "Oh, if you like."

"I'll call for you at nine o'clock," I managed to get in before she put the phone down.

*   *   *

She seemed sustained by a determined cheerfulness when I arrived in Sassari the next morning.

"I'm sorry I spoke like that on the phone. You called just after Gavino. I hoped ... he might be calling back again. He was in one of his moods."

The sun shone weakly through a slight haze, as though in promise of later glory—a reminder, somehow, that our relationship was only second best. We drove down the *Scala di Giocca*, with its broad concrete curves standing out sharply against the indistinct background of the valley below, almost a different road from the one masked in blackness a few nights before.

"I'm having lunch with this man Ruggiero. You can come along if you'd like. I'll be going back to his office afterward to deal with business."

Mischievous: "And what will he think of me? That I'm your mistress, I expect."

"Probably. It'll add to my prestige!"

It was midday when we reached Cagliari, where the streets were even more crowded, hotter, than I remembered. Some time during the morning the haze had given way to an unclouded sun, which was now oppressing the city, but the glimpses of sea still provided a distant hope of salvation.

Ruggiero, an expansive businessman in an impeccably styled suit, was most impressed with Anna. "I must congratulate you," he said to me as we sat down for the meal, "on your choice of … companion, shall we say?"

Anna smiled at him seductively.

He talked more to her than to me and insisted on paying for both of us.

"We could almost be a respectable married couple," she whispered while Ruggiero was settling the bill. "I could be the wife who charms her husband's business friends into giving him the best opportunities. Could you see me in that role?"

"You're not respectable enough. People would admire me for having you as my mistress—"

"But look down on you if you married me? Like the rich man who marries a chorus girl?"

"Something like that."

Ruggiero returned. "Shall we go then?" He turned to Anna. "It was indeed a pleasure to meet you, Signorina Lorcas." He held her hand just a little too long.

At half past four when, my business completed, I found Anna again, she was hot and tired from wandering around the shops. I wanted to take her to the beach where I'd been with Jim. Perhaps it was a form of superstition, as though the atmosphere there would work in my favour.

We went to the same bar under the wickerwork shelter with its jukebox, in front of the same beach huts.

I changed alone. Anna didn't want to swim. She had her period. I wasn't even to see her in a sexy bathing suit.

"You know," I said, grasping at my memories, "one of my conclusions about you? With you one can be natural, reveal those dark secrets in one's life of which one's normally ashamed."

She brightened suddenly. "Funny, Gavino said that too. Perhaps I even fell in love with him instead of you because he told me all his secrets first."

"Perhaps I'd better tell you some of mine then."

"All right. Let me see … how many mistresses have you had?"

I looked at her, wanting her. I was uneasy though. My darkest secret was that at my age I'd had relatively few.

"You see, to start with I was bothered by the morality of it, and by fears of getting the girl pregnant. And I held back because of this ridiculous idea of saving something for marriage."

"And I've never made love completely at all!" she confessed. "I'm still a virgin—isn't that terrible?"

"I wouldn't have expected it."

"Oh, it wasn't on moral grounds. There've been a number of reasons—mainly not many men I've felt strongly enough about. With one I was going to, though. We tried but it was too difficult. And then the last occasion I wanted to … it was an inconvenient time, like today."

A month ago. With Gavino in Amalfi.

I went for a swim, plunging into the water and striking out energetically.

After dressing, I drove back with Anna in near silence to the town and, without stopping, turned onto the road for Sassari.

The sun was setting now and the landscape was as beautiful as all landscapes are at that hour. I remember telling myself melodramatically that it was like the sun going down over the Sardinian hills for good as far as I was concerned. Yet there was no real pain. Just a mild anger, perhaps, and nostalgia.

We stopped at a bar near Oristano. I ordered Sardinian Silver for us both. The memory of something beautiful.

Anna turned to me in excitement, then was suddenly embarrassed.

"What is it?"

"It's only that that's one of Gavino's favourite wines."

"Gavino is, was, and ever shall be, amen!" Then I remembered. "Of course, it was Gavino who brought it to our party. With a bottle of Sardinian Gold as well."

"That's so typical of him! If he has to make a present he always chooses a bottle of each. But he never drinks the Gold himself."

It was as though Gavino had been ahead of me in everything, with Anna belonging to him before any of us had ever met. It occurred to me that they were both Sard and I was the foreigner, who only thought he'd become assimilated. As I drank in thoughtful reminiscence, I was aware of a couple of bats vibrating around each other, swirling up higher into the dusk and approaching again as if their whole lives consisted of nothing but a short-lived dance.

"I wish I *could* love you," she said suddenly. "I've said it before, I know. I like you, admire you—"

"You admire me, but you love Gavino."

"But I admire Gavino, too, even if he needs my help so much. You probably don't realize what a genuine, worthwhile person he is. Do you think it's for nothing that I feel like this about him? It may not be love—there I'm only confused—but there's admiration! But, yes, I *do* love him. What drew me to him, I suppose, is that he stands apart from others."

So do I, I wanted to say.

"Not from his own choice perhaps. He's obstinate, won't accommodate himself to their ways, and for this I admire him. It's because I understand this, because he's not lonely with me, because we both want to be different, that I feel I have to give him what I can." She took a long drink of her wine.

We seemed to have been talking about Gavino all day. All three of us wanted to be different. Why, then, were we fighting? The clash of three individualities. Dim lights, flies above on the ceiling, long rows of bottles behind the bar, some marked with the rugged square shape of Sardinia. When was all this going to finish?

"But then he doesn't trust me, shuts himself off from me, tells me to leave him in peace."

It was dark when we left. The headlights picked out feebly the curves of the road taking us toward the north. Toward England, too, I thought. Another world.

She gave me a quick kiss on the cheek. "Just to show you I'm still your friend. Don't get the wrong idea."

She rested her hand on my knee. Then she made a suggestion that startled me, so that I wondered if it were entirely unpremeditated.

"Arthur, why don't you go and see him? I so much want to know what he really feels. You might be able to talk to him where I can't."

"I doubt if he'd say anything to me."

"He might."

I kept my eyes on the road ahead. At first I rejected her suggestion, but wasn't there something in it that appealed to me? Was this, then, the turning point?

Vaguely I sensed a solution toward which Maurice's phone call and this day in Cagliari had been leading. I was tired of these useless car journeys and constant maudlin conversations. But why go to see

Gavino against my own interests? Or *was* it against them? In my mind I pictured a reconciliation with him, the two of us reunited in a shared love for Anna.

I still needed convincing. "What time is it? I *could* go, I suppose."

"Now?"

"It's not too late."

Gradually, my depression was being encroached upon by the simplest of vanities: the enjoyment of feeling myself a hero. The thought of action appealed to me, although I couldn't then imagine how it would turn out. It's perhaps difficult to know exactly why I made that effort to see Gavino, although I'd like to think it revealed something good about myself. But as I glanced at Anna sitting beside me, I felt I might never see her again.

There was still a long drive, plenty of time to think. For an hour we scarcely spoke.

At last we reached the cement works that marked the approach to Sassari, before the ascent of the hairpins of the *Scala di Giocca*, once again in darkness. As I began steering the car up the rising curves, I was aware of a sense of inevitability. In an hour's time it would all be over, and the result ... well, let that take care of itself. I was even looking forward to seeing Gavino again.

We passed the large board announcing "Sassari." I took Anna home.

Sixteen

"You'll probably find him with some friends in the bar on the Via Roma."

I crossed the Piazza d'Italia to the street beyond and its large bar on the left-hand side. Looking through the window, I saw a whole crowd of them sitting around two tables pushed together. Gavino sat at one end, talking; his gloomy doctor friend listened with the others. Claudia, looking bored, sat a few places away from him.

I stopped outside, waiting for my breathing to become slower as I observed my former friend: the same pleasant, triangular face with glasses, a neat blue suit, no different from when I'd last seen him. Perhaps we might yet become friends again. I opened the door.

Gavino looked up and saw me. For a second he said nothing, taken by surprise, but then he jumped up.

"Mr. Arthur! How good to see you again! What have you been doing with yourself all this time?" He grasped my hand with the usual friendly Sard welcome. "Come and join us. We'll pull up another chair." His eyes avoided mine, though: it was an act for the benefit of the others.

Claudia looked interested. "Greetings," she said with a strange intonation.

Gavino placed the chair for me some distance from his own.

More formalities, introductions, and shouts of welcome followed, as though Gavino and I were the most intimate of friends. He called over the waiter to order another drink and was most attentive. Then he continued telling everyone about the Rome trip, while they all encouraged him. "Eh, Gavino, take me along next time, eh?"

Suddenly I found myself part of a group of men enjoying themselves in lively conversation. It wasn't what I'd intended. Gavino was still avoiding looking at me directly, and I watched him, thinking how he'd been in bed with Anna, how he'd written beautiful letters to her. There was no hint of it in his appearance, with his pleasant, shy, intellectual face. Anna was so different that I couldn't really see them together. Later we'd both be able to talk; Gavino would manage to stay behind.

After he'd finished talking about Rome, there was a moment of awkwardness before individuals began conversing. Claudia was looking at Gavino and me in turn, as if waiting for something to happen. A subtle change had taken place in him, as he'd consciously withdrawn into the background. Only when there seemed to be a chance that I might be left out of the conversation did he make an effort, again, to ensure my participation.

"You must tell my friends here all about your job, Mr. Arthur." A moment later, "And what do you think of us Sards?" As soon as I'd become the new centre of attention, Gavino sat back and depression spread over him, stiffening his muscles so that he seemed uncoordinated, like a self-conscious actor.

Impatient for the opportunity of seeing him alone, I was more and more forced into conversation, telling the others of my impressions of Sardinia. While trying to answer their questions, I manoeuvred to catch Gavino's eye, to suggest somehow that we might leave. But Gavino was growing ever more sullen, sitting now half turned away from the table, watching the waiter preparing coffee behind the bar.

Finally he got up. "I'll get some more drinks."

"The girls in England, they are all right, yes?" one man asked insistently. "Like Claudia here?"

She scowled.

I watched Gavino. He came over with the drinks and handed them around. There was one short.

"Aren't you having one?"

"Me? No, Mr. Arthur, I am tired. I am going home to bed."

"But ... "

Gavino returned to the bar and stood waiting for his change.

"So you can do what you like with most girls?"

"Not exactly ... "

Gavino said *buona notte* to the waiter.

"But they'll let you make love to them?"

"Damn!"

Gavino had hurried out of the door without even looking back at the table. Of the others, only Claudia had noticed, and an expression of bored contempt suddenly showed on her face. The rest were still engrossed in their stupid questions.

I couldn't believe it. Like a frightened puppy, I thought, scuttling away out of reach when it knows it's wetted the carpet.

Ten minutes later I finally managed to leave, asking Gavino's doctor friend to tell him to phone me at the hotel the next day. I walked to the car feeling angry and bewildered. Gavino, of course, hadn't understood. But how could I help someone who ran away? My sympathy for him had vanished.

I got into the car. There was nothing to do but return to Alghero. But I hesitated, not yet reconciled to driving away. Slowly I turned the key, thinking of all my wasted good intentions. And yet wasn't I enjoying it too? Haven't I said that in many ways Gavino and I were alike? Yet here was a situation that confirmed my self-respect, for I'd never have run away like that. Frightened puppies ran away; the cats, too, were terrified of humans in Sassari and Alghero; but men didn't behave that way. So I told myself.

Soon, though, I was to find my respect for him growing again, in a rather odd way. There was a knock at the car window. It wasn't Gavino, as for a split second I'd thought, but Claudia.

I leaned over and opened the door.

"Can I get in?"

"What's up?"

She slumped down into the seat and pulled the door shut. "Nothing." She sounded angry.

I grunted. "Are you unhappy because of Gavino too?"

"You're joking! Unhappy because of that fart?"

The unexpected violence of her reaction surprised me. "How much has he told you?"

"About his little girlfriend that he took from you? Not much. I can guess, though. Wasn't that why you came tonight, to have it out with him?"

"Sort of."

"Just like the cowardly weasel he is, to run away with his tail between his legs!" She added, "It's all he's got between his legs anyway. What a man for you! All sham, flowery words, and nothing else. He's empty, a great big vacuum, a puff of air disappearing into space. A fart, as I say." She gave a little chuckle. "Ha! That's rather clever. I hadn't thought of that when I called him that first. Did you know I was at the university? Only Sassari, of course. Never got my degree, though."

Instinctively I rebelled at her unfairness, which I felt almost like an attack on myself. "There's more to manliness than flexing your muscles and showing off in front of others, as most do here. He's very sensitive."

Why, it occurred to me, should I now be defending Gavino to Claudia? I groped for a logical argument. "No other Italian would have walked out tonight, because of his pride. He'd have fought a verbal duel to the very end, overwhelming me perhaps with meaningless pleasantries—"

"You don't know Italians."

"And so as to show the others, and me, too, that he wasn't humiliated." I was exaggerating, letting my ideas run away with me, but I wanted to convince her. "Gavino understands the futility of that kind of pride. I admire him for not doing what everyone else would. It's a private matter. He'll phone me tomorrow instead."

"He's just a fart," she repeated. "He won't phone you. He's no good to anyone."

"Then why are you so concerned about him?" I justified him angrily: "If people are so concerned about him, fall in love with him, doesn't that mean there's something to fall in love *with*?"

What I'd known all along.

"So that's what you think? How stupid you are. I'm getting cold. Start this damn car and drive me somewhere, will you? Up and down the main street if you want."

I started the car and drove it back along the Via Roma.

"Why are you so upset?"

She leaned back against the door facing me. "You think it's because of Gavino? No! He's the most spineless man I've ever come across. I'm upset because I'm bored! Bored, do you understand? When I'm with people, men that is, Gavino or anyone else, I occasionally, just once in a while, forget my boredom. But he's hardly a man anyway, no use to a woman at all. In public you're ashamed of him, and in the bedroom he's like a frenzied rhinoceros, except that his horn's not as big. For six and a half minutes—I timed him once—and then it's all over. That's one mercy, I suppose."

"You're probably no good to him as a woman." I turned a corner, screaming the tires in the approved Italian manner. "Anna, I gather, has more sex appeal."

"Want to try me?"

I ignored her.

"Here, turn left here. Then keep going straight. Oh, yes, Anna. Don't tell me. There are plenty of women with maternal instincts who just love a child to play with. I bet he sucks her tits and tries to get milk out of them. 'Oh, mummy, mummy, I do love you so, please play with my little willie. It feels so good when it gets all hard.' I had a brother like that when I was ten!"

"But you're still upset about him."

"Because I'm still bored, damn it! I thought this evening there'd be some entertainment, at least. Here, turn right."

"If all you say is true, why do you go with him so much?"

"Why do you think?" She drummed her fingers on her knees, looking ahead at the houses we were approaching. "He pays well. He's got money, our Gavino, or hadn't you realized? It's the one thing he's got going for him. But what a fool! How I despise him! If I were paying what he pays me, I wouldn't turn over and go to sleep after five minutes—or rather six and a half."

Something else was troubling me. "Tonight," I asked, "had he 'engaged' you for tonight?"

For the first time she was disconcerted. "No, he hasn't since he came back from Rome. I turned up at the bar myself, just before you came." She almost shouted at me before I could comment: "Because I was bored, do you understand! I'm a woman too. I'm not one of your cheap streetwalkers. I'm not used to being rejected by men, particularly for amateurs like Anna Lorcas. That's my form of pride, I suppose. No man has ever been dissatisfied with me. Now stop the car on the right, behind my Giulietta. Or are you going to reject me too?"

"Well—"

"Oh, you don't have to pay, if that's what you're thinking. I don't work that way. I'm not a streetwalker, I've told you. Have one on Gavino. He's paid enough for you ten times over. Twenty if you include taking your girl away from you."

I followed her into the house, still resenting what she'd said about Gavino. Again, I half identified with him perhaps. Somewhere within, I was aware of a grudging respect.

Claudia, when she'd taken her clothes off, was certainly beautiful, and I'd no intention of resisting. Perhaps I'd known it would finish like this from the moment I'd seen her at the car window. That night was one glorious release from my frustrations—and I hadn't realized how much I needed it. There's no point in describing it, for Claudia was, after all, a professional, and I imagine all good professionals are alike. But, apart from being my first one, she was also one of the best, and I'll long remember the sheer physical bliss of that gorgeous body, which knew how to re-create desire in me again and again. Oh, there was no hypocrisy. She didn't pretend to have climaxes to comfort my male pride, but I could flatter myself that she enjoyed it.

"I always enjoy myself when I'm appreciated," she said.

We rested or slept at intervals.

"You know," Claudia said at one point, "I'm curious as to whether Gavino ever really made it, completely, with our little Anna."

"Why?"

"Well, even with me he's nervous. Comes too quickly. Too anxious to please—to please *me*, imagine. He'd be far worse with someone he's fond of, terribly overanxious. I'd almost bet on it that he never went the whole way with her."

Which applied to both Gavino and myself. The odd thing is that I still wasn't going to let Gavino down in front of Claudia. I lied about it. "You're wrong. They made it all right. More often than I care to think."

"I'd never have thought it. Perhaps Anna was the right girl for him after all."

Hadn't Anna told me that herself? I was uneasy but proud of myself for showing Claudia she was wrong, even by lying. I turned to her once more, searching with my mouth for her rich breasts, and then rolled over to push my way into her again.

Seventeen

The next morning I got up early, took a last regretful look at Claudia's sleeping nakedness—she lay on her back, with legs sprawled apart—and drove back to Alghero. I was eager to be available in my hotel, since Gavino would hardly phone a second time if he missed me.

After breakfast I went to sit in the hall and picked up the paper.

"Good morning to you, young man."

I looked up to see the man with the moustache.

"No work to do. What a wonderful life you must lead!" I was about to grunt a reply, but he went on. "Things are going very nicely for me, you know, with Teresa."

He sat down beside me. "Every time I see her walking past with that shape of hers, I feel like a young man again! Haven't you ever thought of having a bit of fun with her?"

"She's not really my type."

"Oh, she's a rough, peasant sort, I'll grant you. *Earthy* is the word, don't you think?" He gave a nasty snigger. "But I think I'm getting somewhere. We talked quite a while yesterday. She laughed most of the time at my few words of the lingo, it's true, but looking at me in a certain way ... "

The telephone rang.

"I don't think it'll be long."

"Excuse me, I think I'm wanted." I went over to the porter's desk. "For me?"

Franco, speaking into the phone, shook his head.

I sat down again. For another half an hour I had to listen to the guest's comments on Teresa and his thoughts on what she'd be like in bed.

By half past ten I was less convinced that Gavino would phone, and I had to visit hotels. I asked Franco to take a message if necessary so I could call Gavino back later. I walked from one hotel to another, reflecting gloomily that for a whole day I'd feel obliged to wait for this call, which mightn't come.

By chance I met Maria. "Mister Arthur, how are you?" Her dark features smiled at me pleasantly. "I haven't seen you for a long time."

She actually agreed to have a coffee with me.

"Tell me what's been happening to you. You seem sadder than when I last saw you."

"Have I changed that much?"

She smiled. "No, just a little."

It seemed odd now that I'd once wanted to take her out. We hadn't much to say to each other, and I soon said goodbye to her to go back to the hotel again.

"Any phone calls for me, Franco?"

"No, Mister Arturo."

I stayed in my room the rest of the morning. When finally I went down to the kitchen for lunch, Teresa was telling the others excitedly about her admiring tourist—"the lecherous old man," as she called him—shrieking with laughter as she described how eagerly he'd responded to being made a fool of.

"He made me tickle his moustache this morning. Then he started chasing me around the room … "

She rushed around the kitchen, copying his actions and speaking gibberish in a deep, panting voice to imitate his English.

" … and sweating all over his stinking face, his fly buttons shooting off under the strain." She demonstrated with her hand: "Whiz! Ping! as they hit the ceiling!"

"Teresa!" the old woman said strictly. "Don't be vulgar."

But the girl had thrown herself down onto a chair and was cackling uncontrollably.

For the afternoon I stayed in my room as well, giving instructions to let me know if the phone call came. I read, wrote letters, and became more and more bored but was determined to give Gavino every opportunity to reach me.

Later there was a knock on the door. "Mister Arturo," Carlo said, "there's a young lady to see you downstairs."

I rushed down. But it wasn't Anna, only Caterina, nervous and looking out of place in the luxury of the hotel. When she saw me she was embarrassed and kept giggling while she asked me how I was. Finally she said, "A group of us in a few weeks' time, we're thinking of organizing another excursion. I … wanted to know if you'd like to come."

I smiled. "I suppose so."

"Oh, good. You'll come then?"

"Yes."

She didn't have any more to say, just stood there waiting for me to say something and looking around nervously. "I'm glad you can come," she said at last.

"I'll enjoy it."

"Well, I'd better be going," she said doubtfully. We shook hands. "Goodbye."

She turned around at the doorway to ask once more if I'd be coming. Perhaps I should, I thought.

Eventually, I phoned Anna to tell her what had happened.

"Gavino won't call you," she said. "Did you really expect him to? I'm afraid he's just like that. It's the way he makes me so unhappy myself." She paused, then added, "Thank you anyway. I'm just sorry it turned out as it did."

I hadn't told her about Claudia.

"Can I see you tomorrow evening if you're not doing anything?" I said.

"Would you like to take me to the theatre? There's a visiting company here from Milan."

"Of course."

I went to find Jim for a drink.

"Keep on with the fight," Jim said cheerfully. "You might still win Anna back. You never know."

*   *   *

Outside the theatre people stood in excited, gesticulating clusters, and for once I felt nostalgic for London and its social life: the small, plush foyers throbbing with loud English voices, the queues outside hugging the wall to the stone steps of the gallery, cars and taxis drawing up in the street, where the commissionaire would step grandly forward to open the door.

But this was a Sardinian social occasion. The narrow entrance was no more than a cinema box office, the foyer a bare stone room with a bar at one end, and the audience spread with dangerous unconcern over the roadway outside, jostling restlessly in their delight at the unusual. But the richer families arrived in cars and furs just the same. Students talked knowingly about the play—which should have started half an hour ago—all aspiring to be part of the cultured, continental world.

I looked round with curiosity, remembering how I'd been to the carnival ball in the same theatre, looking very different then, with Gavino. We made our way to our places in the balcony. A number of people greeted Anna.

"Yes," she said, "they all say hello, even if they go into huddles afterward to think of unpleasant things to say about me."

The seats, made of creaking wood, left no room for the knees: the Sard environment asserted itself with apologetic but enthusiastic charm. At first the production seemed amateur, and for a while I looked down condescendingly. But then I found myself laughing with the actors, until I perceived that their skill lay in their apparent lack of it, for in this way they avoided identification with their characters and, by stylizing them, identified with the audience instead. My generally low spirits had, this evening, suddenly disappeared in the serenity that the theatre atmosphere brought me. I enjoyed having Anna beside me for the company.

"Arthur," she asked mischievously during the interval, "have you a stamp you could give me for a letter?" She took an envelope from her bag. "You see who it's to? I'm brazen enough to ask you for a stamp for a letter to my other lover!"

I found one in my wallet, and we both laughed about it.

I caught sight of Claudia looking bored with another man. She saw me and blew me a kiss, making a provocative though barely perceptible movement of her hips. I grinned back. Anna pointedly turned her back.

Oh, the excitement of all that is woman. For within all individuals is the microcosm of the entire sex, so that it's quite legitimate for a man to say, "I want a woman"—any woman with qualities that appeal. And similarly, a woman may want a man. Those who talk only of being faithful, legitimizing one's passions by restricting them to a wife or husband, ignore the appeal of the universal and the fact that individuals have differing qualities, differing limitations. To say that one cannot be attracted to, or indeed be in love with, more than one woman at the same time is the most utter nonsense imaginable.

We returned to our seats. Sitting next to Anna as the play continued, I found I still wanted her as a means of expressing my excitement of the evening. There are times when one needs to make love not for the sake of the person concerned, nor for the purely physical gratification, but as the natural culmination of something enjoyed, as the confirmation of a spiritually shared experience. To limit sex to what was normally thought of as "love" is surely to belittle its role.

After the play we went to a club that had recently opened in a cellar not far from the Piazza d'Italia.

"I know why you wanted to bring me here!" Anna whispered.

We could distinguish little more than the silhouettes of the dancers, and the weak red light in the middle scarcely penetrated to the recesses in the walls, where the tables had been placed. In the darkness we kissed a little as an expression of our shared pleasure, like two strangers necking at a party.

"You're bad for me," Anna said. "You appeal too much to the woman in me."

"I'm in love with you."

"No, not any longer. You like me because I'm 'sexy,' and you still think you're in love. Perhaps it's the same with Gavino. I don't know. I love both of you a little, because of the same things in you."

She took from her bag the letter addressed to Gavino and showed me a single sheet—I had to light a match to see it—with the words "I love you" scrawled across it. She shrugged her shoulders and tore it up. Carefully she tore the stamp from the envelope and gave it back. "For your next letter to me."

"You mean there's some hope?" I was almost alarmed. Perhaps I no longer wanted her after all.

"I don't mean anything. In this moment it isn't true that I love Gavino, that's all. I don't love anyone. I don't know what I feel. Now I'm just halfway between you. I'll go back to Rome in a short time, and none of it will make any difference. You've nearly tired of all this. It won't be long now before you give up."

I denied it, of course.

The next day brought large numbers of arrivals and a growing excitement at the prospect of new work and interest. After the interruption brought by Anna, it was like going to a resort at the beginning of the season again—with crowds of tourists off the trains that connected with the night boats from Genoa and Civitavecchia, more off the Milan plane in the afternoon, and a few from Rome at a later hour. For two days I hardly missed her.

But the next morning I woke up thinking of her, and at five o'clock, with less to do, I decided to go over and see her. I was relatively lighthearted about it, though, feeling simply I had to justify my outwardly crazy behaviour by continuing it for a while longer yet. I enjoyed the journey to Sassari precisely because it seemed irresponsible to take off impulsively. It was like the last day of a two-week holiday I'd taken from my over-strong sense of duty.

"Arthur! I didn't expect you. You'd better come in for a minute. Just let me finish doing my hair." Anna disappeared into the bathroom. "You shouldn't have come," she said when she returned. "I've got to leave in half an hour to meet Gavino."

I'd almost expected it, and wasn't even disappointed. "I thought you'd be seeing him tomorrow."

"No, he has to work late. I'm seeing him today instead. I'm going to Porto Torres to meet him. He had to go there to draw up some contract or something."

"I'll take you there in the car."

"No, he's meeting me off the train."

"All right, I'll come with you then, for the ride."

"If it gives you any pleasure. But he mustn't see you. He's meeting me at the port. You'll have to get off at the town station, all right?"

We went by the little one-coach diesel car. Inside it was difficult to talk because of the noise. I felt isolated from Anna, but I was still elated at the thought of my impulsive behaviour—rendered all the more ridiculous by the fact that she was going to meet my rival. She remained apologetic but was excited about seeing Gavino.

I tried to hold her hand, but she wouldn't let me. "I don't want to get your scent on me. It wouldn't be fair to him."

"You can't tell another person's scent!"

"Gavino can. He's very sensitive to things like that."

The train arrived at Porto Torres, and I left her as it took her on to the port. I'd been with her for not quite an hour, and now, if I returned to Sassari by the next train, there'd still be something left of the evening to enjoy in Alghero.

During the half-hour wait, I amused myself by walking around the Roman ruins on either side of the station, watching the lizards as they slithered over the stones in the evening sun. Sometimes I'd come upon one without disturbing it: lying there in four or five inches of green and grey splendour, blinking so as not to go to sleep. I'd let my shadow fall on it, and in a moment it was gone, with only a brief rustling in the undergrowth to say that it had been there at all.

In the train I dozed contentedly, thinking how I'd enjoyed the trip in spite of Anna. Driving along the road from Sassari to Alghero in the early dusk, I understood more clearly that for some time now it had been the excitement of my adventure rather than Anna's company that had appealed to me. I didn't particularly care that she was going to see Gavino. I just enjoyed the thought that I was in love with her and had to do irrational things for her sake.

It was still early when I arrived back at the hotel, and I met the man who'd been interested in Teresa. He said a curt "Good evening" and brushed past to go upstairs to his room. I wondered what had happened. Meeting him a little later coming out of the bathroom, I noticed that the moustache had disappeared.

"Yes," the man said sheepishly, "Teresa."

At dinner I heard the story as Teresa told it to the others. "I persuaded him that his moustache needed trimming ... And then one side was longer than the other, so I had to make them equal ... But I cut off too much, and I had to shorten the other side too."

"Teresa, you're a dreadful girl!" the old lady interrupted.

Laughing with all of them, I found once again that I desired this coarse girl, who made a mockery of everyone. In my room that night I imagined her peasant body, rough, dirty even, struggling violently beside me, rather than the sophisticated, smooth warmth of Anna Lorcas.

* * *

"Thank you for all you've done, Fraser." The guest with what had once been a moustache heartily shook my hand. "And watch out for that girl Teresa. She's got quite a spirit in her!"

I watched the airport coach bump along the road toward Fertilia, then slowly started walking in the direction of the first hotel I had to visit. Crowds were still arriving, but my enthusiasm about returning to work hadn't lasted. Now, as always when someone memorable was leaving, I was oppressed by the weight of the departure, imperceptibly bringing the season nearer to its end. I'd long been used to this business of arrivals and departures, continuing and overlapping every few days throughout the summer. It wasn't until the last few weeks, when numbers got noticeably smaller and hotels began to close, that I'd acknowledge the dreary end of another tourist year.

But occasionally before then were reminders that sooner or later would follow that initial period of tired loneliness in England, when suddenly there was no one clamouring for attention all through the day. It was then that the photographs sent to me would go into yet another album, as a silent record of the people I'd known. Today was July 27, still early to think ahead; but in spite of the summer heat and the new guests arriving, there was a gnawing loneliness. So much of this season, which was to have been so different, now seemed to have been wasted by my obsession with Anna.

I could still go to her, of course. Yet now I hesitated, wondering if there weren't better ways to spend the rest of my time in Sardinia. One day these seasons abroad would finish, and I'd have nothing but the photographs to remind me of the emptiness of my past experiences.

Jim was waiting back at the hotel in his shirtsleeves and sweating around the sides of his moustache. "I've just ordered an iced beer on your account."

"Better add one for me." I sat down. "Anything new?"

"Anything new!" The usual exaggerated pause. "Every hotel I've been to I've been harassed by hordes of irate Americans wanting to know where their rep is. Isabelle's disappeared."

"Disappeared? Where to?"

"God knows. She was last seen three days ago on the coach to Tempio and no one's heard of her since. The manager at her hotel's livid—it seems she owes him ninety thousand lire. Quite what you'd expect of her, of course."

"Has anyone thought of phoning Tempio?"

There was an odd pleasure in mentioning Tempio. I remembered how Isabelle and Larry—Renzo—had sat there with Anna and me, as though the four of us had been on an illicit holiday.

"They phoned one of the hotels, but no one's seen her."

I almost felt like going and searching for her myself, in a gesture of pointless nostalgia.

Later that day, when Caterina visited again to ask if I remembered about the excursion and was still going to come, I felt a moment's genuine regret. But I assured her I would and sent her away quickly, pretending not to notice her adoring glances.

In the evening Jim and I went to the pictures to see a thriller.

Eighteen

"So here you are again!" I shook hands with Maurice and turned to Margaret. "How does he manage it? Every time he arrives he persuades you to come over with him from Olbia."

Margaret seemed pleased to see me. "Oh, yes, you've got a real rival for my affections there. You should hear the things he says when he's alone with me."

Maurice gave his usual cackle. "Come off it. You know I wouldn't stand a chance among all your admirers in Olbia. Or with this lover boy here, for that matter. Though I gather his attentions have strayed a bit recently. Perhaps we can have a private talk for a few minutes. There's a small matter I have to discuss with you."

It was about how I'd been neglecting my work. A couple of guests had complained to the London office that they'd hardly seen me, and their letter had been passed on to Maurice. I explained what had happened and apologized, feeling terrible.

"One of those times in life when one has to decide between two priorities, eh? In this case you decided personal matters were more important. Well, as your manager, I can't say I approve, but I'd probably have done the same. Don't do it again, though, will you? I'll write back and say you were busy seeing Ruggiero for me—no one's to know it was only on the one occasion. Now, any parties arranged for us?"

I grinned. "Not at the moment."

"Now that's what I call lack of initiative, far more serious! It's all very well chasing an Italian wench all over the country, but you mustn't neglect the important things. Good thing we're staying tomorrow as well. Give us time to get something fixed up."

In the afternoon Maurice disappeared and returned to say that the three of us, plus Jim and Marcella, had been invited by a friend of his to a dance the following evening. "Just as well he happened to think of it, wasn't it?"

The friend lived in a small villa overlooking a valley dense with the olives for which the province of Sassari was famous. The villa itself, though, was surrounded by cherry trees, all bearing fruit and filtering the sun's rays through their branches. A crowd of young people, gathered together with carefree informality, danced lazily on a terrace outside the house. I was determined to enjoy myself; but as always Margaret was in demand, and I didn't dance much except once or twice with Marcella when she was tired of Jim's inability. Instead, I found a bottle of genuine Scotch and, content to watch the others, savoured its warmth as it trickled down my throat, spreading to my stomach, and creating an agreeable laziness in my senses. Again I felt the appeal of Sardinia itself, a country that was still unexplored, exciting.

"Aren't you going to dance with me, my love?" Margaret was extravagantly waving a glass of Vernaccia in front of her.

Keeping our glasses, we clutched each other in an exaggerated hug, consciously attempting to recapture our former ease together by making an exhibition of it. Perhaps I was trying to show her I was still fond of her despite an irrational feeling of having been unfaithful.

"Oh, come live with me and be my love!" I quoted to her as we whirled around the terrace.

She answered with the first quotation to come into her head: "Gather ye rosebuds while ye may." Then she followed it randomly with a few more: "A thing of beauty is a joy forever! A draught of wine, a book of verse, and thou beside me in the wilderness are paradise enow! We must go down to the seas again … "

"To the lonely sea and the sky. And all I ask is a bottle of beer and a wench to drink it by!"

We stopped at the table with the drinks. "Another draught of wine?"

"Oh, for a draught of vintage, that hath been cooled … damn, I've forgotten it."

We drank, then wandered away to pick cherries.

The sun was lower now so that its light streamed into the orchard from the side, forming a mottled pattern of elongated shadows on the ground below. I was serious for a moment, watching the dark shadow of my arm shoot away from me as I reached up for the cherries. "Odd how the shadows become distorted."

Margaret, too, reached up, then nearly overbalanced, so I had to support her—and suddenly we were laughing and kissing as we realized how tipsy we were.

"Come on, lover," she said after I'd kissed her some more, "don't let the others think we're being serious."

The cherries were good and we ate too many.

Margaret departed with Maurice the next morning. I felt jubilant about our kissing, almost as attracted to her as I had been to Anna, whom I now hadn't seen for five days.

The next day there were two letters in my pigeonhole. The first was just a note from Jim. "Called to see if you wanted to drown your sorrows again, but couldn't find you. Isabelle's back but won't say anything except that all men are dishonest swines. Will call tomorrow."

I obviously hadn't been the only one making a fool of myself. Life suddenly seemed absurdly normal—until I opened the second letter, which took me a few minutes to understand:

> Alghero 1 august
>   Dear sir, if you think that in Alghero
> you can give yourself airs with the wimmen your
> mistaken—Youve already made one mistake with my
> sister—With your fine talk and manners of a yunuck
> inglishman youve made my sister beleive youll marry
> her and take her to Ingland or who knows where—
> She thinks your an inglish Lord with property and a
> castle or who knows what great person and this has
> made her beleive you but I know your a miserable
> bugger whose no intention of marrying a girl from
> Alghero but whose out to spend the time with the first
> woman to fall into your arms diluding herself shell
> make a posh marriage—but in decieving my sister
> youve made a big mistake—Id thought of making
> you taste the bullets of my pistol but then I thought
> Id warn you first—Now youve been warned—If
> after tomorrow you dare speak with my sister and
> invite her to your hotel or to go out with you or to
> go dancing as youve done or if you try to pretend to
> her again that youll marry her Ill put 5 bullets in your
> stomach! If you want to stay in Alghero to work work
> and leave the girls alone otherwise Ill make you stay in
> Alghero but in the Public Cemitary
> So long …

"Carlo, have a look at this a minute, will you?"

I watched nervously as Carlo read it with little expressions of disdain. "Don't worry. It's a joke. But if I find out who wrote it, I'll break his balls for him."

"Why should whoever it is write to me?" I thought of the primitive jealousies, the bandits in Orgosolo, and wondered whether I might indeed be in danger.

"Some bloody cuckold with a twisted sense of humour, that's all. Have you any idea who the 'sister' might be?"

"None at all." Neither Anna nor Claudia qualified. Unless, it occurred to me, Gavino … but no, I could never believe that of him.

"There's nothing to worry about then. There *are* some dangerous people in Sardinia, in the backward parts. But that type wouldn't bother to write. They'd just shoot. It's probably some local idiot."

Enrico, whom I saw the next day, was of the same opinion. He was upset about it, though, almost tearful that any Sard should have shown such bad manners and stupidity to a foreigner. "Believe me, Mister Arturo, we have some delinquents here, but please don't think … This grieves me deeply. And look at the way it's written: even I can write better than that!"

He agreed with my feeling that it had nothing to do with Anna, who wasn't from Alghero and had no brother.

"And with girls like that … Mister Arturo, I'm so glad you're rid of her."

I was still uneasy. The letter, stupid as it was, was a personal reproach, as though I were as foreign to Sardinia as the tourists, who—paradoxically perhaps, because they had no pretensions to be anything but foreigners—suddenly seemed to belong more than I did.

Now, however, I determined that for the rest of the season I'd make up for lost time—sticking to English girls in case the letter had been serious.

It wasn't particularly difficult to find a girlfriend among the tourists. She was an eighteen-year-old office girl from Birmingham named Irene, whom I'd never have considered in a normal season. But she was easy, and I was in no mood for conquests requiring an effort. Her accent made me shudder, and she had no interests except jiving, twisting, and petting; but she did the latter rather well and didn't speak much while it was in progress. Afterward she'd become talkative and want to discuss sentimental ideas, but for a week she was tolerable.

When she left, there arrived a pseudo-intellectual from Oxford named Clara, who quoted poetry at all the vital moments and whose ethereal yet nonetheless passionate caresses were for her of profound, mystical significance. I found the satisfying of her physical appetite a more demanding task. I made the most of it, revelled in it, for it was so uncomplicated with these girls who wanted their clitorises rather than their emotions stimulated. Clara tried to hide a lack of any real emotion behind a camouflage of sophistication. She'd indulge in soaring flights of feeling, pretending hardly to notice what was happening physically—then would shudder with delight when I entered her.

On August 18, after Clara's departure, Jenny arrived for her second holiday.

I'd forgotten she was coming. But it was a pleasant surprise, and I was reminded of the fun we'd had together, before I'd even met Anna. I took her to dinner on the first evening, and we talked obscurely, with hidden meanings, imagining our more intimate reunion in an hour or so's time.

Because of our haste we returned much earlier to her room.

"You'd better lock the door," she said with an unexpectedly infuriating giggle. "Light it for me, will you?" She casually put a cigarette in her mouth. "Thanks."

She undressed while she was smoking, methodically laying her clothes on a chair. Then she turned toward me and stood waiting, plump and naked with deep red marks where her bra and the elastic of her panties had cut into her. I looked at her less excited by her willingness than disappointed at seeing how ordinary she was after all. When I made no move toward her, she put out her cigarette, came over to me, and sat on my knee, starting to undress me as well, rubbing herself against me. When we got into bed we were quite passionate, but it was over too quickly and seemed rather pointless.

After talking for a while, I began to think of returning to my own room, but then in what I'd intended as a final goodnight kiss I succeeded in arousing her again, and I was forced to give an encore of the complete performance.

Every night was the same. Even when I thought I was too tired to make love, she was so unwilling to let me go and so insistent with her hands that I was always persuaded to stay until both of us had been physically relieved. When she left, I rejoiced that I could have my nights to myself, and my three weeks of determined self-gratification finished in a long, relaxed sleep.

Still, I wasn't complaining. But funnily, I still wanted Anna. For her effect on me produced a vague dissatisfaction with the Jennies and the Claras. And yet, what was the difference? Just that they were ordinary, accepting the drabness of the everyday and coming alive only during their one or two brief holidays a year, whereas Anna tried to understand her life and consequently was more deeply unhappy, on a higher plane altogether, like the tragic actress compared with the trivial leads of a drawing-room comedy. It wasn't so much what one did that was important, but who one was.

Thinking, too, of Gavino, I began to understand more of what he must have felt toward her. I sensed how dissatisfied he must have been with the girls he'd gone with—although I felt there might have been something of tragedy in Claudia, too, behind her professional façade, which he hadn't appreciated. His encounter with Anna must have been overwhelming. Perhaps he was the perfect tragi-hero for her, and it was merely a piece of stage irony that I'd had a near alter ego as my rival. I felt like writing to him, making friends with him again. But it would have to wait until Anna had left Sardinia—or until I had left. That, I realized, was only four weeks away.

On the one hand I was ready for a change; on the other, unsure whether I wanted to return to my own civilization. I wondered whether, once home, I'd see Margaret again—and, in fact, I determined to do so, for she was someone with whom I could share my reminiscences of this place I now loved. I would never forget the contrasts and paradoxes that gave the island its fascination. It seemed that to return to England would be like abandoning a mistress one loves too much to want her to become one's wife.

I recalled Anna's words: "*Il matrimonio è la tomba dell'amore.*"

Another letter came, as stupid as the first, saying I was still seeing the anonymous writer's sister. There was nothing to do but ignore it.

But that night something quite unforgettable took place. My one dream from the beginning of the season was about to be realized.

Nineteen

Teresa, at my bedroom door, gave an aggressively mocking smile. "Can I come in?"

With cautious but rising excitement, I stared at her ragged dressing gown and bare feet. "Of course."

She looked around my room for a moment, then down at the floor, oddly nervous. "Mister Arturo," she said. She hesitated, then was aggressive again. "I can't sleep tonight. I haven't … had a man for a long time. Do me a service, will you?"

"You mean … ?"

"Oh, the Englishman! All talk and no action. I need that thing of yours there up inside me, right? Then you can go back to sleep."

She came over to me, rubbed herself against me—she had very little on underneath the dressing gown—and gave me a long, rough kiss. She slipped her hand inside my pyjamas, starting to groan as she felt my hardness. After all these months, the feel of her body, her hand fondling me, prepared me for a violent Sardinian climax.

But there were a couple of things I hadn't counted on. She struggled out of her dressing gown to reveal a rather dirty bra and panties. Her breasts strained forward excitingly, and I could hardly wait to get them in my hands and mouth. I fumbled eagerly with the clasp. But as I pulled the bra away, her breasts flopped down like two unrolled fire hoses, with her nipples reaching below her navel. They were large all right. Perhaps *long* would have been a better word. You could almost pick them up and weigh them. Teresa pulled me over to the bed, where, when she rolled onto her back, her teats hung over on either side of her.

The second thing was that she smelled. Not strong, just a vague, unpleasant odour. Her breath smelled too. My penis had dipped noticeably, and now I was no longer sure I wanted to put it inside her, where all kinds of germs might be hiding.

"But screw your courage to the sticking place, and we'll not fail," I said to myself, thinking how Anna would have understood and perhaps even recognized it as a quotation from *Macbeth*.

Teresa, of course, didn't know English. "Hurry up," she moaned.

Well, I managed it, to screw my courage where it was required, that is. Even so I came too quickly, in one of those despairing, warm bursts of nervousness, then felt myself shrinking out of her. That didn't satisfy Teresa at all, of course, and for the next half hour I had to submit to her indignation and mockery.

"Is that all the English are good for? Look at it!" She shook my limp penis, not realizing I'd already come. "A rag, not a cock. Oh, so big, the great English hero, and then what's he like in bed? Just hangs there. Can't even keep it up. Now I know! Perhaps he prefers boys?"

On and on. I didn't bother to defend myself. Eventually it finished with her masturbating—which did succeed in arousing me again—but now she'd no longer have anything to do with me and left in disgust.

The next morning I felt depressed and none too pleased with myself. Hell, though, at least I did it with her and didn't have to regard her as another lost opportunity.

That afternoon, in a wistful mood, I went out to Fertilia and spent two or three hours sitting in the sun near the Roman bridge. I watched the changing light on its crouched form, which stretched over several long, low arches into the middle of the river, where—whether it had collapsed or been destroyed—it cascaded into the water. Soon, I thought, the whole island would be no more than a memory of past glory. I recalled the places I'd visited: Cagliari in the south, like any other stately Italian city; Macomer, surrounded by its sinister hosts of nuraghi; the smooth sea contrasting with the rugged, changing coasts of the north and west; the serene statue of the Redeemer giving his lonely blessing from the heights above Nuoro, aware of the unseen menace of Orgosolo a few kilometres away.

Within me was the realization of understanding so much, yet the knowledge that I could never understand completely. In a few years' time Sardinia would be the fashionable place for tourists, not just the select few who came at present. It would be catalogued, publicized in gaudy posters, reduced to photographs and homemade films thrust eagerly onto friends with explanations of what it was like. It would become as commonplace as Switzerland, with the nuraghic civilization taking the place of William Tell. Everyone would know everything about Sardinia. But I'd continue to love it because it was an enigma, a phenomenon that for me would remain incomprehensible.

Back in Alghero more urgent matters intruded on my speculations. Jim was waiting at the hotel.

"Something rather serious has happened," he said, delaying in his usual manner. "Isabelle decided to commit suicide."

I reacted with disbelief, while Jim was an odd mixture of concern and excitement at the drama.

"Fortunately, she seems to have decided she wanted a death in the limelight, too, like most of her performances. She went rushing all over her hotel shouting, 'My God, what have I done!' at the top of her voice. The doctor's still with her, but I gather she'll be all right."

"I suppose I can't say typical of Isabelle this time, can I?" I consciously had to impress on myself that it was serious and not yet another piece of comedy.

"Let's have a drink, shall we? We've got to hang around, I suppose, in case there's anything we can do."

"Does anyone know what it's all about?"

"No."

Theories were soon forthcoming. Within an hour all the hotels in Alghero had heard about it. There was talk of another broken affair and, without any evidence, a suggestion that Isabelle was pregnant. In the kitchen that evening—where Teresa ignored me—everyone seemed to think it quite in accordance with Isabelle's character, showing little surprise and even less sympathy.

"Just seeking attention," Franco said. "I can't say I'm sorry for her."

"But something still drove her to it."

"We all know she's half crazy."

I was uneasy. In later years, too, I'd be astonished at people's reactions to suicide. Invariably, people would say, "How could he do it to his wife and children?" with hardly any concern about the person's own despair. Sympathy only for those who remained, who were still "the same as us," "normal," as opposed to someone "obviously unbalanced." Let no one expect to get sympathy from others by suicide. You'll only get bewilderment and anger at the insult you've paid to their lifestyle.

Enrico, at least, who rushed in to see me, was genuinely horrified. "Oh, the poor woman! How much she must have been suffering." But then he spoilt it all by adding, "I don't understand it, do you? When she had everything!"

I remembered Enrico's judgment of Anna, and my resentment exploded. "A Christian who doesn't understand! It's your *business* to understand! If Christians can't understand the suicides, the murders, the violence, the sex crimes, all the ugliness, all the vice, then how can they ever show charity? That's the trouble with most Christians—all they do is condemn what they don't like, without trying to understand."

"Oh, no, Mr. Arturo," Enrico went on. "Please don't think ... But do *you* understand her?"

"I think so." My own instinct would always be to fight, but I could sense how, in natures different from mine, frustration or despair could lead a person to try to take his or her own life. "Yes, I understand her."

I was still upset with Enrico after he left. That question "But do *you* understand?" has been put to me often enough by life itself, not just of the petty crimes we all indulge in—like fiddling our expenses or verbally murdering someone—but of the most horrible of human actions, the mass atrocities, the deliberate slaughter of children. "Do you understand?" has been asked of things I could never take part in myself. And the answer, to be hoped, is yes. It must always be yes, because I'm one of humanity, and if I'm honest I can recognize the same drives in myself that others have. I may be no sadist, but I can see how sadism lies within humans and can easily become a driving force. If in my life it takes only the form of occasionally saying something to hurt someone, that's my good fortune. In me, thank God, it's overshadowed by other considerations, not all of them praiseworthy, like fearing what others might think of me. As a human being I can understand the mass murderer, although I find it difficult to kill an ant in cold blood. The commandant at Auschwitz wasn't a monster but a methodical civil servant, who in peace time would have made a perfect warehouse or dispatch manager. But he *didn't* understand and was therefore happy to file people away as Aryans or Jews.

So, Enrico, don't you dare say as a Christian that you don't understand the suicides, the godless, the vandals, the murderers, or anyone else. As a human being, let alone as a Christian, it's your duty to understand.

*   *   *

There was a final visit from Caterina, simple, naive, and utterly charming. She came with mortified, exaggerated apologies to say that the proposed school outing had been cancelled. "If we arrange another one, will you come?"

I explained that I'd be leaving in three weeks.

"Leaving?" She looked lost, unbelieving.

"I'm afraid so."

"Oh." She glanced timidly into my eyes, ashamed of asking. "When?"

"September 22nd."

"But you're really leaving?" she insisted, looking away again.

I nodded.

"And when are you coming back?"

"I doubt if I will be."

"Never?" Her face showed pained surprise, and then incomprehension. She was pretty, I thought, looking at her young and typically Sard features.

I shook my head.

She repeated flatly, "Never."

The realization suddenly hit me. "Caterina, do you have a brother?"

Her expression of frightened shock told me the answer. "What's he done now?"

"I think he wrote to me."

"Oh, no! He just doesn't understand anything!" She started to cry, and it was some minutes before she could tell me what had happened.

"I feel so ashamed. I just mentioned your name on a couple of occasions. That was all! I wanted to talk about you. But then he started getting ideas." Tears rolled down her face. "He's always thinking things involve his honour. He just doesn't understand. I exaggerated a bit, I suppose, but you are an important person in England, aren't you?"

An English lord with property and a castle, I remembered from the letter. "What did he say?"

"Nothing very much."

That he'd kill me, that's all.

"He didn't want me to see you." She was still crying. "I'm so sorry. How can you forgive me?"

I tried to reassure her. Her visit, I realized, had brought me considerable pleasure, even if I wouldn't see her again.

She turned to go, then came back and said timidly, "Will you give me your address? You'll let me write to you?"

I wrote it down, knowing I'd never hear from her—and hoping I wouldn't hear from her brother either.

*　　*　　*

I got daily reports of Isabelle's recovery from Jim, who delighted in visiting her in the hospital so he could make fun of the nuns who ran it. I was too depressed about it to visit her myself. Only a minor figure in my Sardinian drama, Isabelle had an importance that I hadn't before recognized, for so often the character of a place or period is established by those who at the time seem insignificant: Jim, Marcella, Maurice, Enrico—and Isabelle.

Now, the promise of the beginning of the season—I thought of that first excursion with her in the car—had unaccountably been betrayed. Isabelle, a comic figure, had become a tragic one instead. Her eccentricities had to be taken seriously. Never remotely interested in her personally, not even liking her very much, I recognized that Sardinia would have been poorer without her. She was a flamboyant, unashamed contrast to society's morality, perhaps, unlike the timid, sullen defiance of Anna. Isabelle, with all her faults, was *alive*, which, paradoxically, she'd now asserted by trying to kill herself.

I was depressed in other ways too. Gavino, my friend from the first day, had needlessly become a stranger. Teresa, in bed, had been a disappointment. Caterina, in her innocence, had brought me into ugly conflict with local prejudice, stupid though it was. The one girl I *hadn't* wanted to seduce could have got me killed.

Soon I would be leaving. Nothing, it seemed, remained from the season that had passed. Except Anna, from whom there now arrived a postcard saying she was leaving in four days' time.

My final visit to her started as an evening of humiliating domesticity.

"Come over tomorrow," she told me on the phone when I called her. "You can have dinner here if you like. I've got a friend from Tempio staying with me, so you can see what my cooking's like."

"Who is it?"

A giggle at the other end of the line. "Female, don't worry. The maid from the hotel, do you remember? You should like her. She has middle-class ideas that should appeal to you. None of my complications."

"Now that's unfair—" but she'd already put the phone down.

Jim had the car again, so I went by train.

"Hello, dear," Anna called from the kitchen as I went in. "Go ahead and read the paper. We're busy."

I sat down on her neatly made bed. The table was already laid. As I picked up the paper, a girl of four or five wandered into the room, stared at me shyly for a moment, then asked me who I was.

I answered awkwardly, not sure how to talk to children. "And who are you?"

"Tina." She came closer. "Are you Aunt Anna's friend? The other one?"

The innocent "*L'altro?*" bothered me. "I'm Anna's friend, yes."

"Uncle Gavino plays with me," she said, looking at me doubtfully. "I *like* him."

Go away, I wanted to say, and let me read the paper. But she got up onto the bed with me, which was embarrassing. I let her climb over me for a while, tickling her when she asked me to. Finally, I escaped into the kitchen to see if I could help, only to find Anna in a girlish, giggling mood with her friend Nella, who I hadn't realized was married, let alone with a daughter. So I had to listen to the confidences of women together, about children and apartments—the strange world of family and household life, which one day, inevitably, would be mine as well.

Anna made fun of me. "He's quite the dutiful Englishman." A loud whisper to Nella: "We'll get him to do the washing up for us afterward. Do you know that men help with the housework in England? You should have seen the husband when I was working there. I couldn't bear it, could you? A man loses all his masculinity in an apron!"

"Anna, that's stupid."

"But he's awfully sweet, really. It's a pity Gavino's not so house-trained. Go on, back to the other room, where you won't be in our way. You can keep Tina amused. Besides, I've got some secrets to tell Nella you mustn't hear."

For another half an hour I had to stay there, a cuddling father now to whichever of Tina's three dolls she decided needed my attention. I listened sullenly to the shrieks of laughter from the kitchen.

At last the meal was ready, but the conversation still revolved around the child as she sat stating her desires or talking about everything she'd done that day. I kept looking at Anna, trying to convey mentally to her, "But I don't want this. I want to be alone with you. I want excitement, fun with you—not weary domesticity."

My annoyance was still with me when the meal was over, and I was again banished from the kitchen while Anna and Nella cleared away. Finally, Tina was hauled off for a bath and Anna returned to me.

We said little, almost embarrassed now to be alone together.

She took my hand. "How are you? It's a long time since I've seen you."

"All right." My annoyance had vanished, but my depression at seeing a more domestic Anna remained.

"You're different today, dear. What's the matter?"

"Nothing."

"Things have changed?"

I didn't want to admit it.

"They were bound to, Arthur."

Sitting on the bed, I wanted to hold her. "When I see you again, I'm still not sure."

"You will be. You'll get over it." She kissed me lightly on the forehead. "I've probably been stupid to choose Gavino. I know that."

"You're still going out with him?"

"Of course. But I leave on Thursday, you know."

We sat for a long time—she wouldn't lie back—holding hands, while she told me of how she and Gavino had continued seeing each other. Nothing was new: her attitudes, the reasons why she tried not to care about things. At first with Gavino this seemed to have changed, but now she just wanted it to finish.

"He hit me once, you know."

"Oh?"

"He was angry with me."

"Of course."

"You're going to find it easier than I shall afterward," she said finally.

We went out to the familiar bar on the Via Roma, where Gavino had run away from me.

"I've got something for you. For you to remember me by." She gave me back the letter I'd written to her.

There was an odd nostalgia, even the same physical desire, returning now after that alienating meal, so that we found ourselves touching each other under the table. I wanted her more than ever.

I had to catch a train back to Alghero. We walked through the old streets of the town to the tree-lined avenue near the station. There, for a little, we necked in the shadows. My mouth on her neck, biting at her ears, bending them gently. That fresh, sultry aroma of sex, which has always aroused me. But she stopped me. I felt lost, in need of relief.

We went into the station. Twenty minutes to wait, so we sat on a bench in the entrance hall.

"Poor Arthur," she said, understanding me as always. "You want a woman very much tonight, don't you?"

"I want you."

"Or someone else like me."

I thought of Claudia. I glanced round at the lonely booking office, the closed bookstall, the out-of-date timetables on the walls, which reminded me of how I'd been delayed in Domodossola on my way to Sardinia in the first place. With Anna it wasn't the traditional goodbye on the platform, but sitting in a bare railway entrance hall. From being with her in the cabin of a ship on the Mediterranean, to Sassari station at night, in the company now of a cleaner, who'd started sweeping rubbish from one corner to another.

I felt miserable. The end had come, but I didn't want it to. I wanted to get into bed with her even now. Or perhaps she was right: I needed any attractive woman. For a moment I considered going to see if Claudia were home, but I'd told Anna I was catching that train and it would spoil my departure to walk back up the Corso again.

It was almost time. I shook her hand, didn't kiss her—my one last futile attempt to make her want me by not giving her what she expected.

"All the best, Arthur."

I went onto the platform without looking back.

She'd be walking across the avenue now, then up the steep Corso. Probably close to tears. It was unlikely I'd ever see Sassari again. There'd be no reason for coming here. Goodbye, Sassari. Goodbye, Anna.

The train jolted its way out of the station, the dimness of its lights encouraging me to sleep and yet somehow perpetuating my sleeplessness on this mournful, late-night journey. Now she'd be crossing the Piazza d'Italia. But I was too tired for my desire to last except as a vague, dutiful memory. I tried to imagine being with her in bed, but I couldn't and it would never happen. I tried to remember how we'd caressed each other, but images of Gavino doing the same disturbed me. My thoughts mingled with other, unimportant ones. When the train reached Alghero, I was asleep.

"Oh, *ciao*, Mister Arturo!" Leaving the station I met Enrico, emerging from the direction of the port. "What are you doing returning so late?"

"I've been to see … a friend in Sassari. You?"

"Oh, the most exciting news! One of my friends has decided to offer himself for the priesthood. We've been celebrating."

I tried to hide a grin.

"You know, when something like this happens, it makes you think how wonderful life is. Only then you feel ashamed because you haven't got it in you to do the same. How beautiful it must be, to live a life dedicated to everything that's above worldly things. To have one's greatest joy in the service of one's God!"

I couldn't be angry with him. But couldn't one serve God in the worldly things too? I wanted to laugh and cry at the same time. To deny the things of the world, to pretend they weren't important and strive blindly toward an ideal: it was as shortsighted as a pursuit of purely material happiness. Religion was far too important to turn into romantic, spiritual nonsense. I thought of Anna's courageous acceptance of things as they were, and I felt sorry for Enrico. I left him without disturbing his naive enthusiasm.

In my room, with its blue ceiling patterned with angels, turning out my pockets, I came across an old ticket. It was for the Lido in Cagliari, for a cubicle to change in.

I hesitated a little before throwing it into the wastepaper basket.

Twenty

A little over two weeks later I sat with Jim on a headland of the Golfo d'Aranci, looking over a flat expanse of water toward the massive hump of the island of Tavolara. To the left, in a slight haze, was a narrow gap where the mountains gave way to the open sea. In the other direction the town of Olbia lay like a rugged, fossilized starfish taking its siesta on the shore of the gulf, with a long, straight shaft reaching from its centre into the water and terminating in an indistinct blob of angular forms. Looking at this directly, it was possible to distinguish a pier head and a motionless ship riding beside it, but if you looked ahead, toward Tavolara, you perceived the pier as an arrow with an irregular tail that had been shot by some sea god into the starfish's primitive body, leaving it exposed to the consuming rays from the sun. Night perhaps would bring refreshment and the creature would revive; its five limbs would begin to move a little. But now it seemed already dead, its hard, knobbly skin glaring a dirty white and cracking with the heat. You could imagine it lying there for many days, until in some distant future the sea would rise higher onto the beach, would sweep around it, and carry it away.

Jim spoke with a mixture of sarcasm and envy. "I suppose Maurice wants to leave all this now, to be in England still after his eventful week there. Who'd have expected he'd come back engaged?"

"At least we're having a pleasant weekend as a result." I lay back on the grass to look at the nothingness of the sky above. "I'm very happy for him. Very convenient this new hotel being opened, too, giving us the chance to celebrate with him."

"Typically Italian, though. Have you ever heard of opening a new hotel at this time in the season?"

Jim took a while lighting up a new pipe, and the smell of tobacco drifted pleasantly above. "Oh, dear, he wants to leave, and I want to stay, for similar reasons."

"Marcella?"

He paused, puffing contentedly. "I've grown very fond of her. But I'm leaving only a few days after you, and she'll stay, of course. What can you do about it?"

"Could you see yourself marrying her?"

"I don't know. That's the trouble."

Jim, sweating on his neck and around his moustache, was in a mood for talking. I listened, half amused, half envious of his happiness with Marcella.

"It's getting too hot. Let's change our position."

We scrambled down the cliff to settle again on the grass in the shade of a large rock. We leaned back against it lazily, looking down at the water not far below.

Jim pointed out a dung beetle busy rolling a large lump ten times its own size through the turf, and for a while we said nothing, watching its progress. "Look how it keeps running away from it to get its bearings," he said, "and then returns to edge it again in the right direction."

"And its whole existence is limited to a few square yards or so of this coast. Perhaps it says to itself, 'I'll go over to Sunny Rock this afternoon, then I'll have tea in Lizard Gully before returning to Dung.' What a lovely existence."

"You forget it's an Italian beetle. It'll be *Gola delle Lucertole*, and it won't be having tea there either."

"Don't be pedantic."

It was still making steady progress, working hard.

"At least it knows where it's going, which is more than most humans do."

"Downhill."

A few minutes later Jim sighed again. "Oh, Arthur, I wonder if it's got an Italian girl beetle it's building a house for."

"It wouldn't have any problems. Just love 'em and leave 'em."

"In a glorious bed of dung."

For another ten minutes we watched the insect, shifting its load with patient determination and unworried by the number of times it fell on its back. At last it disappeared out of sight into the long grass.

"You know," Jim said suddenly, "have you ever thought much about Margaret?"

"What about her?"

"Well, you always seem to be fond of her. And she of you, for that matter."

I was cautious. Margaret had left Sardinia the previous day; we had kissed again. I was to see her in London. "I don't know. If there hadn't been Anna … "

"How did things turn out with her finally? You never really told me."

"It finished."

"And she stayed with Gavino?"

"Until she went back to Rome."

"He was a pleasant fellow."

I looked at the sea. I still hadn't written to him. Didn't quite know how to. Gavino with Anna: it was easier to picture them now, in the stillness of my own emotions. Understanding required only imagination.

I pictured Gavino on the square in Sassari, parading Anna up and down, angrily defiant of those who shunned her. Half wanting her, half resentful that she'd disrupted the isolation he'd become used to. I envisioned him holding her arm, squeezing her fingers in his. Hands that he found too smooth, with neatly manicured nails. Anna was a foreigner; Rome, not Sardinia, was her home. Perhaps she pitied him, felt affection, but she was too far above him for anything to come of it. He loved her in his way. He could never live, though, with someone to whom he'd always remain inferior. Sardinia's remorseless shackles would always hang from his limbs, even when he walked the streets of Rome.

Lying on that grassy headland, I indulged in a further imagined scene where Gavino lay on his bed, watching Anna as she walked with fastidious curiosity around his room. Even her clothes were not Sard, he was thinking. She still belonged to Arthur and the continental world, which patronized the more primitive parts of its empire—like a Roman patrician who might sometimes give herself to a slave like him but could dismiss him imperiously when she was finished.

Anna undressed in silence. God, he worshipped her when she was naked. Submissively, he removed his own clothes.

She clambered on top of him. "Gavino! Do it to me now. Everything!"

"I haven't the right!"

"Oh, don't say that!"

With a burst of impatience she seized him, bending her fingers around him, jerking his foreskin up and down. Then she stretched up, her breasts thrust forward, and forced herself down toward him, pushing, struggling against the pain. She cried out as she sank down onto him.

He let it happen. Joy, relief, despair: he felt them all.

"There," she said when it was over. "You're my *first*. Do you believe now that I love you?" She lay beside him as his hands lightly stroked her breasts.

Had it really been like that? I'd always fictionalized my own life, and here, in the warmth of the afternoon, I was doing the same for Gavino.

I imagined him afraid of his own happiness, saying bitterly, "You'd better not tell Arthur."

"Oh!" Anna pushed him away from her.

Gavino got up and started dressing. "Here!" He threw her her underclothes, feeling like a thief.

"Gavino, I love you. I'm yours, not his!"

How could a continental fall in love with a Gavino? Hadn't Arthur said that? No, worse, how could *anyone* fall in love with him? Suddenly he remembered. "Why did Arthur try to see me the other day? Did he expect me to apologize? Why should I apologize to *him*? He's had all the chances."

"It wasn't that."

"Oh no?" He wished she'd put her clothes on. He hated her for feeling sorry for him, for expecting him to change, making demands, wanting to lift him up to her level. For making love to him when he wouldn't to her. At least when he paid for it he could do it his way.

She put on her bra and sat sullenly now. Let her!

"Arthur's got more self-confidence, but that isn't important. If only you'd see!"

He'd heard it before, from Claudia, from others. "No, be quiet! I know."

"Gavino, I won't be quiet! I love you and you've got to believe that. You've got to trust yourself."

"Be quiet!"

"At least pretend like other men."

"I *won't* pretend. You're just like my mother, going on and on with all her foolish sentimental chatter."

"I know, you've told me before. It was your mother who ruined your life. You're glad she's dead!"

"No!" All his past frustrations lifted his hand and brought down a stinging reprimand against her face.

She said nothing. Didn't even raise her hand to her cheek. Instead, she punished him with her love, making him ashamed.

"Leave me," he said. "For God's sake, leave me."

*   *   *

There was a sudden shower of earth from above as Maurice scrambled down the cliff.

"So that's where you've got to. I've been looking for you both for half an hour." He sat down beside me so he could lean back against the rock. "What an afternoon, eh? Enough to make them dash to the doctor's complaining of sunstroke at home." His forehead was covered in sweat, and he had to screw up his eyes to prevent it trickling in at the corners. Despite his discomfort, he still carried his relaxed manner around with him.

"Where have you been?" I asked.

"I had to look at some land with the hotel manager and couldn't get away from him." He unbuttoned his shirt contentedly. "So what are the latest scandals? You haven't told me yet." He stuck his chin forward, blinking through his glasses. "I haven't heard any juicy bits of gossip for a long time."

Jim chuckled. "Nothing except Isabelle. She's suddenly gone religious. Taking mass in the hospital every day and God knows what."

"And I told you about my anonymous letters, didn't I?" I broke in. "Nothing came of it, thank God. I thought it was all nonsense, but then do you know what Carlo said to me the other day? 'Mister Arturo, the difference between you English and us Italians is that if your sister slept with a man you'd do absolutely nothing. If mine did, I'd kill her, and the man too.'

"'Sure,' I said, 'but in the meantime you're busy trying to sleep with everyone else's sister, aren't you?'

"'Of course,' he replied, 'I'm a man, aren't I?'"

A snort from Jim. "It's distasteful, isn't it? It's the church, of course, which encourages such attitudes."

"Oh, come now," Maurice objected.

I was content to listen as the two of them got into an argument—with some uneasiness, perhaps, for I was still insecure about religion, tied emotionally to the belief that I had to accept everything the church taught or reject it all. But I couldn't be bothered with arguing. I was aware of the beauty of the bay below, the feeling of well-being that the warmth of the sun instilled.

When Jim and Maurice stopped talking, the silence was almost complete: only the sound of an odd motorcar far away in the streets of Olbia and insect noises in the grass. A ship had entered the gulf now and was moving silently toward the pier, leaving two regular diverging furrows of water behind it.

"I've nothing against having fun while you're young," Maurice's voice came to me. "But you still need an absolute morality to aspire to one day. Responsibility, I agree, is fine, but people can't take so much responsibility."

Jim started making fun of him. "Now that he's getting married he's thinking more of becoming respectable!"

"Which reminds me," Maurice replied, "do you remember that frightful flirt Carmen who came to our party? Someone from Cagliari told me she's getting married, all rather in a hurry. She may have acted in all responsibility, although I doubt it, but she obviously neglected the basic precaution of remembering the date."

"Who was it?"

"That's one of the difficulties."

We stayed talking until late afternoon, then finally got up to return to Olbia for the *passeggio*.

Under a more restful heat now the town still lay undisturbed, its limbs stretching across the shore and the arrow that pierced its crusted surface lying in the same position from the sea from where it had come. Unconcerned and strangely lifeless, a desiccated sea monster, baked by the sun—although one could imagine the tiny insects that were beginning to swarm along its cracks. If that same god that had fired the arrow were now to lift its victim up and throw it, struggling, out to sea, there would be shock, cries of anguish, talk of catastrophe. But that was unlikely. It would stay where it had always been. Its colony of inhabitants would crawl about it, eat, sleep, and make love within it, never thinking, in the habit of their lives, of how soon everything could end.

*   *   *

Teresa's departure when I returned to Alghero was a further stage in the gradual process of disintegration. This time it was final: she'd left a note saying she was going to live on the continent, which was confirmed at the local travel agency, where she'd bought a ticket for Rome.

"What's happening to this place?" the old lady said in the kitchen that evening, shaking her head. "First this American friend of yours almost kills herself, then Teresa says she's going to Rome. What will a girl without education do in Rome, I ask you? Go on the streets, without a doubt. After all, she's slept with a good many men, and they must all have given her something. Everything's changing. I'm too old for it to happen like this, all at once. And you'll be going at the end of next week, and then that nice friend of yours with the ugly moustache. And next time you come I doubt if I'll be here any longer either."

Jim's arrival with the next progress report on Isabelle did little to cheer me up. "They're keeping her in hospital for a while, then she's decided to return to the States."

"Poor woman."

"Oh, she's quite cheerful about it all, thriving on all the attention." He was unconcerned as always. "And now this religious business—amazing what those nuns can do. She's as full of enthusiasm and as neurotic about it as she is over a new lover. Just imagine the effect she'll have on the convents if she becomes a nun herself. It hardly bears thinking about!"

His visit was interrupted by Franco, bringing in a postcard for me. It was from Anna, in Rome.

* * *

"Come on in, come on in!" Isabelle, surrounded by grapes she was stuffing into her mouth, was sitting up in bed looking like a rather frumpy Roman empress giving an audience. "Great to see you again, Art!"

"How are you?" The only chair was piled high with women's magazines, so I sat on the bed. The nun who'd let me in silently disappeared.

"Since they emptied my stomach for me I've been just fine! Takes more than a bit of barbiturate to get me under the ground, I guess."

"Jim says you're going back to the States?"

"Yeah, it's still the best place for finding rich husbands. I'm sick of having no money."

I chuckled. "We thought you were going into the church."

She broke off another stalk of grapes. "That didn't last long. For a while I thought there'd be some ... some security in it. And it might have saved me money on my analyst's bills. But it wasn't for me." Licking her fingers voraciously, she continued, "You know, it was the cannibalism of it that got to me in the end."

"*Cannibalism?*"

"Yeah, you know. This is my body given for you. It suddenly occurred to me in the middle of mass: here I am eating someone. I'm just a fucking cannibal! I almost choked on it. I had to run out and barf. The nuns have been hostile to me ever since."

Isabelle pushed another handful of grapes into her mouth and chomped down on them so that the juice trickled out of the sides of her mouth. "God, these are good! So, Art, when are you leaving?"

"Saturday."

For the first time she looked genuinely sad. "Gee, that really is too bad. What can I say?" She looked around her desperately. "Here, take the rest of the grapes for your journey." She loaded three enormous bunches into my arms. "Wait, give me half a dozen more." She pulled a number off, dripping juice over the sheets. "You'll like them. They only give me the runs anyway. I'm in and out of bed the whole goddamn day!"

I held them awkwardly until it was time to leave.

"Goodbye, Arthur," she said as I went out, tears flooding over her cheeks.

The end came as an anticlimax—although even at this stage I'd decided to indulge my love of the exotic and return via Sicily and then up the length of Italy. I went by plane to Cagliari rather than take the slower train. Only Jim and Enrico came to the airport to see me off, Jim talking casually about meeting in London, Enrico asking emotionally when I'd be coming back to Sardinia. I felt distant, conscious of the anonymous barren grassland where the plane was to arrive, a lonely field unconnected with Sardinia. Just over an hour later I was in the terminal in Cagliari waiting for the shipping office to open so I could get my ticket for Palermo. On board the atmosphere was Sicilian; Sardinia was of no importance. I stood on deck eating the rest of Isabelle's grapes, watching the port and town gradually vanish into the distance.

The next morning brought the Sicilian coastline, the southern elegance of Palermo, then the train meandering lazily through the plains of the interior toward Catania on the other coast. I stayed there that day and went up Etna the next; then caught the night train for the north, crossing by the ferry from Messina to the Italian continent. I visited Naples and the arrested civilization of Pompeii, its nobility held captive by the elemental flow of the earth, with plaster casts of bodies still displaying yesterday's frozen emotion. From Naples I took a direct train to Milan, thus avoiding stopping in Rome, where I would only have thought of Anna.

In London it was already autumn, dull and lonely as I'd foreseen, and for some reason I didn't see Margaret. I heard of her doings occasionally the following season, when she was back in Sardinia, while I, for my final year as a tourist rep, had been sent to Sorrento. For a while I kept in touch with Jim and Maurice, both of whom got married—Jim disastrously, to Marcella; Maurice ordinarily.

It wasn't until three years later that I met Margaret again.

Epilogue

So much for my memories. The photo albums lie open haphazardly in front of me, the flat, two-dimensional, black-and-white images no more than abstract symbols of the events they represent. Getting them out has done nothing but encourage useless speculation about what might have been.

There's nothing I have to do or want to do. It's been three days now since wife and children took off to visit grandparents, but after three days of work—reading until all hours, eating and drinking when I feel like it—with the arrival of the weekend the euphoria has passed.

This morning dawned bright and clear as summer mornings are supposed to; there was an extra hour in bed, time to come to terms with the expectancy of what the day would bring. But that soon faded, and I sit looking at my photos, asking myself what has happened since my early years. My students now think of me as an "older man," and life, as on this Saturday, becomes no more than a tedious afternoon after a morning that was promising. I rarely think now about Sardinia, the one place, the one time, when the expectancy of youth seemed constantly on the point of fulfilment.

Putting the album aside, I get up and stare out at our large garden, neatly fenced off from the neighbours. Soon the view will be different, since we've just bought a new house. It makes sense; I want it too. It's larger, more elegant, more suitable for family and status. It takes more courage than I possess, though, to have a blue ceiling with pictures of angels on it. What's the use of rebelling now, with unconventional ideas, if the life I lead exactly parallels the lives of my neighbours?

I have, they all say, a good life: security, an interesting job at the university, which I perform competently, a reasonable income. Some prestige through being departmental head and a past president of my particular scholarly society, and through the recent publication of my book, a major work of scholarship on a minor writer of fiction.

Depressions like this aren't new to me. I had them in my bachelor days too. And yet in Sardinia at least there was *something*, even if it was only the expectancy. A year later, when I told my parents I was going back into academic work, they were delighted. "We were afraid you were going to stay permanently with that travel agency," they said. I agreed with them that it was hardly work for someone with a university degree—although nowadays people think differently. I'd considered it and rejected it, influenced no doubt by what others might think.

Sardinia. The memories continue, edited by time and by memory's failings. Things have apparently changed there, and it seems incredible that the Sards could ever have come to accept topless women tourists on their beaches, which in my time would have been considered as impossibly immoral. But some things in the past can't be changed.

* * *

"Did you manage all right without me?"

The children are in bed after the excitement of the homecoming, and now we have the evening to ourselves.

"Of course. Got a lot of work done." And spent a lot of time dreaming about the past.

"Enjoyed every minute of it, I know."

"I'm glad you're back, though." Warm, comfortable. The reassuring, secure side of marriage, providing a haven for one's adventurous soul.

"I went to look at the house again. I think we'll enjoy it."

"As long as you're happy. You'll have a good study."

"How are your parents?"

"They're fine. Mum went on a bit about Bob and Janice. She can't accept their deciding to live together."

"I know: 'We tried so hard to bring her up properly!'"

Both of us laugh, aware of the old, unending dichotomy between individual responsibility and authoritarian paternalism. Sometimes I, too, resent that young people can have similar liberal attitudes to my own, just by picking them up off the street, without the personal struggle.

Margaret gives one of her little smiles. "I've got something to show you."

She takes a newspaper cutting from her bag and hands it to me. It's just a small item, under the headline, "Englishmen murdered in Sardinia."

"The bodies of two Englishmen," I read, "identified as James Bradley, 22, and Philip Johnson, 20, both of Romford, Essex, have been found in the mountains of a remote area of Sardinia, near Orgosolo, a village famous for its bandits. The two men, who were on holiday, had been shot in the head. They are believed to have been mistaken for someone else."

"I remember that day, you know," she says. "Just the idea of possible danger. It was that which made it all so real."

"We were living in the present that day. Most of the time we're looking forward to something else, or reminiscing about the past."

"You in particular!"

"I admit it."

"You were in love with that other girl then."

"Yes."

"Just think how exciting it would have been to marry a Sard!"

"Well, Jim did, only it didn't work out. As for Anna ... well, yes, she seemed exciting, for a while. Exotic. But when it came down to it, she was just like anyone else. Well, perhaps not quite ... "

"So instead you ended up with me!"

For a moment I'm lost in my dreams again, then I remember something quite trivial about my time in Sardinia. "You know what turned out to be my biggest mistake while I was there? I could have bought land on the coast. A man in Tempio offered it to me, but I refused. With all the tourist developments, we'd have financial security by now. I didn't even consider it in my anxiety to find Anna."

"You and your women! They've always been more important to you than money, haven't they? They still are."

I consider adding, "In a sense I still love all of them, if that's what you mean. I've never really abandoned them. I would still like to see most of them."

But that would lead into a long discussion of love and those things I consider important in life, which I should approach cautiously. Margaret has heard it all before anyway and does her best to accept me as I am, helped by the fact that she's not entirely without a past herself. But perhaps she's unaware of how strong is the ongoing conflict within. Even now, when my ideas on morality and responsibility are clearer than they were in Sardinia—basically I know what I believe— it's almost impossible to practise what I preach. The inhibitions from my upbringing remain, and I'm unable, openly at least, to step across society's boundaries. I lecture my students on the eternal problem of man's eating the apple from the tree of knowledge of good and evil, with an awareness of both; of Faust wrestling with the universe to rival God and eventually, in Goethe, to be saved because of his constant striving. I tell them that, in the ancient Jewish view, there's a fundamental unity between God and the devil; that without both of them life is barren. But however easy this is to discuss in the literary terms with which I've been dealing for most of my career, it remains far more difficult to live such ideas in practice.

For a long time I thought I'd behaved stupidly over Anna, as any "mature" person would have told me. But at some stage I came to understand that those genuine feelings, which we learn to hide in our attempts at self-protection, were part of the very best in me, painful though they were, and I should celebrate them.

"I wonder what happened to all the people we knew there," Margaret continues. "An odd bunch, weren't they?"

"They've all disappeared. Except for you, thank God."

Yet who knows? Just two weeks ago, by one of those coincidences that form life's pattern, I met a man I'd known at school. Might not Sardinia be similarly resurrected one day, if only in the shape of Isabelle, coming out of a field with a soldier or something? At unknown places in Europe and America, perhaps even farther away, are those who had a shared experience of a few months there. Who have Alghero, Sassari, Porto Torres, Olbia, Cagliari in their consciousness, together with thousands of other memories that make up individual lives.

There's a slightly odd postscript to that season in Sardinia. It's odd because I'm not sure whether it's something that happened or not, whether it's a genuine memory or only the recollection of a dream that was vivid enough to have seemed real.

It's like this. I never saw Anna again, but I may have seen Gavino. It would be nice to finish this story with a reconciliation, friendship even; but it didn't happen that way. I'd written to him, finally, from London. For a while I thought a lot about him, hoping perhaps that one day I'd go back and visit him. But he didn't reply. And although I thought of him again the next year, when I went to Sorrento, by then he'd become like so many acquaintances who've just taken their place, irrecoverably, in memory.

However, it seems that one afternoon—it's here that my recollections are confused—I was at a fun fair or circus or something. It must have been in Naples; perhaps I'd taken a group of tourists there. And I found myself in one of those haunted houses full of mirrors where you had to find your way through. Now that much is certainly real, but it's impossible to say whether what followed actually happened or whether the mirrors so impressed my mind that I just dreamed of it afterward.

Anyway, I recall groping my way through in the half darkness, with the reflections going on endlessly, some of them distorted. Grotesque as a nightmare, difficult to make much sense of it. I'd reached one of those impasses where I didn't know which way to go. I looked in the glass in front of me, and there was Gavino. The same triangular face, the same intelligent expression—but not looking at me directly because of the angle of the mirror and the others it reflected. No matter which way I looked, I couldn't get him to look at me face on. I turned around, but there was no one there. I turned back again, and his head turned away as though he'd seen me when I was looking in another direction. I stood quite still, certain it was him. I tried trickery, suddenly moving my head, but no matter what I did it seemed he'd only look at me when my eyes were turned away. I pushed forward, thinking there must be a way through ahead of me, but found only a glass wall. Was he behind it? I tried to call him, but the sound didn't penetrate.

Eventually, I found the way ahead, and turning a corner there was a huge, distorted Gavino in a mirror above. A step forward and I appeared there instead; backward, and Gavino was there again.

Then he was gone. I struggled on, trying to find a way out, calling to him. One further reflection in a distant mirror, and that was all. I can't remember emerging into daylight, but of course I didn't find him there either. Could I really have seen him? Why, then, didn't I try going to Amalfi, where I knew he had relatives, and which wasn't very far away? The answer remains locked in those inaccessibly distant recesses of my soul.

Somewhere there remains a fleeting memory of something beautiful: a young man's description of a wine called Sardinian Silver. In suburbia I look at the rows of individual havens and wonder what has happened to all those venturesome souls who once were young. In youth there's always something to look forward to, a path upward, a career, success, fulfilment, marriage perhaps. Until one day you realize that you've already crossed over the summit, an unmarked mountain pass you'd expected to be higher but which, in fact, could have been one of several high points on the road—so that looking back you're not even sure which one it was. And then you're going downhill again, and any achievement, such as it was, is behind you. Oh, there are still the lesser rises to the tops of foothills, but the summit is gone for good and was disappointing. So you continue onto the plain, travelling level now, speeding up perhaps to reach the odd hillock—and all you can hope for is that one of them might lead to further, new mountains beyond, invisible in the clouds that invariably cover the road of life's travellers.

Was Sardinia the mountain pass of my journey from youth to middle age? Perhaps not. There were other high points too. But it was somewhere near the top.

"Should we go back there, for a holiday?" Margaret suggests, interrupting my musing.

I hesitate, wondering whether it could ever be the same. "We might find it disappointing. Interesting, perhaps, but … "

But will I ever return, I think, to the Sardinia of my soul?

Afterword

Sardinian Silver *is a work of fiction but based very much on my experience of the island in 1962, as a teacher of English in Sassari. I returned there in 2004, after an absence of forty-two years. I naturally expected changes, but I was astonished by their magnitude, to the extent that Sardinia hardly seemed the same place.*

Some changes, of course, were the result of natural growth over time. Sardinia is now indeed a tourist destination and has been developed accordingly. Where once were isolated beaches and empty fields, one now finds crowded resort areas, marinas with expensive yachts, and a proliferation of cafés and shops. This was particularly striking in Olbia, where essentially a new town, far larger, has arisen alongside the old. There, as elsewhere, a huge new port has been built. In Porto Torres, too, where there was once a single pier to accommodate one small ship arriving once a day, there are now large docks and a constant coming and going of car ferries. Modern roads make travelling easier, but there is a great deal more traffic. Sassari and Cagliari are large, modern cities (albeit still with their old towns), while Orgosolo is now a rather ordinary village like any other, better known for its more recently painted murals than for its once infamous bandits and its atmosphere of fear and suspicion.

Above all, the "southern mentality"—women always having to be chaperoned and young people unable to go out together unless engaged— seems to have disappeared. Although I constantly complained of this in 1962 and can hardly regret the change, I was nevertheless shocked to see young people (the locals, not just the tourists) kissing in public. For most the new ways have become normal and generally accepted. Perhaps, inevitably, Sardinia has become ordinary: still beautiful, but no longer unique.

Or is this no more on my part than simple nostalgia for a past that was, frankly, somewhat squalid? There are, at least, two things that I regret, justifiably. I was looking forward to going to Sassari and strolling on the Piazza d'Italia for the passeggio. *Who knows? Perhaps I might even* meet someone who still knew me. Alas, the passeggio no longer takes place, although people still congregate in the cafés. I had also planned to buy a bottle of Sardinian Silver and Sardinian Gold. But no one had heard of them: they, too, have disappeared.

Thus, this novel evokes a Sardinia that no longer exists, but which had a quality of its own that is worth remembering.

—A. Colin Wright

41716355R00118

Made in the USA
Middletown, DE
20 March 2017